W9-CEC-970

The Lady Flirts with Death

A SIMON & ELIZABETH MYSTERY

THE LADY FLIRTS WITH DEATH

PEG HERRING

FIVE STAR
A part of Gale, Cengage Learning

Detroit • New York • San Francisco • New Haven, Conn • Waterville, Maine • London

GALE
CENGAGE Learning

LIBRARY OF CONGRESS CATALOGING-IN-PUBLICATION DATA

Herring, Peg.
The lady flirts with death : a Simon & Elizabeth mystery / Peg Herring. — First edition.
pages cm
ISBN 978-1-4328-2712-0 (hardcover) — ISBN 1-4328-2712-X (hardcover)
1. Elizabeth I, Queen of England, 1533-1603—Fiction. 2. Tower of London (London, England)—Fiction. 3. Mystery fiction. 4. Historical fiction. I. Title.
PS3558.E7548L33 2013
813'.54—dc23 2012051193

First Edition. First Printing: May 2013
Find us on Facebook– https://www.facebook.com/FiveStarCengage
Visit our website– http://www.gale.cengage.com/fivestar/
Contact Five Star™ Publishing at FiveStar@cengage.com

Printed in Mexico
1 2 3 4 5 6 7 17 16 15 14 13

The Lady Flirts with Death

Chapter One

"You should not have come." Elizabeth Tudor whispered the words hastily as her visitor entered the cheerless room and made the sign of the cross. Simon felt some—though not much—of the tension in his spine lessen. Dressed as a priest, he had covered his head with the hood to shade his long, plain face, pulled the right sleeve down to hide his crippled arm, and bent his body, apparently against the cold of the March day that invaded the room's corners and chilled the floor to ice. Despite that, the princess had recognized her old friend immediately. He might have smiled if dread-tightened lips had allowed it. Elizabeth Tudor's first thought at his unannounced appearance was for his safety.

"I am here on orders from our monarch, lady." Simon handed Elizabeth a rolled sheet of vellum, the same one he had shown at the front entrance and at several succeeding checkpoints. The message was brief: *The bearer acts on my orders. Assist him in all possible ways.* The document was legitimate, to a point. Simon had, however, carefully scraped Henry VIII's signature from the bottom and replaced it with "Mary," the simple signature used by their new queen. Simon gambled no one would look closely at the royal seal pressed into a splash of wax next to the signature and see that its design was hardly current.

Elizabeth reacted to the words and the handwriting with a quick frown, momentary surprise, and recognition. She had been present when her father wrote the note for Simon, many years ago, ordering him to help investigate a series of murders. Now the note had provided Simon entry to her prison cell, where he intended to do what he could to free her, even if it meant planning an escape.

He had chosen early morning for his visit, when the lowliest guards were on duty. Such men were likely to accept an official-looking document and do as it ordered rather than investigate one unimportant visitor. As for Mary Tudor, their new monarch had much to keep her occupied in these early days of her reign. While she had no idea who Simon Maldon was or where he was, she would hardly approve if she knew.

Elizabeth was up early, or perhaps had not slept, Simon thought, noting that her face was even paler than usual and her eyes tinged with red. She wore unrelieved black, a stark contrast to her sister, who these days weighed herself down with every sort of bauble and frippery, perhaps to banish memories of years of deprivation. Elizabeth dressed plainly and behaved modestly, probably hoping to convince the world she had no desire for the throne. It had not worked.

Though Simon was sorry to see Elizabeth in a nervous state, it worked to his advantage. The surprise of a visit from a priest, followed quickly by the realization that he was not a priest at all, hardly showed on his old friend's face.

"I have come to instruct you in the way of the True Church, daughter," Simon said in a mumbled attempt at a Spanish accent. "Your sister the queen is most anxious that your soul be turned from any remaining bent toward the heretical teachings of the past." With his back to the guard, he raised his eyebrows to indicate she should play along. "I am Father Stefano."

Elizabeth's face took on an expression of polite acceptance. "I am ready to hear your instruction, Holy Father." She added with quiet emphasis, "And to make my confession."

With all the authority he could muster, Simon nodded at the

guard at his elbow. Confession was sacred, and although the man undoubtedly wanted to hear what juicy, treasonous sins "Boleyn's Bastard" might confess, he reluctantly backed away.

Knowing well the game she must play, Elizabeth retreated as far as she could into a corner and knelt on the cold stone floor. With a curt gesture, she indicated the three women in attendance should leave her with the supposed priest. They bowed slightly in acknowledgment and retreated with a rustle of skirts, regarding Simon with suspicion. The women were no doubt spies who reported everything Elizabeth said, heard, and did in her prison cell. Even as he carefully maintained his priestly demeanor, the tingle of fear along Simon's spine increased. He had entered dangerous territory. *For Elizabeth,* he reminded himself.

He surveyed the rooms Elizabeth occupied, comparing her prison to the cozy home he occupied. Small, drafty, and sparsely furnished, it was still better than some homes he had seen. A window let in light, and a brazier added warmth to the cold morning if a person stood close enough to it. Not as bad as he'd feared, but it was inside the dreaded Tower of London. He imagined Elizabeth's terror at being ordered to the place where her mother had been held while her father and his council decided what to do with her. Sixteen years ago, Anne Boleyn had been led onto the Tower Green and beheaded. She was no more, but her daughter, not yet twenty, had experienced since then a lifetime of rejection, sorrow, and danger.

Remembering his charade, Simon raised his hands over Elizabeth's head and began a singsong chant. Despite the gravity of the situation, he saw a glint of humor in her eyes. He spoke in Latin, a language the two of them had practiced together in the early days of their acquaintance, when he had been charged with perfecting her skill at languages. However, their collaboration twice in the past to solve murders was what had created something like friendship between them.

"How did this happen?" Simon intoned, raising his hands in what he hoped was a convincing benediction. The guard watched with interest, peering across the space poorly lit by a single candle. It was likely he knew little of Catholic practice, since England had been a Protestant nation for decades. All that changed with Mary's ascension to the throne.

Elizabeth was here due to a rebellion planned by one Thomas Wyatt. Despite her support of Mary's claim to the throne, she had been the focus of the plot. Wyatt disagreed with Mary's intent to return the nation to Catholicism and her plan to marry Philip, the Catholic future king of Spain. Wyatt and others like him feared the marriage would reduce England to a Spanish fief, a galling idea to those who recalled Henry VIII, father of both Mary and Elizabeth, freeing England from foreign influence, religious and otherwise.

According to rumor, if the rebellion had been successful Elizabeth would have married Thomas Courtenay, an Englishman with some claim to the throne. Most believed a woman could not rule the land alone, but a woman married to a noble Englishman would be acceptable. Elizabeth was well-loved, too, being like her father in coloring and bearing. There was even, Simon thought now, a tenor to her speech like Henry's, confident and commanding.

"I had nothing to do with Wyatt and his plans." Elizabeth spoke with head bent as if in meditation. She had switched to Greek, and Simon's lips curved in a smile. She was testing him.

He had expected her denial. To admit she had knowledge of the plot would be fatal. Her presence in the Bell Tower indicated she was believed guilty. If judged so officially by Mary's council, she faced death by beheading. Since that would put an end to one of Queen Mary's greatest problems, she would be tempted to order her sister's death, guilty or not.

Simon thought not. His acquaintance with Elizabeth had revealed a mind so quick he often marveled at it. She would have been wise enough to stay out of all plots against Mary.

Members of the noble class had to think ahead, like chess players, and gamble on the future. The gamble of late was whether to support the restoration of the Catholic Church or hold to the Reformation. Each family, each person of influence, had to make that choice. How long could one afford to waffle? How much could he dissemble? Henry's will called for his three living children to succeed him. When Edward VI died at sixteen, his sister Mary had overcome an attempted coup and now reigned. But at thirty-seven years old, she might be too old to have an heir. If Elizabeth outlived Mary, she might become queen. The trick was to avoid beheading in the meantime, and it was a difficult trick these days.

Simon asked the question that brought him here. "How can I help?"

Elizabeth raised her face and said in clear English, "Pray for me."

Simon maintained his chanting cadence with some difficulty. "You are in grave danger."

"I will trust in God and in England," Elizabeth said in Latin, "I am the daughter of Henry the Eighth, and my sister will not fail me, for the same blood runs in our veins."

Simon said very softly, "I must do something, Highness."

"It has helped more than you know to see you, Simon." There was a note of distress in her voice, but she conquered it before continuing. "How goes the world with you?"

His petty life should have been of no concern to her, but he recognized genuine interest. "I am well. The apothecary shop prospers, and Hannah is now my wife."

Remembering his role, Simon again made the sign of the cross, and Elizabeth bowed her head in apparent piety. He wondered what the guard thought, but it did not matter. He would do as ordered. They had all been Protestants only a few months ago. Now they must all be Catholics. He added, "At least I am not penned like a beast."

With a grim smile, Elizabeth said, "I am allowed out of here quite regularly. There are three latrines down the hall, built to hang over the moat, that I may visit whenever I like."

Unable to see the humor, Simon merely grunted in response.

Elizabeth glanced around at the thick stone walls. "When they brought me here on Palm Sunday, on a barge and through the Traitor's Gate, I was so distressed that I sat down on the lawn in tears. Although my jailer, John Brydges, lives in this place, he is not a bad man. He spoke quite kindly and convinced me that sitting out in the rain would do no good when I could be inside, dry and"—her lips twitched with humor—"relatively warm."

"Most beneficent." Simon's tone was flat, but his brow rose sarcastically.

"He let me walk outside for the first few days too, but people would approach and give me things, flowers fashioned from paper or sweet-smelling pomanders. When it was observed that some still love me, my excursions outdoors ended."

"The queen—"

Elizabeth's eyes rose to Simon's in warning, though her voice remained calm. "The queen is my sister and your sovereign. If she receives bad advice from her councilors, it is not her fault. A ruler must have honest men about or just rule is impossible."

"And the queen's advisers think only of the nearest way to their goals."

Her lip curled. "Renard, the worst of them, wants my head separated from my shoulders."

Simon shuffled his feet, trying to banish the cold that seeped upward through the stones. "You could leave England. There are those who would help you, men with power."

"Men like Robin, who languishes in this very prison with a death sentence hanging over him?" Robert Dudley, "Robin," was one of Elizabeth's oldest friends. Vibrant and energetic, Dudley would soon die because his father had tried to set Mary aside and put his own daughter-in-law, Jane Grey, on the throne. The elder Dudley had already met his fate, as had Robert's brother Guilford and Jane, an unwilling pawn in Dudley's play for power.

Simon met Elizabeth's eyes squarely. "There are others who would come to your aid."

She shook her head, glancing at the women who whispered in the opposite corner. "My sister is the lawful queen. We must count on her goodness."

Simon did not, but he could not argue with Elizabeth, who seemed to him Henry VIII's rightful heir: strong where her brother had not been and fair where her sister could not be. The ways of the powerful were far beyond him, however. He would do as she asked. Still, it made him sad to see her pushed aside, her talents unappreciated, her potential wasted.

"Shall I come again tomorrow?"

She rose and put her hands over his in a gesture that might have been inspired by religious fervor. They were cold, and a tightening of her fingers revealed her reluctance to have him leave her friendless in this awful place. But she said firmly, "It is too dangerous. I prefer you live, Simon." She would have smiled, he thought, but a glance at the eavesdropping guard stopped her. "I endangered your life more than once. I would not do it again."

"Visits from a priest are no threat," he said, pulling the hood forward to hide his face again. "In fact, it might be said you have set your feet on the right path."

Elizabeth bowed, probably to conceal from the others her bitter expression. "My feet do not matter," she said softly. "It is my head that must concern me."

Chapter Two

Hannah Maldon listened patiently, green eyes lowered to hide impatience as her customer explained in detail the workings of his bowels. She had already provided him with physic made of treacle, but he seemed unable to resist fully describing his problems. Reminding herself of Simon's belief that a good listener was often better than a physician, she managed to make small murmurs of sympathy and understanding when appropriate.

When the man finally left, Hannah returned to the worktable and began bottling medicines Simon had prepared that morning. Adjusting the coif she wore over her mass of brown curls, she tried to concentrate, tried not to worry about what would happen if Simon's charade as a priest was discovered. She was unsuccessful.

Hannah wished Elizabeth well, of course. The princess had been kind to them both, and the dangers they had shared together made them closer than a princess royal and two commoners had any right to be. But no one could protect Elizabeth from her sister the queen, and while visiting her in the Tower was dangerous enough, Simon was certain to suffer a traitor's death if he followed his conscience and tried to help her escape England.

Hearing a clink in her pocket, Hannah was reminded she had put the money for the medicine there as her customer talked. She transferred the coins to the money box kept in a drawer under the table. Putting stoppers in the last of the bottles she had filled, she set them on a shelf and went into the living quarters behind the shop to see to supper.

The place she and Simon called home was not large, but it was more than Hannah had ever dared hope for. An orphan, she'd been lucky to be taken on as a scullery maid at Hampstead Castle and content sharing a tiny room off the kitchens with two other girls. But Simon Maldon changed all that when he came to Hampstead and became friends with the Princess Elizabeth. There he and Hannah had fallen in love. Several years later Simon had inherited his master's shop when the old man died, allowing the two of them to marry.

Along with Simon, Hannah had gained a family. Simon's father Jacob was unfailingly kind though distant; his brothers and sisters were welcoming, and his mother, Mary Maldon, was helpful if a little bossy. It did not matter, for Hannah felt blessed. The orphan was now an apothecary's wife, with a business to run and a home of her own in the back, a large room with a loft for children when they came.

If they came. So far Hannah's womb had not quickened, and none of Simon's learning could explain why. It was not for lack of love between them, she thought as she surveyed the silent room. She was happy with Simon, but a baby would add so much to her life: a tiny body to cuddle and hold, a growing child to cherish and guide. She had prayed and prayed. Chiding herself for questioning what God had given, Hannah set the thought of children aside. Again.

Stirring the soup that hung far enough off the fire to simmer but not scorch, she turned to the small loaves of bread she had made that morning and left under a cloth on the hearth. Frowning, she counted them. She had made six loaves. Now there were only five.

For a few minutes she stood, stupidly counting the loaves

over and over. Five. She pictured them in her mind as she had shaped them and put them in to bake. Six. There had been six loaves. She returned to the shop, but her mind remained on the bread. Was she certain there had been six loaves? The more she thought about it, the less sure she became. A happy thought occurred. Newly pregnant women were said to suffer tangled thoughts. Perhaps she was finally going to have a child! A miscounted loaf of bread would be nothing compared to that.

Simon paused outside the Tower gate, attempting to put his thoughts into some sort of order. He had meant to see Elizabeth then return home, but now he changed his mind. He would visit St. James's Palace first. His friend Calkin, a guardsman there, might know something about Elizabeth's future. If she had one, he thought grimly.

In no time he was swallowed in the mass of shops and homes that was London, their random placement making it difficult to travel directly from one place to any other. The streets were filling with people headed somewhere, some with heads up and eyes forward, looking toward to their destination, others with shoulders hunched and faces turned down. The noise level rose as peddlers began hawking their wares and others raised their voices in competition. Simon kept to the center of the bumpy street as much as possible to avoid stepping in—or possibly being doused with—night soil as chamber pots were emptied into the street from balconies above.

Once he was away from the Tower, he stepped into a deserted alley, took off the cassock he wore, and stuffed it into his medicine bag. It had served well, and now he had daily entry to the princess' company in the guise of giving her religious instruction. In addition to the disguise, Simon had further assured his welcome by offering to bring medicine for one of the guards, having noticed the man rubbed his stomach as if it caused him pain. Priests and monks had for centuries provided physic to ease minor discomforts. And, Simon thought with a smile, so could apothecaries disguised as priests.

He kept a small store of costumes in the loft of their home, despite Hannah's contention that their days of investigating crimes were over. The priest's robe had once been the property of a man Simon was forced to kill. Despite its past usage, the robe paired with a sedate manner presented a convincing Father Stefano.

Simon admitted to himself that he enjoyed playing different roles. He could become a sailor or a scholar, a peddler or a felon, just by a change of clothing, some makeup, and an adopted attitude. In rare moments of privacy, he practiced walking with the sailor's roll or the beggar's slink. Even the princess had at times entered into his playacting, giving him advice on how to behave, speak, and walk to be convincing in different roles.

The day was fine, and the world welcomed spring everywhere he looked. Flowers grew uninvited in the cracks of walls and at the edges of streets. Birds flew back and forth with sprigs in their beaks, set on nest building. As Simon approached St. James's Palace, he heard the sounds of men practicing the soldiering arts on the green. A commanding voice ordered them left and right, forward and back. Though the speaker tried for a stern note and the men answered smartly, he heard in their voices a note of joy. Winter was over. They were free of the castle and the cold.

In the Royal Guard, the men charged with protecting the king or queen and family, only Calkin was left of three guardsmen Simon once knew. Looking up as Simon approached the practice field, Calkin seemed unsurprised by his reappearance after several years. Leaving his men to their drills, he met his old friend halfway. "Simon, how goes it?"

"Well enough, Sergeant, well enough." Simon reached out his left hand and Calkin took it and pulled him in, adding a clap on the back that almost hurt.

"It is good to see you! I hear you have taken a wife."

"Hannah and I are married, yes."

"That state is not for me, as you well know, but your Hannah is a jewel." Calkin pointed a finger at Simon. "Do you recall her courage when they said the princess poisoned old Amberson?" He slapped a hand against his thigh. "I knew then she was one of a kind."

For a while they caught each other up on the events of their lives since their last meeting. "Do you still practice with the knife?" Calkin asked, raised brows adding import to the question.

"When I can." Though skill with a knife had served him well, Simon was no soldier, and in dreams he often relived the moment when he'd killed a man. The dreams were not pleasant.

The finger Calkin pointed at him now was admonishing. "Your skill is remarkable, but it must be practiced faithfully."

"I know, but Hannah does not like to see me at it."

"It saved her life." Calkin shook his head at the mystery of a woman's mind. Simon might have suggested that to understand a woman one should concentrate on a single one and not a succession of them. He did not, knowing he would never convince Calkin of that.

Turning advice into action, Calkin said, "Let us throw a few times at the butts." Simon thought of arguing he had things to do, but he wanted to learn what Calkin knew of current gossip. "All right, as long as you don't pule like a babe when I best you."

"Are you asleep, man? It's a dream you describe."

He led Simon across the practice ground where men grunted and swore as they sparred with swords, wrestled, and practiced a variety of other exercises meant to keep their skills sharp. Finding a target not in use, Calkin took a stand some twenty feet away and threw his knife at it. The blade stuck in the outermost edge, almost off the target completely. "Do you take my meaning now?" he joked. "Lack of practice makes the throw wide."

Simon pulled his own knife from his belt and examined it. Of late it had been used as a tool rather than a weapon, and the blade was slightly dull. Wiping it on his shirttail, he took a stance, pulled in a deep breath and let it all out, and threw. His knife stuck in the target's inner ring, almost at center.

"The best eye I ever trained; that's you."

With a flush of pride, Simon resolved to spend more time practicing. His crippled arm made it impossible for him to compete with other men in many areas of physical activity, but a knife required different skills—and only one good arm.

As they walked forward to retrieve their knives and try again, he asked, "Have you heard what might become of the princess?"

The man's expression sobered. "Elizabeth?"

"I understand she is imprisoned in the Tower."

"She is." Calkin put a hand on Simon's shoulder. "I know you are fond of her, but it is unlikely she will live out the year." He added more softly, "Perhaps not the month."

The words were like a blow, though he had tried to prepare himself. "I feared as much."

Looking around to assure no one was listening, Calkin lowered his voice even more. "It is said Mary and her council are decided. It is only a matter of framing the pronouncement to convince the people Elizabeth plotted against her sister."

Simon felt sick. "Is there no hope the queen might change her mind?"

Calkin's reply sounded bitter. "The Spanish bridegroom comes soon, they say. Perhaps she will wait to hear what he thinks on the matter."

That did not make Simon feel any better. Why would Philip want an extra princess around, especially one who could be the focal point for rebellion among England's Protestants?

"When does he arrive?"

"Only a matter of weather, they say." Calkin looked sharply at his friend. "Stay away from her, Simon. Your princess is a doomed ship that will drag those nearby under as she goes."

Unwilling to lie to Calkin, Simon said simply, "I understand."

They continued throwing, but Simon's mind was elsewhere. In a dozen throws, Calkin bested him seven of twelve times. "See!" he crowed. "Your first shot was mere luck!"

Simon shrugged, smiling ruefully. "I am rusty, but I must return home. Hannah is minding the shop."

"Come again when you find the time." Calkin patted his stomach. "I need the practice after lying about all winter."

"How could Mary order her own sister to the block?" Hannah asked, aghast at Simon's news.

"The queen is convinced, I think, that everything she does is for the good of England. Her faith was her support through years of turmoil, and now she feels justified in getting rid of anything in the way of her church's return to prominence."

Hearing himself say "her church," Simon realized he did not consider himself a Catholic. More highly educated than most due to his father's influence, he was unable to close his eyes to logic and questioned, at least in his own mind, the bastions of power. Simon identified with those who believed the Bible should be read by anyone who wanted to undertake it. He liked the passionate arguments he had heard among reformers, the earnest questions of what is faith, what is religion, what is man. Although he did not participate in reform, he approved of the idea that a person's immortal soul was in his own hands, not in the judgment of a priest.

Hannah began the tale of her morning's activities. As she talked, her busy fingers searched for weevils in the flour she had bought that day. When she found one, she cast it into the fire, all the while explaining she was sure there had been six loaves. Listening patiently, Simon chuckled to himself at the juxtaposition of a commoner's life with the affairs of the mighty. Elizabeth might lose her head, and Hannah was puzzling out the loss of a bit of bread.

Sensing that his thoughts strayed, Hannah left off her report and asked, "Will you go to see her again?"

"I think it is safe to do so," he answered, hedging the question a little. "If this John Brydges hears she has been visited by a priest, he will no doubt conclude she hopes to save herself by embracing the queen's faith. The priest himself will not be in danger."

Hannah's expression revealed she was not completely convinced, and Simon added with a grin, "I also promised the head guard some physic for his bilious gut. If he finds my remedy effective, he will have all the more reason to allow my visits."

"Well, then," she replied, her tone still doubtful, "take our best concoction. Your visits to the Tower seem to me like a man I saw once at a fair, putting his head into a lion's mouth."

Chapter Three

"Do they speak languages other than their own?" Simon asked Elizabeth the second day, noting the baleful glances of the women in her cell. When allowed to choose, the princess had always chosen women of learning, but these were not her usual attendants.

"No," she answered in Latin, "though I think the homely one knows a few words in Spanish." She glanced at the coterie huddled in the opposite corner, working diligently to repair a musty-smelling tapestry. "We must be grateful my sister thought less about their learning and more about their loyalty to her."

Simon indeed thanked God for the queen's single-minded choices. In all the time he had known her, Elizabeth had been spied upon, every move reported to someone: her father, her brother, her enemies. She seemed used to it and had a hundred ways to thwart spies. Simon, however, was unused to being constantly observed. He felt the hairs on the back of his neck prickle when he considered what news might be carried to the queen by someone they underestimated.

"I was sad to hear of the young king's death," he said, and Elizabeth lowered her eyes at the doubly troubling memory. Not only had Edward VI's death resulted in political danger for Elizabeth, but she had also truly loved her younger half brother. Now she had only Mary, hardly someone to cling to as one's only remaining family member.

Elizabeth asked, "Have you children?"

"Not yet, but there is plenty of time" Simon answered with the automatic addition he used when Hannah despaired of getting pregnant: *There is plenty of time.*

"Of course." Elizabeth's eyes told him she understood more than he would say. A childless wife was a curse to most men.

"Hannah is most anxious to have children, of course. Women care so much about such things." He paused, embarrassed to have spoken to the princess about the desires of women. She was a woman, he knew, but she seemed somehow different.

Her answer confirmed that she was. "I suppose some do," she said. "I have never found babies particularly attractive. Still, I ask you to carry my good wishes to your wife, and my hopes that children might come soon, as many as you can afford." Her smile was genuine, and with a glance at her watchers, she quickly pressed her hands together to indicate it was religious fervor that brought pleasure, not something else.

Hannah made another unnerving discovery that morning. The stew she had made on Monday had been both tasty and hearty. It should have been enough for a second supper, but when she looked into the pot, it was almost empty. Perhaps Simon had woken hungry in the night and helped himself, but that was not like him. She looked around the room nervously. Bread missing yesterday, and today her stew was depleted. What if there was a thief in the neighborhood?

The door leading to their back garden had no lock, only a latch that operated from both sides. Beyond that door, the newly planted vegetable garden lay. Hannah pulled back the window covering and peered out, assuring herself that all was as it should be. At one corner, beyond the row of turnips, was a dovecote, up against a small fence separating their space from the neighbors'. The dovecote was little more than a raised wooden box that allowed the birds to get out of the weather. Common folk were not usually allowed to raise doves, since the business was a profitable enterprise for many noble estates. But the medicines of an apothecary required eggs, and allowances were made as long as they kept less than two dozen birds, used the eggs for physic, and did not sell the birds for meat.

There were footprints in the soft soil around the dovecote, but she herself had probably made those going out to feed and water the birds. The area was empty and quiet. No one lurked outside their home. Vague hope stirred in her a second time. Perhaps pregnant women, known to behave oddly, walked in their sleep and ate portions of stew as well.

Simon left the Tower the way he had come, his step slow and stately as befitted the priest he portrayed. He spoke briefly with the guard, repeating instructions about when and how to take the medicine he had provided. Then he headed for the Outer Ward, which meant crossing a green space flanked by some of the less desirable housings of London's Tower.

The day was young. Damp clung to the stone walls around him, and dew wet his shoes as he crossed the expanse of new grass growing slowly inside the dark, high walls. If he had been less concerned about getting free of the place, Simon might have stopped to gaze at the maze of buildings that made up what was simply called The Tower. William the Conqueror had built the original structure, meant as a fortress and royal residence. Henry III later had the place whitewashed. After many additions, the White Tower was now thirteen towers, and while the royal family at some times and the Crown Jewels all the time could be found there, it was more and more these days a place of sorrow and despair. Beheadings, torture, and years of imprisoning people from all walks of life seemed to have stamped its mark on the place. Simon could almost hear the screams of the condemned and the roar of the crowds when their appetite for death was appeased. At the Outer Ward, he glanced backward to where the towers rose within a solid wall of stone like tombstones in a massive churchyard. How demoralizing it must be for Elizabeth to look daily upon those walls and know she might never again see outside them!

"Good day to you, Father." It took a moment for Simon to realize someone addressed him. He turned to see a man just inside the ward with a guard at either side of him.

Simon lowered his head, hiding his face with a bow. "Good day, my son."

He meant to go on, but something about the man stopped him. His face was familiar, though dried blood obscured his features, and one eye was closed with swelling. Despite that, he seemed slightly amused. A prisoner who had not yet lost his sense of humor?

"I wonder, if these fellows will allow it, do you have leisure to hear my confession?"

Simon felt dismayed. It was one thing for Elizabeth to pretend she was confessing as they conversed in secret. It was quite another to shrive a man with serious crimes to his charge.

He looked again at the face and the knowing expression. Recognition hit, and he almost said the name aloud. Peto! A feeling close to joy rose in his chest, but he managed to remain outwardly stoical. A hundred questions demanded answers, and he could ask none of them.

Some of the answers were obvious. Like Elizabeth, Peto was a prisoner here, apparently newly arrived. And somehow, the criminal who had years before become Simon's friend had recognized him despite his disguise.

Another thought made him hesitate to answer the question Peto asked. Did the officers of the law know they had Peto the Pope in custody? Peto took great pains to keep his identity secret from the world's so-called honest men. Those who knew him protected him due to affection and appreciation of his generosity. But he had been brought to the Tower, not the Clink, the prison nearest his usual haunts. The authorities in Southwark must have turned him over to the Crown, probably to absolve themselves of responsibility for so slippery a criminal. That argued the guards knew their prisoner's identity.

Peto seemed to read Simon's thoughts. "I was arrested last night in Southwark." He indicated his guards. "My friends here will find me a cell, no doubt, and provide me with worst bread every other day until I tell them everything I know." He spoke with a casual knowledge of prison procedure. Despite understanding what lay before him, his voice was firm, his tone natural. "Before I confess to these fellows, I would like to confess to God."

Worst bread, a coarse bread made of bran and ground peas, was an unimportant prisoner's only sustenance. It was given every other day; on intervening days he got only a drink of water from the nearest pond or puddle. The practice was meant to make a man confess quickly. Prison was not itself a punishment, only a stopping place until the deserved sentence was meted out. If starvation did not make a man confess, there was always torture.

Simon repressed a shudder at the thought of what awaited his friend. Peto's gaze seemed to will him to agree, however, so he made the sign of the cross. "I will hear your confession, my son." He turned to the guard. "Where can this man absolve himself of sin, in private?"

"His sins are not easily dealt with, Priest," said the guard. "This is Peto the Pope, who has plagued the law in and around London for years." The guard stopped, waiting for Simon to look impressed.

"Most clever of you to have caught him." He tried to sound congratulatory.

The guard looked at his companion, who shrugged. "Well, he gave us no trouble, and it behooves a man to make things right with God before he is hanged. Come. He is to have a place of his own, away from friends who might help him escape."

The guard led the way to a tower smaller than the one Simon had just left, took a flight of stairs leading downward, then opened a low door with a large iron key. Replacing the key on his belt with a metallic clink, he indicated the dark space beyond. "Call when you finish." He added with a chuckle, "I expect he will shine with goodness when you're done with him!"

The door closed behind them with a scrape and a bang, and Simon could not help but shiver at the finality of the sound. As the stench in the place assailed his nostrils, he almost gagged. The room was little more than a closet with a bucket in one corner—no doubt the source of the evil smell—and a pallet in another. The door, solid and banded with metal, had a slit in the center just large enough for meals to be handed through. The room's single window was barely large enough to see out, and the view only a small patch of grass and the encircling wall. There was nothing in the cell: no furniture, no means of passing the time. It was the most miserable place Simon could imagine. Even the common cells, though overcrowded, might be better than this solitary place where a man had nothing to do but ponder his very short future.

Peto seemed unconcerned with any of that. Looking to see that the guard had moved away, he grasped Simon's shoulders. "Simon Maldon! It is good to see you."

"I wish we met in better circumstances, Peto." The cold once again seeped into Simon's feet through his thin leather boots. How did one survive in this place?

A wave of one hand banished that subject. "I will live, or I will not. Death has no terror for me, for I have seen it."

Simon knew Peto had killed men. He also knew why. In the

underworld of London, there were hunters and there was prey. Peto was a hunter, and his methods of making his living were outside the law. Still, Simon liked to think Peto was more than a common criminal.

"How did you come to be arrested?"

"Ill luck. And ill will, I suspect." Peto sat on a projecting ledge of stone and made his own observation. "You came to see the princess."

Simon had no fear of Peto giving away his secrets. "I did."

"Will you help her escape this place?" Criminal or not, Peto was an Englishman, and the English in general liked Elizabeth.

Simon made a rueful grimace. "She says she trusts in her sister's goodness."

Peto frowned, disbelieving. "Trust that mad old maid? Mary will have her head from her shoulders in a fortnight."

"I hope you are wrong."

Peto huffed a sigh. "I have been wrong quite often of late."

"Is that how you came here?"

"It is." Leaning his back against the rough stone wall, Peto grimaced at its roughness and instead leaned forward, elbows on his knees. "I am charged with murder, which is hardly beyond belief. What is odd is that I am innocent in this case." He shook his head ruefully. "It was neatly arranged, and now I face the derrick." His casual term for the hangman jarred Simon's nerves.

"Who would plot against you?"

"One who knows me well, no doubt, for the trap was well laid." Peto frowned. "The plague on it is this: I am uncertain who can be trusted to help me out of this coil."

More than once, Peto had escaped custody with the help of loyal friends. But if one of his close associates had turned against him, a request for help might be useless, even dangerous.

Simon considered his odd situation. Two people he liked and

respected were imprisoned in the Tower. Both faced death, and neither deserved that fate, at least if one believed them, which Simon did. He had come here to see Elizabeth, putting himself in danger. Could he do less for Peto? With a sigh he could not quite suppress, he asked, "What can I do to help?"

Peto's forehead relaxed, and Simon realized he had been hoping for such an offer. "I will not ask you to endanger yourself for me." He indicated the cassock Simon wore. "You seem determined to do that on your own. But you might take a message to Pen."

Penitence Brook, an odd fellow who claimed to be a fool, was Peto's friend and ally, as unlikely a betrayer as Simon could imagine. "That I will gladly do."

Peto's smile was wry. "You would assist a murderer?"

"You say you are innocent of the crime, and I know you do not lie."

The other bowed his head slightly. "I thank you for that, Simon. While I am not known as an honest man, I would like to think that my word, at least, is honest."

They were an unlikely pair to have become friends, a businessman who respected the law and a man guilty of many crimes. But from the first there had been an affinity between them.

Almost from the first, Simon silently amended, admitting to himself that for a few moments when they first met, he had thought Peto intended to kill him. That fear was long gone. "Will you tell me how you came to be arrested?"

Peto raised his eyes to the window overhead, where the patch of blue sky seemed designed to torture rather than inspire the cell's inhabitant. It certainly was not designed to air the place out, Simon thought, his nose wrinkling.

Peto let out a long breath. "I was called last night to the Bull's Horn, an inn on Dagger Lane in Paris Garden."

Paris Garden, an area of Southwark on the south bank of the Thames, was known for wildness, and it was where men like Peto thrived. "What took you to this place?"

"A boy from the neighborhood who often carries messages came to my lodgings to tell me a friend, Red John Cooper, was at the Bull's Horn and wanted to meet with me on a matter of some secrecy." Peto raised his brows as he avoided mention of the meeting's purpose. "When I arrived, the host, a fellow named Saddler, pointed me to a room at the back. He keeps his supplies there, but a cot in one corner gives rest to those who seek a haven for a night or two. John often slept there when he wanted privacy."

He paused again, perhaps waiting for Simon to question why a man might sleep in the back room of an alehouse. Knowing the reputation such places had, Simon thought he knew.

Springing up like leeks on the other side of the Thames, alehouses, cheaper versions of taverns, provided ale to those who could not afford wine. By law, proprietors were to serve only noblemen and visitors, and even then, their beer was to be watered to prevent drunkenness. Such establishments were forbidden to allow gaming, which might encourage men to stray from decorous behavior. The laws were clear. But there was almost no enforcement of them.

To supplement their income, alehouse keepers often ignored the laws, serving strong beer to all who entered their doors and providing additional entertainments as well. It was said that all it took to open an alehouse in Southwark was a front door for customers to enter and a back door for them to escape when the law showed up. Not that it happened often.

Many alehouse keepers overlooked their patrons' sins as long as they were discreet. Peto and men like him were no doubt welcomed in a place such as the Bull's Horn, whatever their reasons for being there. They had money, and they were generous about spending it.

When Simon did not seek details of Red John's purpose, Peto continued. "When I arrived, just after dark, Saddler reported John was asleep. This was not surprising, for his work is mostly done at night. Saddler gave me a candle and went back to pouring drinks."

Simon's natural inquisitiveness made him ask, "Did anyone seem to be watching you?"

"I did not think so. But I was wrong."

Peto had a gift for blending into his surroundings. Most people's gaze passed right over him, which was exactly as he liked it. Only his eyes were extraordinary. On the rare occasions when Peto looked at a person directly, it seemed those gray eyes looked straight into his soul.

The pause that followed was so long Simon wondered if his friend meant to go on. Knowing they would not be left alone for much longer, he prompted, "You went into the room to meet your friend."

"Yes." The word dragged, as if he did not want to get to the next one. "The room was dark when I entered, but I knew it well enough. I set the candle on the table. As I did, a sound came from the corner that I first thought was John rising to meet me." He paused again, clenched his fists, and finished. "But I have heard a death rattle before."

Simon grimaced. He had heard the sound too, and it never failed to affect him.

"I took up the candle again and went to the cot. When I reached him, John was a corpse, though still warm." He looked at his hands, spreading them palms up before his face. "His blood—" Peto's face, usually almost expressionless, revealed shock and sorrow.

Simon shivered at the image and said gently, "This man was a good friend?"

"The one I most trusted and my right hand in business."

"Then your loss is doubled."

Peto's smile was grim. "In work such as mine, one learns to deal with many men but not to count on all men's loyalty." His tone indicated how he felt about such people. "I had of late two men I counted on, Red John and William Brewer. William died two weeks ago in what at the time seemed an accident. John's death makes me reconsider that." His eyes met Simon's. "Someone is maneuvering to take my place."

A revolution in the gritty streets of Southwark? Was Peto, long a sort of king among the felons of the area, in danger of losing his position, even his life? In Simon's view, an enemy of Peto must be a lesser man, and therefore no boon to Southwark.

Although a criminal in the eyes of the law, Peto the Pope shielded those who worked for him from life's worst buffets. He righted wrongs, at least as he saw them. He provided for widows and orphans. He offered employment, though the authorities would not recognize his smuggling operations as beneficial to the economy. Within Peto's schemes, people were treated fairly, made money to feed their families, and had recourse when they were bullied or cheated. It was more than the nation's council had done for a dozen years—more than they cared to attempt.

Simon took a seat on the hard pallet bed. "What did you do when you saw your friend was dead?"

"I saw the trap at once. There was a back door to the alley, but it would not open. Something was wedged against it. There was no other way out. As I stood there like a fool, the host entered, a candle in one hand and a tray of ale in the other. Behind him, a roomful of witnesses saw me, alone with a corpse and with blood on my hands."

"But—" Simon stopped, unable to think of what to say. It was a fortunate pause, for they heard the guard's step outside the cell. Peto quickly knelt, and Simon assumed a posture of patient listening. As the guard paused, Simon spoke a Latin phrase in a singsong voice, *"Et Spiritus Sancti."* The steps passed on.

Peto rose and picked up where they had left off. "The most unlucky part is that the local constable and three of his men, hooded and quiet, sat facing the storeroom and drinking their fill of Saddler's wares. I was immediately arrested, and no one present dared offer help with the law in the house." He tilted his head to the side with a faint grin. "I tried to tell them I was James Smith, but someone in the crowd said my name. The constable clapped hands on me, so pleased with himself he could hardly believe it."

"Who said your name? Surely everyone there was your friend, or should be."

"It was a woman, but I did not see her face."

Simon turned away for a moment, adding up the elements of the story and running a hand absently through his hair. A dead body in a locked room, officers of the law conveniently present, and a purposeful revelation of the captive's name. It was too much for coincidence. He turned back to Peto. "There is indeed a plot against you." He glanced at the door, wondering how far the scheme extended. Was a spy even now outside the cell, listening to their conversation?

Peto nodded grimly. "Someone made it look as if I killed Red John."

"To be rid of both of you."

"Exactly. John is dead. The law will deal with me. The plotter will step into my place with no one to stop him and with no blood on his hands, at least to appearances."

Simon reminded himself that Peto chose the life he led, chose to live among those to whom murder was an acceptable business practice. Surely it was not his affair to right their wrongs.

Despite that he asked, “What message would you have me carry to Pen?”

Peto looked again at the window. Seeming almost embarrassed, he said, “There is a woman at my lodgings who must be warned. She might be arrested, though she has done nothing to deserve it.”

“A woman.”

“My luck.” He gave a bitter grin. “Or so I thought.”

Simon recalled Peto’s belief that blonde women brought him good luck. Apparently this one had not. “Shall I go to her? I can say I have seen you alive and”—he indicated Peto’s bruised face—“almost well.”

Peto shifted his feet, touching his damaged face lightly. “She will do better with Pen. She is excitable and often distrustful.”

“I see. What message should he take, then?”

Peto considered. “She must go with Pen to his house. His sister will take her in, knowing I will reward her when I can.”

“Very well. I will send Pen—”

A scrape sounded at the door, and the guard peered in. “Father?”

“I have done what I could for this man,” Simon answered in a pious tone. To Peto he said, “God has heard your cries, my son. Wait patiently for his mercy.”

Peto kept a solemn expression, but his undamaged eye glinted. “Thank you, Father.”

Simon left the Tower aware of the things buzzing around him without really seeing them. The place was a bustle of activity: goods delivered by carts pulled by everything from men to goats. Visitors coming and going, many with heads lowered as if the view of the towers was bad luck. Guards stood at their posts, some watchful, some less so, as is the case when men stand all day with nothing to do but observe. No one paid any attention to Simon, and he remained deep in thought. Two of his friends were in trouble, and he had no idea how to help either, much less both. Elizabeth asked nothing of him but seemed to enjoy his visits. Peto's request was simple, and Simon resolved to visit Pen immediately.

Once he had decided his course, Simon paused for a moment to observe some boys idling nearby. Choosing one who seemed likely, he gave the lad a mission and a halfpenny. "Go to the apothecary street near the Moorgate and see the lady at the shop with the blue door. Say her husband has some business in town and will return late. She will give you something to eat for your pains." When the boy ran off in the proper direction, Simon turned toward the Thames Bridge and to Southwark.

Chapter Four

When a boy came to say that Simon was delayed in the city, Hannah felt both nervous and proud, guessing he was on some mission for the princess. Although she feared trouble, she could not fault her husband's loyalty. It was what she loved about him, part of what made him a good man.

For a while she worked in the shop, arranging the items for sale and cleaning the corners. Simon made the medicines at a table at the back of the large room, wearing a glass mask when handling the more potent substances. Once he was finished, Hannah helped him package and display them. It was she who suggested he add sweet-smelling oils to their cosmetics and common medicines when possible. She even got him to color some of the creams with henna so they were an inviting, soft pink rather than dull gray. He had done it to humor her at first, but it soon became clear that, given a choice, people bought the products that smelled and looked best.

A noise in their living area startled Hannah. She stopped to listen, but there was no further sound. Moving quickly to the curtained doorway, she peeped through. The room was as she had left it.

No. It was not. There had been four figs in a bowl on the table, two for her and two for Simon. Now there were only three.

Angry at the thief she now knew had been in their home several times, Hannah strode into the room and began a search.

A glance out the window revealed no sign of anyone outside. There was no miscreant hiding in the hearth corner or under the table. There was no one in the loft, nor the trunk where she kept their blankets. She searched the room for a hiding place she had not considered. None. Yet someone had been here. Where could that person have gone?

Going to the door, Hannah stepped outside. The day had grown almost warm, and a slight breeze ruffled her clothes as she surveyed the neighborhood. Her neighbor Catherine was at work on her vegetable plot, her back to Hannah and her face close to the ground. Two children, probably the tinsmith's twins, shrieked playfully somewhere out of sight. No one there who might have come into her house to steal from her. As she stood wondering what she was missing, Hannah's ears picked up an unusual sound from the dovecote. Several birds visible from where she stood seemed fretful. Her favorite, Guinevere, fluttered anxiously, cooing her mournful sound. Hannah approached slowly in order to avoid further frightening the birds.

The dovecote had been the work of Simon's master Carthburt, the former owner of the house. It was round, about eight feet in diameter, and raised a few feet off the ground to protect the creatures inside from predators. Its base was rough planks, which Hannah kept covered with straw to make cleaning easier. Rough, lapped boards formed the sides, enclosing all but a few feet of the circle and leaving a space for the birds to come and go. A wooden door, now propped open, provided protection for them in foul weather. Inside were roosts at various levels, along with water and feeding troughs. The steeply pitched roof was topped with a fanciful representation of a dove made of iron, its wings spread as if in flight.

Hannah's doves were like friends to her. Each had a name and a personality. Some came readily to her hand when she brought food. Others held back, somewhat shy. She approached the cote now, watching the nervous birds. They seemed almost resentful of something, and Hannah moved slowly, wondering if a fox or a cat had somehow climbed in among them.

What she saw when she peered into the dark recess was surprising. A woman lay curled along the rounded edge of the wall, her clothes covered with straw and a half-eaten fig in her hand. The interloper in Hannah's dovecote was blonde, pretty, and very advanced in pregnancy.

Southwark, and the Paris Garden section where Peto lodged, was like a stepchild to London. It was no easy matter to get there. Only one bridge crossed the Thames, and it was crowded all day with carts, animals, pedestrians, carriages, and businessmen plying their wares. Only twenty-six feet wide, the bridge was lined with over two hundred shops, each about seven feet deep, which reduced the usable space of the bridge way to about twelve feet. Divided in two to make a lane going each way, six feet of actual travel space remained. Traffic was always dense, often totally gridlocked. Crossing inch by inch, or so it seemed, and hemmed in by fellow travelers of various types and degrees of body odor, Simon saw glimpses ahead of him of the area that was London and not London, exciting and yet repugnant.

Teeming with life, Southwark was safe enough in the daytime, although he knew Hannah would crinkle her nose at the thought of his going there. There was no clear authority south of the river, and the justices of the peace and constables responsible for enforcing the law had little control. As a result, Southwark was both a wonder and a terror. Activities frowned upon in London itself—bullbaiting, plays, and prostitution—operated across the Thames almost unbothered by officialdom. Southwark provided all sorts of sights and amusements, but it was a place where one should guard his purse and his life.

It was mid-morning when he finally stepped off the crowded

bridge and entered Southwark. Parting from him at the Tower, Peto had murmured the name of the street where Penitence Brook lived. Stopping often to ask directions, Simon made his way there. As he walked, he passed idlers sitting, standing, and lying in the streets, men who eyed him as if judging where on his person his purse was secured. He avoided their eyes, looking instead at houses in various states of disrepair and decrepitude. Southwark was, these days, home to much of London's poorest housing, though it had not always been so. Fine homes once lined the river, but gradually they had been deserted by the nobility. Now, dozens of poor people dwelt in places where one wealthy family once lived.

Trades in Southwark were the same as in London and yet different. Tradesmen who could not operate under the rules of London's city fathers often took up residence in Southwark, where shoddy practices went unnoticed. In London proper, apprentices were strictly regulated, but Southwark had a surfeit of shiftless ones attached to masters who failed to oversee their behavior, professional or personal. Unemployed soldiers with no skills except killing roamed Southwark as well, looking for easy prey. And prostitutes, the "Dutch widows" once regulated by the church, these days operated freely south of the river. In short, scoundrels and idlers of all classes and backgrounds made Southwark their home, and noisy fights went almost disregarded among those who preferred continued health to a knife between the ribs.

Of course, Simon told himself as he walked, there must be respectable people and reputable businesses here. But the lack of clear authority—the city and the county argued continuously about who was responsible for the area—made Southwark a welcoming place for those outside the law and possibly outside any moral code at all.

Penitence Brook was known as a lack-wit who wandered the

streets with no apparent purpose, and there was certainly an oddness about the man that might be seen as idiocy. However, Simon knew, as Peto did, that Pen was in fact a keen observer of people. People spoke freely in front of Pen, never suspecting he reported whatever was of interest to Peto the Pope.

Navigating the warren of buildings that was Paris Garden, Simon found Pen's home, a large house that had once been grand. Its exterior appeared to have been through a minor war or two in the last decade. The front door was scarred and faded, the window glass had been removed—probably taken by the original owner when he relocated—and replaced with linen strips soaked in linseed oil. Gouges along the front wall suggested rocks had been thrown at the house, but he could only guess why that might have happened.

When he knocked at the door and asked for Pen, a razor-faced woman pointed up the stairs. "All the way to the top. And tell my cod's-head brother there's slops to be emptied." Simon tried to see a resemblance to Pen, for this must be his sister. There was some, but where Pen was thin, this woman was stout. Pen's expression was almost always benign, but the sister's was angry, as if life had never given her anything to be happy about.

He stepped inside, into darkness and the smell of leeks. Before him was a stairway that had once been open and impressive. Now it was closed in on both sides with bags, crates, baskets, and jars, apparently a storage area for inhabitants of the home. Who needed a wide staircase, after all? No farthingales here, and no lord descending with his lady daintily holding his arm. All that was needed was enough room to go up or down.

Behind the stairway, a large chimney climbed all the way to the roof. Some lucky tenants might have fireplaces, which undoubtedly meant higher rent. All the tenants, however, would benefit from the cleaner air a chimney provided. Simon had engaged a mason to add one to his own house, believing a chimney was healthier than the usual smoke-hole in the roof that left one's eyes watering and throat burning.

As he made his way up several flights of stairs, he passed through a microcosm of life among the poor. Old faces peered out doorways at him, undoubtedly grandparents charged with caring for the smallest children while parents and older children scrabbled for a living somehow. Some sat in their doorways, apparently eager for any unusual occurrence to mark the day. He noted various signs of disability: a crutch, an eye patch, even a wheeled cart where a man without legs sorted rags into piles. The sounds of children playing were everywhere, and he saw several half-naked toddlers as he passed. One young woman sat in a doorway, cradling an infant as she sang softly. She smiled as he passed, her missing front teeth ruining somewhat the image of Madonna and child.

As he approached the upper story, the noise quieted and the way narrowed. Simon had to crouch to get through. The smell of food receded, and he smelled something else, something woody. Pen's sister apparently let her brother live at the top of the house in exchange for simple labors, but her manner had not suggested he was in any way welcome. She might have a generous heart under that rough exterior, but navigating the rickety stairs, Simon figured Pen's allotted space was too cramped to bring in much rent anyway.

Unwilling to simply appear in the space the man called home, Simon stopped a few steps down and called, "Pen?"

A face appeared, peering at him nearsightedly. Then he heard a cackle of surprise. "Master Simon! So many years since we have met! Come up, do! Come up!"

Simon did as asked and entered a single room with walls that sloped abruptly. There was space to stand upright only in the center. It was lit, although poorly, by an octagon-shaped window of perhaps ten inches in diameter. Under the slope of one wall was a heavy-footed bed too grand and too large for the room. Beside it a stool, where Pen sat. Between his feet was an ancient, broken bucket holding what appeared to be carving paraphernalia: a knife, several pieces of wood, and a small plane for smoothing. Stacked against the opposite wall were several mismatched but tightly lidded jars in a neat row. Each had a smear of color on its lid, and Simon guessed the jars contained paint of various shades.

On a peg hung a leather cap and a long coat that had been patched many times. Other than that and the rough blanket spread across the bed, the room lacked fabric of any kind, no softening pillows, curtains, rugs or clothing. Far from the fireplace and with only one tiny window, the place was sure to be cold in winter and stifling in summer. No wonder Pen spent most of the day moving from tavern to tavern.

Simon's old friend moved to sit on the bed, indicating the stool. "Make it a comfort," he insisted, bobbing his head and waving his hands in his excitement at having a visitor.

As Simon turned to sit down, he saw on the wall behind the stairs an array of wooden birds, each hung from a peg by a thread sent through a tiny hole on its back. Meticulously carved and carefully painted, they seemed ready to spring to life and fly around the room.

"You carved these birds?"

"It passes the time," Pen replied, looking at them disinterestedly.

"But how do you do such fine work?"

"There is a fellow on the second floor who deals in this and that, sometimes in wood. He gives me bits of soft alder or pine." He shrugged. "I like the feel of it, and the birds seem to want to come out from beneath their wooden shell."

"They are wondrous fine. You might sell them and earn

yourself some money."

Pen shrugged. "What would I do with money, Master? I have a roof over my head." He chuckled before going on in the slightly slushy manner of speaking Simon recalled from the early days of their association. "In fact, it is so close overhead I may touch it, should I doubt the fact. I am fed well enough. Whatever else she might be, my sister is an excellent cook, and there is enough to eat if not plenty. And I have friends like you. I have no need of more."

Simon was embarrassed to be called this man's friend when he had made no effort to contact him for years. After brief excuses for his absence, he told Pen his reason for coming. The man's homely face took on a serious expression. "Red John is dead?"

"Yes."

"A likely fellow, he was, fond of women and drinking and laughing." It seemed the most positive eulogy a criminal was apt to receive. "I will do as Peto asks," Pen said, adding with a glance out the window, "though I usually stay well away from that one."

"Peto's woman? Why, Pen?"

The answer came in a whisper. "She is a witch!" Pen looked over his shoulder as if the woman or her avatar might be standing behind him.

"A witch?"

Pen's eyes went wide. "A creature from hell, Master! One minute she is nice as you please, and most fair, too. The next she is like to scare a man to death with her screams and her terrible gaze." He made the sign against the evil eye. "Even Peto treads lightly in her presence."

Simon could hardly believe his ears. "Peto cowed by a woman?"

Pen made a wafting gesture as if to erase his last statement.

"I do not mean he is feared of her, for Peto fears nothing. Still, it is my thinking she has him under a spell of some sort."

"He abides a woman's moods?" Peto did not seem the type to stand for peevish tantrums.

Pen squinted one eye almost closed. "In truth, I do not think he sees the worst of her temper. But I am a fool. She has no use for me, no need to keep my affection."

Simon marveled at the depth of Pen's understanding of people, belied by simple looks and protestations of idiocy. "Do you think the woman false?"

"Oh, no, Master! Not false! Almost crazed with love for Peto, she is. Anyone who does him ill should beware her wrath." His eyes turned to the carved birds as if seeking peace. "But she do fly into rages." He muttered a repetition. "Such rages!"

Simon could not help being curious. "Shall I do as Peto asks, then?"

Pen rose and dusted wood shavings from his lap and backside. "No. I will see to it."

Simon hesitated. "Your sister said you have work to do."

Pen let out a high, cackling laugh Simon remembered well. "How should a lack-wit do as he is bidden, Master Simon? And if I am not a lack-wit, then I needs must find employment and live as witty folk do. I tell you, my friend, I am not for it."

As they started down the stairs together, Simon marveled again at the detail and variety of the birds on Pen's wall. To have an art such as that in one's fingers and to care so little about what it might bring him! Pen was indeed a different sort of man from most.

At the bottom of the stairs, Pen's sister stood, arms akimbo and face like a thundercloud. "Where are you off to?"

"Simon here has brought me important business, Judith."

"Pah! More likely he has enough money in his pockets for a bowl of ale!"

"I will not be long, and by sundown you will have no cause to complain of me."

"No cause!" Spittle escaped Judith's lips as she glared at her brother. "You've more thinking to do if that is what you think, Penitence Brook! I never saw such a man for slipping away when there's work to be done!"

Her comments followed them out of the house, and Simon guessed Judith never lacked complaints or words to give voice to them. For his part, Pen paid no mind whatsoever. Simon wanted to ask why he stayed with his sister when his welcome was so slight. But then, he reminded himself, Judith might have reason to be angry if Pen took his household duties as casually every day as he had today.

As they walked the crowded streets together, dodging tradesmen and skirting buildings that had expanded into the street itself, Simon asked, "Who might have laid this trap for Peto?"

Pen waved a hand as if to swat the question away. "I am not one you should ask such things, Master. You know I am a fool, with a fool's wit and a fool's face."

Simon stopped, grasping Pen's arm so he had to stop, too. "I know you are a cunning judge of men." Recalling Pen's assessment of Peto's companion, he added, "And women."

Pen seemed both distressed and pleased at the estimation of his abilities. "I cannot answer questions of who and why, Master." He leaned toward Simon. "It is not safe."

"Peto is your friend, Pen."

The man's expression turned sorrowful, and his gaze dropped. "He is." His next comment seemed unrelated to what had gone before. "I know where a certain ship is moored. Its crew, Spaniards all, waits for Peto, who was to meet them on a certain matter of business."

After a moment, Simon made the jump and got Pen's meaning. "The men on this ship might know something of this crime?"

Pen shrugged. "They speak naught but their own language. How would they know?"

"But they would know your face, recognize you as Peto's friend?"

"They would."

"Then you must go to them and report what has happened. Will you do that?"

Pen considered, his undersized nose twitching slightly. "I will."

Simon felt a sense of relief. Peto's fate did not rest entirely on his shoulders. "When will you seek them out?"

"Tomorrow after dark was the time Peto was to meet them. Today I will find the woman and see her safe in Judith's spare room."

Simon smiled. "Does this woman not have a name, Pen?"

Pen searched his memory. "I think it is Frances."

"Frances. She sounds a proper lady." In response Pen raised a doubtful eyebrow.

"Now," Simon said. "To learn more about last night's murder, where should I begin?"

Pen shook his head vigorously. "It is not your affair, Master."

"Peto is a prisoner. It might help if I discover what I can." Simon pressed his lips together. "Remember, I have done this sort of thing before. I need only a starting point."

Pen pursed his lips in disapproval but advised, "Go to the Bull's Horn if you must and see it for yourself. They will not shut you out if you have a coin or two."

They parted at the end of the lane. Simon was disappointed at Pen's reluctance to speculate on who had framed Peto, but he understood. In this world, strong men survived and weaker men made themselves invisible.

Pen had pointed the way to the Bull's Horn before setting off for Peto's lodgings. Simon pulled his cap low over his brow and headed for the scene of the crime. It could not hurt, he told himself, to learn what he could by listening to those who had been there.

Chapter Five

"Who are you?"

The woman stared at Hannah for a moment before replying. "Janet. My name is Janet."

"And how do you come to be in my dovecote, Janet?"

The answer was a sob, and from there things deteriorated. The woman's shoulders began to shake and she covered her face with her hands, bawling like a lost calf.

"Here, now, stop," Hannah said. When that had no effect, she repeated it once and then again, until it became a soft crooning. Lifting herself onto the dovecote floor, she scooted sideways until she could touch the woman's shoulder. When she did, the other fell on her, weeping as if she would never stop.

"I'm sorry, I'm sorry!" finally came through.

Hannah patted her back as if she were a child. "It's all right."

She sat up, her tear-streaked face close to Hannah's. "But I t-t-took your bread and I ate your stew and I stole your fig!"

Hannah smiled. "Because you were hungry."

"Y-yes."

"You had only to ask, and we would have offered that and more."

Blue eyes searched Hannah's. "I didn't know. I was afraid to ask."

"Come inside, and we shall talk."

The woman—she was little more than a girl, really—looked down at her filthy clothes. "Inside?" Hay and bird droppings clung to her everywhere, even in her hair.

"I will find something you can wear while I clean your dress."

Inside, Hannah located a loose shirt of Simon's almost ready for the ragbag. Despite its condition, it covered the woman's expanded belly and protected her modesty. Soon she sat near the fire in her underskirt, the shirt billowing almost to her knees, and worked with a brush and a wet cloth to untangle and clear her hair of dirt. Taking up the dress the girl had dropped on the floor, Hannah went to a bucket by the fire, her source of warm water, and poured some into a bowl. Locating a cake of soap and a soft brush, she began cleaning the spots from the dress.

The fabric was of good quality, and Hannah guessed it had been given to her uninvited guest by someone above her in station. There were places on the bodice where decorative pieces had been removed, as such things were deemed unfitting for a commoner's clothing.

As she worked, Hannah eyed her guest. What had made a woman in the last days of pregnancy, a woman who had probably served in one of the great houses of London, go into hiding in their dovecote? Sensing the girl would not explain until she felt safe, Hannah did not press. Instead, setting the dress near the fire so the wet spots would dry, she cut some dried meat and put it on a clean square of cloth with a bit of cheese. "Here. Eat this."

Janet took the food eagerly but ate, Hannah noticed, with decorum, biting delicately and chewing daintily. She reminded Hannah of those she had served at Hampstead Castle, adding weight to her theory that Janet had observed ways of the gentry, possibly even the nobility.

This was further demonstrated when Janet finished her meal and carefully wiped her mouth with the cloth. "I thank you," she said, giving Hannah a shaky smile.

"You can repay me by telling how you came to be in this state." Hannah held the girl's gaze. "I will not judge you. I only want to help."

Looking at her lap, Janet began, "I worked in a fine house; I'll not say which one." Her lips set in stubborn defiance, but Hannah merely nodded. No use pressing for names at this point.

"His Lordship's son took a liking to me, and I was foolish enough to give in to his talk of love. When I became pregnant, I hid it as long as I could, but Her Ladyship noticed and became furious. She sent him to their estate in Lincolnshire, to oversee the planting, she said." Her tone turned angry. "But as soon as he was gone, she sent me away, boasting that she would tell him I ran off with the real father of my child."

Hannah tried to think of something encouraging to say, but all that came out was a murmur of sympathy. How could a serving girl believe she might prevail in such a situation?

Janet turned to Hannah, her face a mask of despair. "She was so cruel! She said if she ever clapped eyes on me again, she would have me sent to prison." Tears rolled down her cheeks unheeded, and she covered her face with smooth, white hands. The rest was unintelligible.

It was a common enough tale. Illegitimate children were handled in different ways. Sometimes the pregnant woman was paid off and sent away. Sometimes the child was raised in the household, an odd mixture of servant and scion. Apparently this family had decided to brand Janet a liar and frighten her into keeping silent.

Hannah's heart went out to the girl. Whatever her mistakes, she was reduced to wandering the streets, stealing food and sleeping in outbuildings. And from the looks of her, the child was due any day. How could any family care so little what happened to a grandchild?

Reaching across the distance between them, Hannah touched Janet's arm. "You will be safe now," she said firmly. "You and your baby are here with us."

★ ★ ★ ★ ★

The Bull's Horn was crowded with people, though the sun was not yet directly overhead. The host, Saddler, obviously reveled in the custom—and the attention—last night's murder had brought. On the way Simon had worried about how he would get the man to tell his story, but Saddler did nothing *but* tell it, over and over. Tall and thin everywhere except for his middle, which pouched as if a puppy was napping beneath his shirt, he stood with one foot on the edge of the hearth, arms resting on his raised knee.

"Breathed his last 'fore I got to 'im," he said solemnly. "I know a corpse when I see one."

"Poor John," a woman said, wiping her eye. "Always a good time when he were nearby."

"His stories was the best," a man chimed in. "Had a way with the telling."

Someone brought Saddler back to his account. "Had 'is throat cut, did he?"

"Head was almost separated from the body," their host said, his tone dark but his eyes shining. "Sliced it right well, our man did."

Simon noted Saddler avoided speaking Peto's name. There seemed to be an almost superstitious feeling in the crowd, for no one else said it aloud, either.

"What did you do?" said a young woman whose suggestive clothing and painted face could not hide her youth. "A murder in your storeroom!" She shuddered, and a man standing nearby moved closer to her. From his clothing and the calculating look on his face, Simon guessed he was a bawde, a pimp interested in adding to his collection a whore who offered at least the appearance of innocence.

"The constable and his men was in here, having a pint. Soon as I saw Red John in that awful state, I called for the law, as a man should." Saddler's emphasis on the last few words did not ring true, and Simon wondered what would have happened had the constable not been on the scene. A body dumped in the Thames brought no trouble to a less-than-honest businessman, which Saddler undoubtedly was. He almost certainly knew what sort of meetings went on in his alehouse but was willing to look the other way. That is, he *had* been willing to, until the meeting between Peto the Pope and Red John resulted in murder.

A young man asked the question Simon wanted to ask. "No one went in there before?"

"Here's how it went," Saddler said, bringing one hand to his chin and rubbing the stubbly beard there. "Red John and Christo Bannon came wanting a place where John could get a bit of rest. John went in there on his own two legs, all alone. I looked in once to see if he wanted something to eat, but when I heard him snoring, I shut the door. That was the last time I saw him alive." Saddler waxed dramatic, dragging the last sentence out and lengthening his already long face with supposed grief. "I don't suppose he cut his own throat now, d'you?"

"Bannon went on his way, then?"

"He did. Said he'd see a certain person was told John had returned."

"And we know who that was." The speaker turned to those around him with brows raised. "Bannon is his cousin, but he never knew there was murder to be done!"

The host took the tale back from the interloper with affronted dignity. "Bannon went, all right, but not without effort. His knee is plaguing him again." He leaned forward, lowering his voice. "For two days now, he's walked like a duck with piles." The audience laughed appreciatively, though Simon noticed a few looked around as if wary of the joke.

When the laughter died, Saddler returned to the subject of murder, repeating, "Red John was well when he went into that room."

"Maybe someone was hiding in there and killed Red John." It was the young woman again. She seemed unwilling to believe Peto was capable of murdering a friend.

"There was nobody in there, and I'll tell you how I know it. Bannon himself looked the place over before he left Red John alone in there." Saddler sniffed in mild disgust. "As if my eyes wasn't good enough, he had to go in and see for himself the room was safe."

"But it wasn't," a man with an unnaturally red face observed with an air of wisdom incongruous with such an obvious statement.

Once again the innocent whore offered an alternative to Peto as murderer. "There's the back. Perhaps Red John let someone in through that door."

Saddler looked disgusted as he ticked his reasons off on his fingers. "First, John was asleep. I said that already. Second, nobody knew he was in there, did they? Just me, the wife, Bannon, and . . . his cousin." Saddler pressed a third and final finger. "We all know who crouched over the body, his hands wet with Red John's blood. Still warm, he was." Even the detached Saddler shivered at the memory, and several customers shifted their feet nervously.

"But Peto did not seem the sort to do such a thing." The girl's comment sent a wave of discomfort through the room, either because she'd said aloud the name of Red John's accused killer or because others agreed with her opinion.

Saddler looked around the room, lowered brows almost meeting over his large nose. "Some o' you were here and could see that door." He pointed to an ill-fitting rectangle at the back of the public room. "Once Red John went in there, no one came out. Only one man went in." He glared around the room, and several heads nodded in agreement. "It had to be him that killed Red John who was his friend and a good friend to many of us."

He waited, and Simon felt the crowd adjusting its loyalties. These people knew Peto the Pope. Many, he guessed, had benefited from his enterprises. But if he murdered a man they apparently liked, almost before their eyes, who would defend him?

Simon wanted a look at the room where Red John had died. There had to be a way for someone to have hidden there and taken the man's life as he slept. He did not approach Saddler directly but took a seat at a corner table, ordering cider and a bowl of the stew that bubbled on the hearth. A girl of twelve or so served him, and he made innocent conversation, identifying himself as an apprentice new to the area. Although Simon was old to be an apprentice, it was not unknown for a person to fall short of his master's expectations and remain in or even be dismissed from apprenticeship. Such men often ended up in Southwark, working for masters not quite so particular.

The lentil stew was surprisingly good. As he ate, Simon picked up a conversation between two women a short distance away. One he heard clearly, since her voice was shrill. The other's tone was lower, and he could only pick out a word here and there.

"—shame he is dead," the louder voice was saying when Simon tuned in. "He was ever light company, and I shall miss him."

Simon heard a few words of the other's opinion: "—murder—" and then "—hang for it."

"Mayhap he should," the other said. "Even he should not be free to kill as he likes."

Next came a question he did not hear, but the first woman answered, "There are others who can do business. Peto was once a good man, but look what he has become!" With a click of her tongue she added, "To cut a friend's throat, and John such a jolly fellow."

After a while, Saddler left the room. His listeners wandered away, some out the door, some to the hearth or to the spigot. The girl came and took Simon's empty bowl away, and he asked for more cider. When she returned he asked, "Were you here when the murder happened?"

"Mother works the nights." Rolling her eyes in a gesture typical of children protected by their parents from things they would like to see, she added, "Father does not want me here when the drinking starts in earnest."

Simon understood the man's concern. A young, pretty daughter was likely to bring trouble, and likely to get into trouble as well.

He glanced around the room. Saddler was not in sight. "Might I see the spot?"

The girl's eyes widened. "Why?"

Making a quick assessment of her character, he said, "Curiosity, I suppose. I understand that the murderer is well known for his many crimes."

It was the right approach. "They say he was something, once," the girl said with the air of one too young to appreciate anything more than six months in the past. "Of late—" She paused. "Men get old, you know, and cannot do as they once did."

Simon tried to hide his shock. Peto? Old? His reputation had indeed suffered if those who once admired him thought he had lost both his power and his sense of honor.

The girl glanced around the room, assuring her father was not present. "Come. You can help me with the kegs."

She moved briskly toward the storeroom, and Simon followed with some misgiving. Moving a keg required two strong arms. Having only one, he would have to admit he could not help. At least he might get a look at the storeroom before he had to confess his disability.

It turned out to be unnecessary. The girl had barely opened the door when her mother called her into the public room. With an impatient "Tsk," she left to see what was wanted.

The storeroom was not large, hardly more than a rough shed. It was square, but not perfectly so, and the walls to the left and right were lined with shelves filled with supplies. The place smelled of earth and vegetables. In the center of the room was a table with two rough benches shoved beneath it. Behind it, in the corner on the right, was a primitive bed, a pile of rushes stacked on a rope frame. There was no blanket spread over it, and Simon imagined the constable's men carrying the corpse out wrapped in rough wool. At one end, a dark stain showed on the rough plank floor. Here Red John had lain, mortally wounded, when Peto entered. Within seconds, he had died. Who had killed him?

The room had no real windows, although a small, square hole cut high in the walls on either end let in some daylight. Each was less than a foot square and covered with greased paper, which was undisturbed. No one had come in or out that way.

In the building's back wall, opposite the doorway where he stood, was a second door, the one Peto had been unable to open. Simon moved to examine it. A latch on the inside was designed to fall into place when the door closed. The outside had no latch at all, and the reason for that was easy to guess. Someone inside the storeroom had to open the door so thieves were prevented from coming in at night and helping themselves to Saddler's goods.

So why was Peto unable to exit through this door last night? What had kept it closed?

Opening the door, Simon stepped through, holding the rough wood frame to keep it from closing and shutting him outside. Against the building a few feet away was a stack of logs, firewood left to season. The logs were of various lengths, some only two feet long, others as long as eight feet. One of the mid-sized ones might make a convenient brace to hold the door closed. Bending close, Simon found a scrape in the weathered wood that appeared recent. He was right. A log set against the door had kept Peto inside with a corpse.

The constable had looked into the room, seen a corpse and a man with bloody hands, and taken at face value what he saw. It was hard to hold the man to blame. Peto was a known criminal; ergo, he murdered Red John. Knowing Peto, Simon looked at other possibilities.

If a man had hidden somewhere in the room, he could have killed Red John as he slept and then escaped through this door, blocking it closed so Peto was unable to leave the same way. When the outcry inside told him the crime had been discovered, the killer would have taken the block away from the door, thrown it back on the pile with the others, and gone on his way down the dark alley, leaving Peto in the hands of the law, an apparent murderer with no other explanation for what had happened. The trap was well planned.

Returning to the storeroom, Simon began looking for possible hiding places, moving sacks of grain and sending at least one mouse squealing and scrabbling for cover. His hopes soon fell. There was no spot where a man could have hidden. The shelves were open and filled with goods. A bin in one corner was almost empty, but it was not big enough for a man to hide in. Was it possible someone crouched in a corner, under the table?

Bending down to examine the space, he could not believe it. The table itself was low, small, and set close to the well-stocked shelves. Only a midget could have hidden beneath it, and even then, he would have been easily visible when Red John entered the room. Simon sighed in frustration. How was it done?

"Here, now! What are you doing in here?"

Saddler stood in the doorway. Behind him, his daughter peeped fearfully under his arm.

Simon took a step toward the host, though his instinct was to do the opposite. "Master, I had such an idea, and I had to see if it might work." He waved a hand at the room behind him. "You must give tours! Charge a penny to let people come in and see where the murder took place, while you tell the story of how you discovered it and caused the arrest of"—he paused dramatically—"a certain person." He grasped the landlord's arm, acting the part of a gushing voyeur. "With your skill in telling and that horrible stain, you could make a nice sum. The very place where *he* was captured." He widened his eyes and nodded slyly at the man.

Saddler glared into the dark corner. "They wouldn't pay, would they?"

"Think how many came today to hear how it happened. Won't they pay to see the spot?"

The man's face was like a book, and Simon easily read his thoughts. Saddler was kicking himself for having told his story for free all morning. He was probably relieved his wife had not yet gotten around to scrubbing away the stain. His lips moved, and Simon guessed he was already rehearsing his patter for when the customers started showing up, making himself even more of a hero than he had done earlier.

The daughter threw Simon a grateful look. He had managed to get himself out of trouble without getting her into it.

"Did Red John often stay here, in this room?"

The question derailed Saddler's plans for future income. "Who are you, anyway?"

"I recently found work in Tinker's Lane," Simon lied. "My father says I am too curious, but I like to know how things happen. And that is how you will make money on this, by telling the story in detail. You must tell it from start to finish, building excitement until you throw open this door"—he banged said door against the wall dramatically—"and show them the place where it happened."

Brows knitted, Saddler fell once more into thought, considering the prospects. Moving past him, Simon headed for the door before the host thought to ask what was in it for an unknown customer.

Chapter Six

Hannah showed her guest the apothecary shop, proudly pointing out the different medicines for sale. "You might help out, if you stay. Each day we start by scrubbing the tables with vinegar, to clean them. And there's sweeping and dusting as well as putting the medicines Simon makes into packets for our customers."

Janet seemed eager. "I can help with the medicines. Show me what to do."

"You might put these digestive powders into papers," Hannah suggested, choosing something that was not strenuous. "We pour so much into a paper and then twist it closed, like this." She demonstrated several times. Janet thought she could do it, so Hannah moved to another task, pleased her guest wanted to earn a place in the household.

But after only a few minutes, Janet's voice rose in shrill protest. "I can't do it!" she complained. "I've spilled it all over!"

It was true. There was powder on the table, on the floor, and on Janet's protruding belly. There was even a dusting of it on her nose where she had rubbed her face with a hand. Hannah tried not to laugh. "It takes practice." She swept the spilled powder into her hand, returning the gritty residue to its original jar.

"I'm so clumsy these days!" Janet's sunny mood was gone. "I'm as big as a farmer's cow, and I'll never be pretty again."

"You are lovely now, but you will soon be yourself again.

Here, you sweep the floor and I'll finish the medicines."

Janet took the broom with obvious reluctance and made only a few desultory movements. She watched Hannah's deft completion of the task with little apparent interest in doing better next time. Instead she asked, "Where is your husband?"

"He had business in the city." Hannah frowned. What would Simon think of Janet's presence? She hoped he would understand there was nothing else she could have done. How could a woman learning midwifery turn away a desperate mother on her very doorstep?

Hannah had become skilled at helping with childbirth over the last two years, working beside an elderly local woman until she was able to work alone with confidence. Along with the midwife's experience, Hannah had Simon, who shared what he knew of practical matters such as controlling bleeding. Having read widely from respected medical texts, he rejected practices that had no rational basis. He did not advocate pressing a hangman's noose to the head for a headache or wearing the skin of a donkey to cure arthritis. Simon believed in the healing properties of plants but lamented the fact that not enough was known about their dangers and their efficacy. From his apothecary master, Carthburt, he had learned a healthy skepticism for magic charms like healing stones for removing warts or red cloth for healing the plague. From Jacob Maldon he learned the human side of medicine, and so encouraged Hannah to consider the emotional aspects of healing as well as available physic.

"My father advises speaking calmly and moving deliberately to soothe a patient," Simon told her. After attending several births, Hannah saw the logic of it. If a woman believed she was in good hands, things usually went better. If she could not have children of her own, Hannah found comfort in helping others come through their travail.

She resolved to keep Janet calm. The girl had many things to worry about, and her emotions seemed to bubble close to the surface. Hannah was certain she could help her, and Janet would be a different person once she held her child in her arms.

Janet's current thoughts were not about the coming birth at all. She leaned on the broom, that task forgotten as she regarded Hannah speculatively. "Is your man a good lover?"

Hannah was so surprised that at first, she could think of nothing to say. Such things were not discussed among the people she knew, although she recalled some women in Elizabeth's household whispering comparisons of men they had lain with. Hannah had no comparisons but was sure Simon was the best man in the world. Setting some jars on the shelf with more force than necessary, she responded, "We are very happy together."

"Mine is a wonder." Janet rolled her eyes suggestively, but her expression turned rueful. "When next he sees me I will no longer be swollen like a milkweed pod."

"Don't talk that way," Hannah said, shocked at Janet's tone.

The girl was unrepentant, casting a scornful glance at her bulging stomach. "Why would a man want to look at this? Why would he not turn to another woman?"

"But it must be this way," Hannah began. "You will—"

Suddenly Janet put a hand on her belly, and her forehead puckered. "Ow!"

"Is the child kicking?"

"No, this is different. It's like—" Janet looked down in horror as a wet spot spread across her skirt. She looked to Hannah, fear in her eyes.

"No need to worry," Hannah soothed as she mentally listed the things that had to be done without delay. "It is only the babe, telling us it is on the way."

★ ★ ★ ★ ★

The constable who had arrested Peto was, according to a succession of people, some amused and some disgusted, hardly a sterling example of his profession. The officer spent most of his time "with his nose in a pot of ale," as one man put it. An hour after leaving the Bull's Horn, he found the constable at another alehouse, lending credence to the observer's words. The alehouse had no lettering on its sign, simply a board cut in the shape of a mug topped with foam. Even those who could not read got the message.

His name was Jenkins, and he was not a bad sort unless a person expected strong upholding of the law and vigorous investigation of crime. Jenkins apparently saw his role as more of a figurehead, appointed to provide the appearance of order.

"Oh, aye," he answered when Simon asked if he was indeed the man who arrested Peto the Pope. His manner revealed pride, a bit of hero worship, and a great love of morbid gossip. "O' course, I didn't know at first it was him." He settled in to telling his story, wriggling his shoulders and leaning toward his listener. "We nosed out that smugglers were meeting at the Bull's Horn, so we went there and waited to see who showed. We couldn't know one of them meant for the other to die." Jenkins snapped his fingers. "Red John, his name was. As dishonest as they come, but they say he liked the ladies and a pint with his friends." He investigated the mug before him and found it empty. "They say he was willing to buy a pint, as well."

Taking the hint, Simon ordered a round. "So you knew R— the man was in that room?"

"I did not. I heard it would benefit me to be at the Bull's Horn last evening, that's all."

"Who told you that?"

The constable's lips pulled tight. "I have my sources."

"And no one went into the room until the man you arrested did?"

"Exactly so." Jenkins took a long drink and belched a cloud of stale breath in Simon's direction.

"And you could see the storeroom door from where you sat?"

"I could. The only one who went in was this thin whip of a man, all dressed in black. I noted it, o' course, but we waited to see if other criminals might fall into our net. In the meantime, Saddler discovered the crime."

"And was the host surprised at what he found?"

"Oh, aye! White as a sheet he was." Jenkins slapped Simon's arm playfully. "Whether 'cause a man was murdered or 'cause he saw no way to keep his house out of it, I can't say."

"So you arrested the man in black. How did you learn his name?"

"Why a woman there said it, plain as plain. She was shocked, y'know, and she says, 'Peto, you didn't kill Red John!' O' course he had."

"Who was the woman?"

Jenkins frowned at the apparent inanity of the question. "I don't recall." He thought about it, scratching the scalp under the leather cap he wore. "Red haired, if I remember correct." He went back to the part of the story that interested him. "Once I knew the killer was Peto the Pope, I made sure to keep good hold of him. They say he is like butter and slips through the law's fingers every time. I sent him to the Tower where they'll keep him locked up tight." Jenkins took another swallow and said proudly, "He did not slip through my fingers. That he did not."

Hannah insisted that Janet lie down on the bed. Her pains came in waves only a few minutes apart. When she had made the girl comfortable, Hannah went about readying the room. She stoked the fire, for a birthing place must be as warm as possible. Next, she brought down some clean linen cloths from the loft and darkened the room by closing the curtains. Luckily, she had no customers that afternoon, for she would have ignored their calls for service. Her mind was fully focused on the coming child.

A sense of regret dogged Hannah's thoughts. She and Simon had discussed a birthing chair and agreed they should have one, but they had seen no need to hurry. Now she wished they had, for she wanted Janet to have the best chance for a quick and trouble-free experience. A birthing chair, with its cutout hole and its upright back, would have been just the thing. Much better than lying in a bed.

When Janet was between pains Hannah went into the shop, where she picked out a jar of almond oil and a poultice to help the process. She was as ready as could be, she thought, returning to the girl's side.

For some time, the only indication when a contraction came was a brief frown on Janet's pretty face. Finally, however, she took in a deep breath and held it, her eyes squeezed shut and her lips taut. "Relax," Hannah said, stroking her cheek gently. "The babe comes more easily if you remain calm."

Janet did not seem able to do as Hannah said. As the pains increased in severity and frequency, she tossed from side to side, howling when the contractions reached their height and panting and groaning as they eased.

Hannah tried to take her mind off the pain, at least temporarily, by asking questions. "Tell me about the place where you worked. What was your place there?"

"The kitchens." Janet's forehead shone with sweat. "I was a scullery maid."

"I was once in such a position," Hannah said. "I know how it is."

"Really?" Still panting, Janet turned to Hannah doubtfully.

"But you have your own house, and a shop."

"I was lucky enough to meet Simon," Hannah told her. "Now we have everything we want—except what you will have very soon."

Another pain began, and Janet's voice became strained. "What's that?"

"Why, a child." As Janet's grip tightened on her hand, Hannah came to a decision that felt absolutely right. "I will have to speak to my husband, of course, but I would like it if you and your babe stay here. We will keep you safe, and you will share your child with us. It could work out well for everyone."

There was no reply for some time, as pain possessed the girl once more. When the spasm eased, she released Hannah's hand, lying back on the bed. "I would like that." Her tone was odd, her expression almost smug. She must have mistaken it, Hannah thought, for another pain came, and Janet gripped her hand tightly, teeth set. Her screams came through, all the same.

The birth proceeded quickly after that, and it was just over an hour from the time Janet's water broke until Hannah handed the child to its mother, wrapped in a clean bit of cloth. The little girl Janet held against her body seemed healthy and content. Once she felt her mother's heartbeat again, she went to sleep, accepting the world without any sign of fear or distress. With practiced movements, Hannah gently shifted mother and child aside, replacing the blanket under them with a clean one.

While Janet rested after her labor, Hannah made a spot on the floor next to the hearth for her and the baby. It was too much to expect Janet to climb up to the loft tonight, but she would make a place up there for them in the morning. When she recovered, Janet would have privacy.

Hannah tiptoed over to look at the newborn. She was so very small! Tufts of brown hair covered her head, sticking out every which way. Hannah settled one of them into place with a petting motion, feeling the silky softness. A miracle, and she had helped. She pulled a chair up by the fire and sat, watching mother and daughter sleep. Before she knew it, she too dozed.

The baby's cries woke her some time later, and Hannah went to the bed. Janet awoke slowly, a frown on her face. "What?"

"Your daughter is hungry." Bringing some extra pillows from the foot of the bed, Hannah helped Janet sit up and arrange herself so the child could feed. She seemed slightly repelled by the process, but the baby went to work, feeding greedily.

Pulling back the curtain that enclosed the bed, Hannah showed Janet the place she had made near the fireplace for her and the baby. The new mother's brow crinkled in a petulant frown. "The floor will be hard." She paused, glanced at Hannah, and began again in a different tone. "It will be uncomfortable for the baby."

"I can get some straw to put under it," Hannah suggested, a little disappointed that her providence was not better received. "As soon as you are able to climb, there is a pallet in the loft for you and your child."

Janet's lips tightened as she glanced at the ladder leading to the half story above. She said nothing, but she settled herself firmly into Hannah's bed, the contented child at her breast.

Chapter Seven

Simon knew he should turn homeward, but he was caught up in the search for information. According to Peto, a boy had brought news of Red John's return to Southwark. Saddler heard Christo Bannon tell Red John he would send word to someone. It seemed logical to Simon that Bannon had sent the boy to Peto, but he wanted to know for sure.

Returning to the Bull's Horn, he was amused to find his suggestion had already been put into action. Saddler stood before a small but attentive group in the doorway of the storeroom, explaining last night's events. Having already heard the story, Simon ordered a bowl of cider from the host's daughter, who seemed willing to talk, or at least willing to delay returning to her work. He led the conversation to the identity of the boy who might have carried news of Red John's arrival to Peto the Pope.

"His name is William," she said. "You will usually find him at the stables across the street this time of day."

William was indeed in the stable, combing a horse as he ran his hand along its back and talked softly to it, assuring the beast he meant it no harm. Simon watched for a moment, taking in the musty, somehow comforting smell of hay, oats, and horse sweat.

"Are you one who takes messages for Peto the Pope?" A fearful look crossed the boy's face when he turned to find a stranger asking questions. Simon hastened to reassure him. "I merely want to know how he was called to the Bull's Horn last night."

When William hesitated, Simon took a penny from his pocket and held it out. "I promise you, no harm will come to you if you tell me, nor to Peto."

William thought about it, his eyes on the penny. "I never told a lie," he asserted. "He said tell him Red John is waiting at the Bull's Horn. That's what I did."

"And who gave you this message to deliver?"

"His cousin," the boy responded. "Bannon said Red John had returned to town, and Peto should meet him at the Bull's Horn after dark."

"You did well," Simon gave the boy the penny and turned back toward the alehouse. Bannon seemed to be an important part of what had happened last night. He'd escorted Red John to the alehouse. He'd sent word to Peto. He might have only been doing what he was supposed to do, but Simon wondered exactly what type of man Peto's cousin was.

Pen was standing outside the Bull's Horn when he returned, distress evident in his manner. He did not seem to notice the people who pushed him this way and that as they passed. Pulling Simon aside, he whispered, "I hoped you might still be on this side of the river, Master Simon. Peto's woman has gone missing."

"Missing?"

"She is not at their lodgings. The girl there said she had gone to a midwife in Millwick, but I went to the place and no one there ever heard of her."

"Could she have heard of Peto's arrest and gone into hiding?"

Pen glared at the ground, shaking his head so that his grizzled hair flopped forward. "She was to come to my house if there was trouble, but Judith has not seen her."

Why had Frances not done as Peto instructed? "Are you

certain this woman would have had nothing to do with Peto's arrest?"

"Half crazy with love for him she is," Pen insisted. "She would never do him harm."

Simon chewed his lip. "I suppose she might have left London, fearing arrest."

Pen considered it. "Perhaps it is as well if she has." He shrugged. "I'm not sure my sister would have abided the woman in her house. The two would not have done well together!"

Simon was surprised. "Yet you said Peto tolerated her moods?"

"Such women are difficult, he says." Pen frowned. "Her absence will try his mind."

"We must hope there is word of her before long." Having no other ideas about Peto's woman and her present location, Simon took up a new topic. "Do you think Peto's cousin might have hatched this plot against him?"

The reaction, Pen's terrified glance at those nearby who might have overheard, was enough to tell Simon that was exactly what Pen thought. "Come away, Master!" he said urgently, turning like a frightened deer and heading away from the alehouse. Moving as quickly as his distinctive gait allowed, Pen led Simon to an open area on the riverbank where children playfully splashed each other with cold, dirty water. He chose a spot near a small clump of trees, surveying the area to be sure there was no one nearby.

Satisfied, he finally spoke what was on his mind. "For months, Bannon has been turning folk against Peto in a sly manner. I believe he killed Red John, though I can't say how, and arranged for Peto to hang for it. Once Peto is gone, Bannon, being his kinsman and a fearsome sort, will take over the business without much trouble at all."

"Why did you not tell me this at the outset?"

Pen cast another glance around them. "It is worth a man's life to speak of such things."

Simon believed Pen, though he couldn't see how Bannon had accomplished the crime. "We must stop him."

Pen's grimace revealed he'd feared Simon would take this path. "Master—"

Simon interrupted the warning with a question. "What do you know of Bannon?"

Moving nervously from one foot to the other, Pen weighed the options. Finally, he sighed, probably accepting that Simon was Peto's only hope. "Bannon was once a soldier for hire." He turned to squint at Simon directly. "He is no stranger to killing."

Simon hid his shiver of dread by gesturing impatiently for Pen to continue.

"He returned to England a year ago. Of course there is little work these days. Men such as he are fit only for the butcher's trade or an outlaw's life. Bannon settled in Southwark and became a good fellow."

"A thief."

"You have heard the term." Pen seemed pleased. "Now if I recall it rightly, Bannon and Peto are second cousins. Their mothers were—"

Simon cut off the genealogy recital with a hand on Pen's bony shoulder. "The people of Paris Garden will not help Peto for fear of this thief's displeasure?"

"Not a thief of the usual sort. I once saw Bannon beat a man half to death because he laughed at his hat." Pen shivered at the memory.

"So why did Peto trust this man, then?"

Pen cackled derisively. "Did I say he trusted Bannon, Master? Bannon is his kinsman. Peto felt obliged to give him work." He raised a finger under Simon's nose. "But he sent you to me, not to Bannon. I wager Peto knows Bannon is behind this."

"But he does not know who has chosen to take Bannon's side."

This time Pen's expression was grim. "Two of his best men are dead. Peto can trust no one." He added a second later, "Only a man foolish enough to be thought useless."

"Peto does trust you, Pen, and he knows your worth."

Pen shook his head vigorously, sending his lank hair further awry. "What shall I do on my own? Those that can be bought, Bannon will buy. The rest will fear for their lives."

"How has it come to this? I thought Peto's people loved him."

Pen hung his head. "He has been somewhat unmindful of late. Bannon saw the weakness and did his dirty work well."

Comments heard at the alehouse returned to Simon's mind. "He spread lies about Peto."

"I have heard them." Pen sounded aggrieved. "They are false, but having no gift for words, I cannot argue against them like a lawyer in the courts."

"Tell me what they say."

Pen shrugged. "Nothing we who know Peto would believe." He counted the lies on his fingers. "That he has gone soft. That he was besotted with the woman and neglected his duties. That he had become greedy, keeping money that would once have been shared with his workers. When a man said these things once, I saw another nod wisely, as if it was fact."

"How do such rumors grow?"

Pen's grin was without humor. "That's what rumors is, Master! A man, or even a woman, says a thing with certainty, as if he knows it is true. Another man hears and passes it on to someone else, who says it again. Repeated often enough, things come to be believed by those who do not—or cannot—think for themselves."

"Not Peto's friends, surely."

"No, no! But the world changes. Men die or leave, and younger ones take their place. Many cannot recall when Peto established order in this corner of Paris Garden, bidding the worst of the bullies to move on or face his justice." Pen sighed. "They believe whoever shouts the loudest." Scrubbing a sleeve across his nose, he added, "Young dogs want to believe an old dog is soft, so they can pretend, even to themselves, they might defeat him."

Simon watched the river, its current a changing scene that was nevertheless unchanging. Peto was once a legend, smuggling into England the goods people were anxious to buy and making the authorities look like fools at the same time. And he'd been generous with the profits, which was all the better.

He could not help but compare Peto's situation to Elizabeth's. Once people showered them both with love and support; now those same people watched their destruction in silence, fearing for their own lives and well-being. Of those Simon had seen in Southwark today, not one but Pen seemed willing to help Peto, and it had not taken much to convince the people of Southwark that he was a murderer. How fickle life was!

Pen moved beside him, a signal he thought their meeting was ending. Simon had a more practical thought. Was Pen capable of communicating with the Spanish smugglers, Peto's best hope of escape? Although neither of them spoke Spanish, Simon knew smatterings of several other languages that might avail. With a sense of dread, he concluded he might convince the smugglers to help where Pen could not. Knowing he was wading into waters better left unexplored, Simon said, "I want to go with you to the Spanish ship."

Pen turned to look at him directly. "Are you sure, Master?"

Simon sighed. He was not, for explicit knowledge of illegal activity made him a party to the crimes. Still, if Peto were able to escape—and he had no idea how that might happen—his friends at the dock might take him to safety outside England. "Yes, Pen. I am." Once it was said, he felt better. "But first, tell me what business these men had with Peto."

Pen nodded, accepting his decision. "Peto and Red John were partners with the crews of several different ships, each with a secret hold somewhere on board. Peto and John see—saw to it that the hidden cargo disappeared into the night before the excise men could tax it."

Simon knew he was hearing things few men knew about the affairs of Peto the Pope. "How was it done?"

"Before the ship arrives at its destination, a stop is made in a deserted place upriver. Red John's part was to meet the ship, take the goods, and bring them to Southwark by land. The ship then went on to the wharf and delivered its legal cargo."

"Clever."

Pen grinned. "Been done that way for a long time, Master." He rubbed his shoulder absently, grimacing in pain, and Simon resolved to bring him a balm for arthritis on his next visit. "Peto managed the selling of the goods. Along the way, he and John provided work for many who now pretend they never heard of them." He sighed. "That is the way of it, I suppose."

Simon did not let himself be distracted again by faithless people. "What goods?"

"Oh, anything that turns a profit. Wine, certainly. I have seen cask after cask unloaded late at night." Pen's eyes rolled as he tried to remember. "Velvets and silks, o' course, for such things are always in demand at a price less than what the Crown says we should pay. Spices from the Spanish islands: pepper, nutmeg, cloves. And sugar. The nobles are mad for the stuff, and they say it is a very healthful addition to a meal."

The profits for such an undertaking would be substantial. "Might the sailors have joined with Bannon in hopes of keeping more of the profits for themselves?"

"I much doubt it. Peto was fair in his dealings, and any fool can see Bannon will squeeze the last coin from them."

Simon made a decision, marked by an abrupt shift from listening posture to readiness. "Then we must report what has happened and ask them to help Peto escape from the Tower."

Pen seemed somewhat cheered by that. "I never would have thought of it, Master, but you have it right. These Spaniards know Peto well, and they have no other connections in London, so Bannon's poison has not been at work among them." He, too, straightened his body for movement, though for Pen, the result was less than truly straight. "Come to the house at sunset tomorrow. I will take you to them and vouch for your honesty."

Simon hid a smile at the idea of being presented to smugglers as an honest man. "We will do what we can, Pen."

With a touch to his cap, Pen walked away, disappearing almost immediately in the surging, noisy crowd of people clogging the street.

Simon was not yet ready to leave Southwark. He wanted to see Peto's cousin, to judge the man for himself. Another trip to the Bull's Horn and some casual questioning might reveal where he could go to get a look at Christo Bannon.

Chapter Eight

Janet's baby seemed content to be in this world, on the north side of London, in Hannah's home. Janet was less serene. Only hours after the birth she was up, despite Hannah's warning that she must stay in bed for three days. Despite her fears and screams, childbirth for Janet had been as quick as Hannah had seen, and she seemed to have returned immediately to health. She paced the room, peering out the window at the dying daylight. "Is your husband often gone so long?"

"Not often." Hannah stole a glance at the sleeping child. "Things have occurred of late that took him into the city."

Janet's eyes grew round with curiosity. "What things?"

"An old friend is in trouble, and Simon wanted to offer what cheer he could."

"He is that sort, then? The kind who will help a friend in trouble?"

"Oh, yes. Simon has often been called to help"—Hannah revised the sentence's end—"friends." She switched to a safer subject. "About the baby's needs—"

Janet waved a careless hand. "I know you will see to everything."

"But you must—"

Suddenly Janet's whole manner changed. Her eyes flashed and she pounded her fists against her own legs. "I will do what I must for this child, but I do not care to prate about it all day long. Tending to a babe is not my single goal in life!"

The look on Hannah's face must have stopped her. Biting her lip, Janet paused, apparently waiting until her breathing calmed. "Hannah," she finally said in a quieter tone. "I will listen to what you say and take your counsel. But you must not press me!"

"Of course," Hannah said through stiff lips. She tried to smile. The returning smile Janet gave her was every bit as false, and neither of them said anything for some time.

The serving girl at the Bull's Horn spoke of Christo Bannon with something like reverence and seemed thrilled that he favored their place of business with his presence from time to time. "He's handsome, Bannon is. Always wears a fancy coat and a hat he got in the war, off'n a Frenchie."

Bannon took his largest meal of the day at midday, she reported, "Either here or at the Rose, just over a way." Since he was not present and the sun was directly overhead, Simon thanked the girl and went to find the tavern called the Rose.

The warmth and dryness of the day held, so the doors to the inns and shops Simon passed stood open. From them spilled noise and a sense of urgency, as if the inhabitants yearned to wring the most enjoyment possible from life. The laughter from the taverns and alehouses seemed to him not genuine humor, but a need to be noticed, to forget present circumstances, or to pretend life was good. Glancing into the doorways, Simon saw a palette of browns, blacks, and grays spotted with occasional color in the form of whatever finery the wearers could manage, a feather, a cheap trinket on a string, a twisted rope of colored fabric.

Arriving at the Rose, Simon saw little difference between it and the Bull's Horn. Both were run-down houses converted to places where cheap ale, cheap food, and the prospect of entertainment drew the poor, giving them meals they could afford, pastimes they could appreciate, and company that asked little of them.

Simon hunched himself to a slouch and entered. The Rose, as inapt a name as one could imagine for the place, had a slightly different setup from the Bull's Horn, an owner more round than tall, but the same general air of dissolution. Typically of such places, everyone looked up as he entered. Within seconds he was appraised, judged, and deemed less than noteworthy. Another poor apprentice, come to drink away his mealtime and his boredom.

Simon met no one's eye as he made his way to a tun at the back of the room where the host stood. He ordered, handed over a penny, and received a quart of ale in a bowl. Although no judge of such things, he thought the ale was stronger than he was used to. Brewers from the Continent, unlicensed to operate in London, often set up shop in Southwark, offering stronger beer at better prices and drawing drinkers from all stations of life. A word to the host proved his theory, for the man's German accent was so thick he could hardly make himself understood.

Once he was served, Simon took a place against a wall, standing since the seats were all taken. He surveyed the room with a casual gaze as he sipped from the bowl. A few dandies sat at one table, throwing dice. No one seemed interested in their flagrant disregard for the law. Across the room several women watched them speculatively, probably wondering if the men would have money left to pay for their companionship when evening came.

The rest of the room was filled with small groups who ate, drank, conversed, laughed, and argued in a good-natured manner. Simon amused himself by trying to guess how each person there earned his living. Was the big man a butcher? He would undoubtedly make short work of a side of pork with those huge upper arms. And the little man who seemed unable to keep still: might he be an acrobat from the outdoor shows common in Southwark? The woman with him looked foreign, dark-eyed and aloof from the conversation around her. Because she did not speak English? Foreigners got only as far north as Southwark if they plied trades deemed unwholesome, like performing.

As he sipped his ale, Simon found what he had come to see. In a corner relatively well-lit by afternoon sunlight through an open window, the man who must be Christopher Bannon sat at a table. With him were a woman and a small boy. He was indeed handsome, striking, in fact. Simon's informant had not given details about the hat, but it was so different from what most Englishmen would wear that it had to be the one.

Bannon dominated the table, and the other two seemed pastels to his paints, sidepieces to his centering presence. What his black trousers and dull red shirt lacked in color, he made up for in accessories. A belt of braided scarves circled his waist, the colors chasing each other in and out like children at play. He wore an earring in one ear, possibly a jewel but more likely a piece of glass cleverly cut to reflect light. The hat, likely once the possession of a foreign nobleman, was unlike anything Simon had ever seen. It looked like nothing more than a failed pancake, half risen and the other half flat. In it Bannon had thrust a peacock feather, which bobbed as he fed himself from a large trencher piled with onions, cheese, bread, and fish. A hearty breakfast, Simon guessed, for men like Bannon traveled late at night and slept half the day away.

The woman on the outlaw's right was almost beautiful. Her face had all the right parts: almond-shaped eyes shadowed by dark brows, high cheekbones tapering to a dainty chin, and pale, unblemished skin. Her mass of red hair was uncovered, the better, Simon supposed, to show off its striking hue. The whole did not complement the parts, however. Simon thought she resembled nothing so much as an alley cat in human form: beautiful but soulless, perhaps even dangerous.

The boy on Bannon's other side was perhaps six years old and so frail that the bones of his arms seemed too large for him to lift. He was pale and almost gaunt; his eyes, when he made the effort to raise them, were listless and blank. A lack-wit, Simon thought.

While Bannon ate, the two waited, the woman watching and assessing, the boy apparently uncaring. When he had his fill, Bannon passed the trencher to the woman, who took it with a studied air of nonchalance. Simon noticed, however, that she quickly finished everything that was left. When the trencher was empty, Bannon turned to the boy, a glint in his eye. His voice carried easily across the room. "She ate your food, boy. What d'you think o' that?"

The boy said nothing, and the woman snickered. "Too stupid to know he's hungry, he is."

"Oh, he is hungry, ain't you?" Bannon said, leaning over the slumped shape.

Simon read the child's lips rather than hearing the words. "A little."

"But we can't have you fat, now, can we?" Bannon asked in a meaningful tone.

"No. Not fat. But—" Argument failed, and the boy lapsed into silence. Simon sensed this was routine. The lad showed little hope of mercy from either adult.

"Here, then. You'll be glad to know I've saved you some," Bannon said cheerfully, and he took from his pocket a piece of bread. "There. Make a meal of it."

The boy reached out a hand for the bread, but Bannon snatched it back. "No word of thanks, then?"

"I-I thank you."

This time Bannon handed it over. The boy ate the dry clump

quickly, obviously fearful it would be taken back for some imaginary misdeed. Watching him, Bannon said again, "Can't have you getting fat now, can we?"

The child remained silent, licking the crumbs from his fingers and making sure he reached each one.

Simon looked to the fire, where a pot of soup bubbled. All his life, he had had enough to eat. His parents had provided plentiful meals, and now he had a wife who loved him and delighted in fixing dishes he especially liked. It was hard to imagine the life this boy led, although what he had seen gave him some idea.

Bannon spoke again, and his voice carried like a beaten drum. "Outside, Hound. Wait on the street. I have business to discuss." With a blank expression, the boy rose and left the room. Bannon turned to the woman. "You, too. Find something to do besides trailing after me."

His companion moved off with what dignity she could muster, pouting as she joined the group of unescorted women near the spigot. They moved aside politely to let her join them. Whatever the drawbacks of being Bannon's woman (and a bruise on her forearm looked as if fingers had pressed into her flesh), in this society, there was apparently some prestige as well.

Simon waited only long enough to see Bannon settle into conversation with a man who looked to be of his ilk, their heads together and a bowl of ale between them. He took a wooden bowl from the hearth, ladled it full of soup, gave the host a coin, and went outside.

The boy sat on the ground, his face blank. Simon crouched beside him, holding out the bowl. "Something to put in your belly, lad."

The child looked first at Simon then at the food, hesitating only a moment before taking it. He drank as fast as he could, chewing nothing, but letting carrots, parsnips, and whatever else slide down his gullet. Only once, when the door opened and someone came out, did he stop, frozen. When a glance revealed it was safe to continue, he wasted no time.

Fearful that the soup would immediately come back up, Simon examined the boy. He was indeed small for his age, and the clothes he wore were much too large. One sleeve was torn in a long gash, and through it Simon saw an odd-shaped bruise, deep purple in the center with the edges fading to yellow. He would have offered salve for it if he'd had any.

When the soup was gone, the boy sighed with content, burped, and turned to Simon. With light behind his eyes and food in his belly, he seemed quite different. "I thank you."

"You are welcome."

Blue eyes looked Simon over, possibly wondering what payment would be demanded for the meal. It seemed he did not care but simply waited to see what was required.

"Does he beat you?"

Thin shoulders rose and fell once. "Sometimes."

Simon almost asked why he did not run away, but that was a foolish question. Any protection was better than being alone on the streets of Southwark, and he guessed that was all the boy knew of the world. Bannon was strong enough, and threatening enough, that his people would be left alone by those who might otherwise take advantage of their weakness. Simon shuddered slightly. This boy would grow up believing brute strength mattered most and that what one could take, he should.

There was nothing he could offer except sympathy. "I'm sorry."

The boy searched Simon's face somewhat wonderingly. Finally he said, " 'S all right."

"What is your name?"

Again the blue eyes examined him, behind them what might

have been shame. "He calls me Hound. But my name is Henry."

"Like our late king." That meant nothing. The child merely shrugged again.

Behind them the door opened, and noise assaulted their backs. They both turned to see Bannon stepping onto the street with the woman close behind.

"Here, now, what are you about?" he growled when he saw the two of them. There was menace in his voice, and the boy's thin body stiffened.

"I beg your leave," Simon said, rising and taking up the bowl the boy had set down. "I brought my dinner out here to eat it, away from the noise. I asked if the boy knew the way to the Bull's Horn." With a guess at Bannon's rules, he added, "He seems unable to speak."

Bannon gave an indistinct grunt, as if unhappy to have no reason to chastise Henry.

Simon plunged ahead, grasping the chance. "I heard there was a murder at that place. I thought I might go and see where it happened."

"Aye, there was murder," Bannon said, his chin rising slightly. "I know something of it."

"Do you?" He let admiration shine in his voice. "Did you know the dead man?"

The sadness on the big man's face was as false as an actor's beard. "I took him there. How was I to know he'd have his throat cut only minutes after I left him?"

"Then it's true the man was killed as he slept?"

Bannon waved his hands widely, strutting a few steps, boots clomping. Again, Simon thought of actors. "It seems they had some disagreement, but how was I to know that?"

Apparently unwilling to be left out of things, the woman added, "Christo was at home 'cause he twisted his knee. Spent the whole night with a poultice on it. He didn't know what happened till I returned home and told him."

Simon felt the boy's body shift at his feet, a nervous movement that seemed a response to the woman's words. He wished he could speak to Henry alone and ask if Bannon had truly been home when the murder occurred. Instinctively he distrusted the red-haired woman's story.

"A terrible thing." Bannon seemed to have said what he cared to about the matter. Over one arm he carried a full-length soldier's coat that looked to be of foreign design, made of good material and in elegant style. Carelessly he dropped it now onto the boy, who teetered under its weight. Giving him a kick that was not a punishment but not gentle, either, he said, "Come on, then, Hound. We must go."

"A fine boy," Simon said. "Is he your son?"

"I love him like a son," Bannon said, "and he's right fond of me, too, aren't you, boy."

"Fond. That I am." The boy rose, balancing the coat carefully to keep its ends from touching the ground. He flashed Simon a glance he interpreted as thanks, both for the food and for saving him further trouble. Then he fell into place behind Bannon, the weight of the coat bending his slight body forward.

As Bannon started off down the street, the woman gave the boy a sharp glance of warning. He fell back, letting her have undisputed second place. Simon watched them go, his heart heavy. He could not alleviate the boy's suffering, any more than he could save the many others like him who lived from hand to mouth, doing whatever it took to stay alive.

As the three disappeared around a corner, Simon decided Christo Bannon was an evil man, not only capable of petty meanness, but also capable of framing his own kinsman for murder. In addition, he noted at the last that only a day after Red John's murder, Bannon's knee seemed perfectly well.

Chapter Nine

Hannah held the baby, crooning softly and caressing the tiny fingers curled around her thumb. The child should be swaddled. The linen bands were ready, but she did not want to cover the little form from head to foot, as custom demanded. "A child's legs will not straighten properly if it is not swaddled," the midwives insisted, "and its back will grow crooked."

They were probably right, being experienced, but one young wife down the lane who had two children in the last three years had not bothered with swaddling. Her children, now toddling happily around their home, were as strong and straight-limbed as any others. Hannah resolved to ask Simon if he thought swaddling necessary. It seemed a miracle that this wee being's perfectly formed legs kicked so energetically, and she was loath to hide them under wrapping.

Janet herself had no opinions about anything concerning her daughter. All day she had fed the child when it cried but kept her face averted, as if she longed to escape that duty. Much to Hannah's dismay, she even asked about a wet nurse. Hannah said she knew none, but in truth the request shocked her. Janet had plenty of milk, and the baby took to nursing as easily as she had come into the world. Of course many noble women did not nurse their children, believing it ruined the shape of their breasts, but Hannah knew women who had nursed with no visible effect on their figures. She did not understand Janet's lack of appreciation for the gift God had bestowed on her. The gift

Hannah herself had not been given.

"What will you call her?" Hannah asked. The day was dying, and the two women sat by the fire, lit only by its glow.

"I don't know." There was a long pause. "Choose something."

"But you are her mother."

Janet's face pinched with irritation. "I want you to. Give her a name, so we can stop fussing about what it will be."

Hannah did not think there had been any fuss at all, but remembering Janet's earlier outburst, she chose to be co-operative. "If you are certain."

A shrug from Janet banished all responsibility. "Whatever you choose."

Hardly daring to say the name lest Janet reject it, Hannah said, "I would call her Susan."

Janet took the child from Hannah's arms, made a mocking gesture of blessing over the her head, and laid her down on the blankets Hannah had spread near the fireplace. "There. Susan she shall be. Now I suppose I should try to sleep, since she is not fussing." With that, she lay down beside the child and turned her back to Hannah.

The sun was peeking over the rooftops when Simon awoke the next morning. He had arrived home late after fighting his way through the crowds heading into Southwark for a night of reveling. Darkness had come early, along with a steady rain that slowed his return, wet his clothes, and made him grumpy. Hannah met him at the door with a candle, nodded when he mumbled a promise to tell her everything on the morrow, and led him to their bed without saying much at all. As the day's events whirled inside his head, she nestled beside him, letting her calming presence drain the tension from his neck and shoulders. After a while, he had slept.

Odd dreams interrupted his rest, dreams that someone was

crying for help, or at least crying. He thought once that Hannah left the bed for a time. She got up early, and he was dimly aware of metal scraping as she stirred the coals of the fire. The smell of the air changed, and he knew she had added fuel to banish the chill of morning. He rolled over gratefully and dozed a while longer. When the fire began crackling merrily, he finally opened his eyes. Hannah's backside was visible through the gap in the bed curtains, bent over something at the fireside. He recalled her saying they needed to talk in the morning.

When she turned and saw that he was awake, Hannah started slightly. Tiptoeing to his side, she asked in a soft voice, "Will you come with me into the shop?"

Simon rose, stretched, and followed her through the still-dark room, curious now that he was fully awake. When he was almost to the doorway, a muted gurgle stopped him and he turned, noticing a bundled form on the floor near the hearth. "What is that?"

Hannah again gestured for him to follow, and he obeyed, casting a suspicious glance backward. "Who is in our house, Hannah?"

She moved around the shop, opening the shutters to let in the morning sunlight. She took her time, making more noise than necessary, perhaps to delay answering his question. "It's a girl I . . . found yesterday," she finally said when she again faced him.

Simon knew Hannah well and could easily read her moods. She tried to sound matter-of-fact, but there was a pleading note to her voice. As she told the story of what had happened the day before, he sensed immediately that his response was important. It would not be enough to agree with whatever she was proposing. His wife wanted him to approve her actions.

Hannah felt the lack of a child more keenly than he did. While Simon *wanted* children, she *longed* for them. He could be patient, hoping time and prayer would provide a family. Hannah despaired each month when her body gave evidence that no baby grew inside her.

"I've never seen a first child come so fast and so easy," she was saying. "It was no more than an hour after her water broke the little one arrived. And there was not much blood, either." Sensing that Simon cared to hear no more of the particulars, Hannah instead launched into a litany of the child's virtues. "She is already beautiful, not ugly like some babies who look red and misshapen for days after birth. Why, the herb-seller's son, born last week, is smaller than she by a good bit, and his cry is not nearly as strong."

Though Simon felt some curiosity about the girl and her child, he was distracted by his own concerns. It might be good, he told himself, to have guests in the house. Their presence would distract Hannah's mind from his activities, which were undoubtedly unwise and possibly dangerous. She would worry less with something else to occupy her mind.

"If you could have seen her, Simon! She was so afraid, and I knew it was right to take her in. And you have often said I should have a girl to help me."

He forced a frown from his brow. It seemed Hannah was thinking into the future, planning that Janet would become a permanent member of the household. Not sure how he felt about that, Simon did not object. So many things might change in a few days or weeks.

On first hearing, he was not convinced that the girl's story was true. A nobleman's child? More likely a man of her own station who could not afford a wife—or perhaps already had one. If Janet had a man somewhere, she might decide to return to him. If she had run away from her parents' home, she might choose to go back to their care. Whatever the truth was, there were a dozen ways in which Hannah's plans for Janet and her child might go awry. He hoped she was not too disappointed when it happened.

Whether she had told the truth or not, Simon could not muster much concern over Janet's situation. Girls got into trouble. It was a fact of life. She would neither hang nor face the headsman, so her problems were less pressing than Elizabeth's or Peto's. Hannah had taken her in and helped birth the child. As long as he would abide two extra mouths to feed, they would fare well. He knew what was wanted. "She is welcome to stay as long as she likes, Hannah."

Her face broke into a smile, and Simon smiled back, wishing the other problems he faced were so easily dealt with. Hannah touched his arm briefly as a signal to wait, disappeared, and a few minutes later pulled a sleepy Janet into the shop, cuddling the woman's child against her own chest.

"Janet, this is Simon." Although she seemed less than warm, Janet nodded politely. She had little choice but to be pleasant, he supposed. He had the right to insist she leave his house, and apparently she had nowhere else to go.

"And Simon, this is Janet's little girl, Susan. Isn't she beautiful?"

"She is," he murmured, having as little choice in the matter as their guest. Hannah's desire to help this woman fairly burst from her, and he decided if she wanted it, then so did he.

He bowed gravely. "Welcome to our home, Janet, to you and your child."

Chapter Ten

Simon spent the first half of the morning in the shop, seeing people who needed his help. Most could not afford a physician, and even those with a little money did not call for a doctor unless the need was dire. Instead they went to the local apothecary, who diagnosed their illnesses as best he could and dosed them with physic.

As a boy, Simon had served as assistant to his father, a respected physician, but his weak arm was problematic. Worse, following his father into a house where the victim of some terrible illness or accident awaited them had always made him sick—not with fear, but with dread of the pain they would not be able to allay. He had never become accustomed to setting bones, sewing up wounds, or working futilely to save a woman dying in childbirth.

The thought of babies brought Hannah and her charges to mind, and as if he had conjured them, the two women appeared from the living area. "Janet is going to do the cleaning while I add scents to the oils I made earlier," Hannah announced. A note in her voice hinted she was happier than she had been in some time. Perhaps another woman's company was what she had been needing. They both worked hard in the shop, but when Simon had tried to encourage Hannah to spend more time with friends, she'd replied, attempting a light tone but not quite succeeding, "All they talk about is their children. I have nothing to add."

The two women went to the front, where Hannah explained what she would be doing. Like most apothecary shops, theirs sold creams and cosmetics as well as medicines, and she was making skin softeners, each with a delicate scent: lemon, rose, lavender, and others designed to please customers. Simon went on with his work, half listening to their talk.

Once she had shown Janet the creams, Hannah said, "Your first job will be crushing these leaves to a very fine powder." The girl nodded assent, took up a pestle, and began the task. As soon as Hannah was absorbed in her work, however, Janet approached Simon and watched him mix ingredients in a bowl. "What is that?"

"Licorice," he replied. "I mix it with comfrey to help with breathing problems."

Surveying the jars on the shelves, she took one down and sniffed it. "What's this?"

"Physic for stomach pain made with wormwood, mint, and balm."

Scrunching her nose distastefully, she replaced the jar on the shelf. "Which of them is a love philter?"

Simon hid a smile. "I don't make such things."

"But you know how, do you not?"

There was no use telling her love charms were mostly wishful thinking. Many apothecaries sold them; Simon preferred not to. "I might have known how once," he said jokingly. "But Hannah insists I have no more to do with them, lest I lure another woman."

Hannah turned to roll her eyes at him in a humorous acknowledgment of his jest, but Janet didn't notice. "It is hard to keep a lover, even after you've captured him."

Recalling Janet's lost nobleman, Simon dropped his teasing and changed the subject. "How does the smallest woman in our household this morning?"

Janet's answer was a careless shrug. "Sleeping. What is that?" she asked, touching a bowl that held a rather noxious substance.

"It's a treatment for gout made of worms, pig's marrow, and herbs boiled together." Some said a red-haired dog should be added to the mixture, but Simon doubted the efficacy of that and liked the local dogs too much to try it. Taking up another jar, he told her, "This is opium, which is helpful in eliminating pain. I measure the doses carefully, for too little is ineffective, and too much might be fatal."

"Why would a person take something that might kill her?" Janet asked in wonder typical of one in possession of both youth and perfect health.

"When pain plagues a person for days or weeks, he might try any remedy. Folk should consult a physician or an apothecary who knows the risks and the proper dosages, but too often they dose themselves, with tragic results."

"I don't think I will like being old," Janet said. "I like neither physic nor pain."

Simon had no answer for that one, so he went on with his task, measuring drams of a safe dose and wrapping them in papers for his customers' convenience.

"What happened to your arm?"

It was not a topic he liked to discuss. "It has been this way from birth."

She regarded the withered limb distastefully. "It must be terrible, having people stare at you all the time. I am glad I was born well and whole, for I could not bear it."

Simon managed only a grunt in response. What did Hannah see in this girl?

He began making minimal responses to Janet's comments, which remained self-centered and shallow. Eventually sensing his lack of interest, she wandered to the doorway, watching the crowds on the street. The half-crushed lavender leaves lay forgotten on the worktable.

The sunlight cast a flattering glow on Janet's face. No doubt she would be called beautiful by any standard, but Simon was not sure he could admire someone so concerned with looks and so convinced of her own importance. Several times when he looked up, she was examining her stomach, apparently anxious to see if her figure had returned to its original shape.

As the morning wore on, Simon also noted Janet was perfectly happy to let Hannah wait on her. She could lean toward the polished metal mirror in the corner to examine her eyelashes but professed herself unable to bend to stir the mush or help with the morning bread making. Hannah seemed not to notice, hurrying through her tasks, and stopping each time she passed the bed to check on the baby, to cuddle the baby, or to simply admire the baby.

As a gurgling sound came from the other room, Hannah now set down the spatula she had been using, wiped her hands on her apron, and left the room. Janet turned to watch her go but did not stir from her place in the sunlit doorway. Soon Hannah was back with the infant in her arms. "Is she not the prettiest child?" she asked.

It might have been the tenth time he had heard that question already this morning. Simon agreed, summoning as much enthusiasm as he could. He glanced at Janet, whose attention was elsewhere, allowing Hannah to care for the child she had borne as if it were her due.

Susan began to fuss, waving her arms and opening her mouth like a fish, Simon thought.

"She wants to be fed," Hannah said. She had to repeat the statement before Janet responded, sulkily turning from the door and taking the baby into the other room.

Unused to such things and a little embarrassed at knowing what Janet must do to quiet her infant, Simon busied himself with replacing medicines sold in his absence over the last few days. He felt mildly angry with Janet, who seemed determined to take advantage of Hannah's kind nature and love of children. She even seemed resentful that Hannah could not feed the baby at her own breast.

Sensing Hannah was happy with the situation, he remained silent, but he resolved to approach his wife later about not letting her guest take advantage of her. It was because of the child, he knew. Hannah was fascinated with her.

While the baby was a miracle, as all babies are, Simon focused his mind on the snarl of troubles his friends faced. Tonight he would do what he could to persuade the Spanish smugglers to rescue Peto. Though certain in his own mind that Christo Bannon had plotted Peto's arrest, Simon knew he was ill-equipped to accuse a man with Bannon's resources and ruthlessness. Should he go to Calkin with his suspicions? The guardsman would know who might go into the depths of Southwark and take on Bannon and his minions. If Calkin took up that cause, Simon could concentrate on helping Elizabeth.

Since the baby came, Hannah seemed unable to fathom Simon's need for justice. When he tried to talk to her, she contributed only vague murmurs of sympathy and hardly looked at him. In the end he concluded that for the time being, he and his wife were focused on different goals. It was probably for the best, because neither had to worry about the other feeling neglected.

With Hannah distracted, Simon wished he could talk to Elizabeth, but she had told him she was to be visited by a doctor this morning. "So I shall be well for my execution," she'd said grimly. He decided he would take the chance of going to the Tower before he left for Southwark and his meeting with Pen. Word of the priest's visits had surely gotten around by now, and the guards would not be surprised to see him.

At mid-afternoon, when he had done what was required in the shop, he took his medicine bag, stuffed the cassock into it, and glanced around, feeling guilty about leaving Hannah to deal with work, the household tasks, and her guests all at once.

He found her sitting by the fireside with the child in her arms. After assuring himself that Janet was nowhere close, he said, "I must go out again."

Hannah ran her finger over the baby's smooth cheek. "Umm."

He bit his bottom lip. "I will probably not return until late."

That caught her attention, and she looked up questioningly. "Where will you go?"

"To the Tower to see the princess. Then with Pen to a meeting this evening."

He did not say why or in what location, but Hannah heard what was not said. He saw in the set of her head, the unconscious tensing, she did not want him to go. Both errands were dangerous, though neither of them mentioned it. Hannah was no doubt aware his risks were now double. Helping Elizabeth might result in arrest, imprisonment, torture, and death. Now he was meddling in the business of Peto the Pope. Had he the right to endanger not only his own life, but all he and Hannah had? Still, he did not know how to ignore his friends' plight. If Hannah asked him not to go, what would he say?

She did not do that. Touching the baby's hair lightly she averted her eyes and said, "We will await your return." Softly she added as he turned to go, "Be careful, Simon."

"You will put your nose into danger, Simon Maldon, no matter the consequences." Elizabeth was not nearly as understanding as Hannah. "You intend to help an infamous criminal prove he did not commit a murder that only he could have committed?" Her tone was a combination of disbelief, reprimand, and a tiny bit of grudging admiration.

Simon had shared the news of Peto's arrest in hopes of providing Elizabeth something to ponder other than the headsman's axe. The strain of imprisonment and threatening death showed in her haunted, bloodshot eyes and her inability to sit still. It did not stop her, however, from sharply insisting he have no more to do with Peto the Pope.

"He is unjustly accused, Highness." He had told her Peto was in the Tower, accused of murder, and how he had been called to visit him in his guise of priest. He neglected to add he had taken on the role of Peto's messenger. She would surely have a great deal to say about that.

"He *says* he is innocent. But you admit he is a criminal many times over. What difference if he hangs for this crime or another?" She glanced at the guard, who seemed already bored with the supposed priest's visits and now dug busily at a spot on his scalp. She lowered her voice, though they spoke in Latin. "And I am not 'Highness' these days. I am the Lady Elizabeth."

Elizabeth's title had often been problematic. As a child she was deemed royal, then not, then royal again. Queen Mary considered her a bastard, since she did not recognize that their father ever divorced Mary's mother, Catherine of Aragon. Anne Boleyn had been of the nobility, however, so Elizabeth had to be treated with some consideration, had to have a title.

"I'm sorry," Simon said, rolling his eyes to show his objection. "My lady."

"That 'lady' at least assures I will die as my mother did." She added with sudden bitterness, "Unless they avoid a trial and poison me here in this awful place."

"Please don't say that!" It would indeed be easier for Mary if Elizabeth died of some vague ailment. She did not even have to order it. Merely making it known she wished it done would probably be enough that some loyal courtiers would see to it. But Simon did not admit in Elizabeth's presence he shared her fear. "The queen will see you are no threat to her."

"But I am, Simon, even if I do not want to be." Elizabeth indicated their dismal surroundings. "I am here not because *I* plotted treason, but because treason was plotted with me in mind. As long as I live, there will be those who believe I would replace my sister if the chance arose." She clasped her hands against her stomach as if poison already burned there. "No matter how much I try to dissuade them."

Hannah stirred from watching Susan sleep, reminding herself she had work to do. She moved to the shop doorway, stopping once to look back at the baby. As she pulled aside the curtain, Janet stood at the worktable, head down and one hand beneath its edge. "Janet?"

With a start, the girl spun around, putting her hands behind her back. "Hannah!"

"What are you doing?"

Janet's eyes did not meet hers. "I thought I could help here in the shop. You and Simon have been good to me."

Hannah smiled. "We are lucky you have brought us a child to love."

"Yes." Janet's tone was flat. "I thought I would dust the shelves."

"All right." A vague feeling of disquiet rose in Hannah's mind as Janet picked up a cloth and began cleaning jars and boxes on the shelves. When her back was turned, Hannah quietly opened the money drawer and checked the coins to see if the amount tallied with what had been there earlier. It did. She felt guilty to be checking on Janet, but told herself it did not pay to be too trusting. The girl apparently noticed nothing as she traced the shelves' edges with her rag. Smiling at her industry, Hannah went to work at her own task, making headache powders from sweet-smelling herbs: rose, lavender, and sage.

Janet gravitated to her side as Hannah deftly twisted a paper and set the finished product on a shelf. Janet scanned the array of boxes, jars, and papers constituting the shop's most popular medicines. "I asked your husband if he makes love potions, but he said he does not."

"Hmmm," Hannah murmured, concentrating on her measurements.

"Do you perhaps know how to make something to keep a man faithful?"

"Simon says there is no such thing."

"But there has to be!" Janet's voice rose in distress.

"What keeps two people together is love, caring, and—in truth, some measure of luck."

"I am lucky, some say," Janet said thoughtfully. After a moment her voice took on a stronger note. "But I want a potion, to be sure."

Hannah regarded the younger woman sympathetically. "This nobleman of yours, Janet. It is best to forget him."

The girl looked at Hannah coyly. "Perhaps if you ask him, Simon will make me a love philter. I promise I will not use it on him, nor will I go to him, even if he asks me to."

Hannah could hardly believe her ears. This girl, less than a day from childbed, could think of nothing but recapturing her man's affection. And she had obviously considered Simon as a lover as well! "I will ask him," Hannah told her, "when the time is right, and if you are attentive to little Susan, as a mother should be."

"Oh, I will be!" Janet assured, her eyes bright. "The man I love is admired by many women, so I must do everything I can to keep him with me."

"But if he is noble—"

"Oh, not him," Janet said with a wave of dismissal. "My lover is a real man, not some mother's boy with soft hands and no spine."

"Oh." Hannah was having a hard time keeping up. Yesterday the girl had seemed brokenhearted about losing the highborn father of her child. Now she claimed to be in love with someone else entirely. Hannah replaced the jar lid, sealing in the scent of lemon. "This man loves you in return?"

"He does. And I pray that he continues to do so." Janet's expression grew serious. "I could not live if I lost him, nor would I want to."

Chapter Eleven

When Simon arrived at the Bull's Horn near sundown, the place was bustling with customers. The landlord's daughter and wife moved briskly through the crowd, hefting trays of ale as they stepped sideways between patrons. The girl recognized Simon and stopped when her tray was empty. "Father has done well with your suggestion he show the scene and tell the story of the murder," she said happily. "Though it makes more work for Mother and me, it has put him in a better humor than I have seen in some time. For that I thank you."

"I am glad to have made your life more pleasant, even for a day," Simon replied. With a saucy wave and a twitch of her skirt, the girl went back to work.

Saddler stood at the tap, measuring ale with a jealous eye and ordering his women about. The door opened, and Simon looked up to see Bannon enter, ducking his head to avoid hitting the rough cross timber. Quickly lowering his own head, Simon looked aslant at the newcomers. He recognized the redhead from the day before, and behind her, the boy Henry.

The host greeted the big man with an obsequious heartiness, and Bannon acknowledged him with a gruff reply. Saddler led the party to a table where two men sat. At a gesture from the host the two men got up and moved, eyes averted, to an empty space along the wall, where they leaned in attempted nonchalance. Undoubtedly aware of the notice of others, Bannon lowered himself onto the stool Saddler pulled out for him. The woman seated herself opposite. There was no third seat, so the boy simply dropped to the floor, resting his back against the table leg.

Simon kept his face down as Bannon surveyed the crowd like a petulant lord, dark brows lowered over equally dark eyes. His gaze lingered for a moment on Simon, who casually leaned his forehead on his hand as if too tired to raise his face. The gaze moved on, but when Saddler approached with a bowl of ale, Bannon asked a question in a low voice. Saddler glanced at Simon and said something, a gesture with his hand indicating the room at the back of the shop. Bannon asked a second question. The host thought about it and answered, causing his guest to look again in Simon's direction.

Saddler moved off to continue his duties, and Simon watched Bannon as unobtrusively as possible. He was an outlaw, as Peto was, but he was not at all the same type of man. Several times Bannon demonstrated casual cruelty to the woman and the boy, obviously enjoying the power he held over them and going out of his way to let them know how little they meant to him. Whenever attractive women passed the table, Bannon spoke to them in tones teasing and suggestive. He even caressed a few of them.

The solicitous Saddler brought a bowl of ale, and Bannon drank deeply before passing it to the redhead. She took several small sips, trying to appear dainty but getting what she could before he took it away again. Nothing was offered to Henry. He seemed used to it, did not look at either of his companions but merely stared at the wall opposite. Simon did not think the boy had seen him but guessed he would not acknowledge it if he had.

A few minutes later, a man Simon had not noticed earlier approached Bannon. His gait suggested arrogance, but he seemed anonymous, like night, coming and going without noise or fanfare. His approach to Bannon was, if not as an equal, at least as a confederate. During their brief conversation, neither looked in Simon's direction, but he could not help but feel their interest. When they finished, the man left with the air of one on an errand.

The host's daughter approached to ask if he wanted more ale. Simon refused politely, saying he must soon leave. "Do you know the large man sitting in the far corner?"

"Of course," the girl replied. "That's Christo Bannon, the one you asked about earlier."

"What is his trade?"

She looked at Simon speculatively. "I couldn't say."

"And is the boy a relative?"

She glanced at the pale figure on the floor. "Christo calls him Cousin sometimes, or more often Hound." Her brows lowered. "I think there was another before this one."

"What became of him?"

The girl looked at him askance. "I couldn't say."

A voice behind him interrupted. "Master, could you spare a penny to buy a drink for a thirsty man? I will be grateful for your generosity and provide jolly company."

Turning, Simon found Pen standing beside his chair, his expression pleasant but not familiar, as if he had seen a stranger and taken the chance that he might be generous. Simon tried to affect an attitude of mild irritation, knowing Pen had provided an excuse for them to talk. Rolling his eyes, Simon ordered more ale. Pen dragged a nearby stool up to the table and sat. As he looked around the room and noticed Bannon, his eyes widened. Like Simon, he lowered his head. "He knows I am Peto's friend, Master. We must tread carefully."

"We are two men having a pint, nothing more." Simon glanced outside. "Half an hour or so, and it will be dark enough to visit your friends at the wharf." Feeling something heavy land in his lap, he looked down to find a purse full of coins. Pen grinned, head bobbing. "Peto gave me that to keep should I ever need it. It might be of use to you now as you work for his good."

Simon acknowledged that he did not have the money to bribe prison guards, should it come to that. "Did you learn where Peto's woman has gone?"

"No. It is as if she disappeared into the air."

It was frustrating that the one thing he might do to put his friend's mind at rest could not be done. Where could the woman be? "Tell me more about her," Simon urged.

Pen's expression revealed a struggle between honesty and loyalty to Peto and, by extension, his woman. "She is passing beautiful," he admitted, giving positive points grudgingly, "but her devotion to Peto would fright a man."

"How so?"

Pen leaned forward, tapping his finger on the tabletop. "For one thing, she will tolerate no other woman near him and makes a great ado at any who approach. Sometimes he tired of it, but you know how he is about his luck." A lock of lank hair left the confinement of Pen's cap and fell onto his forehead. "She plagued him more than any woman since I have known him, but he was patient with her moods."

"And you don't think she could have been involved in the plot against Peto?"

"Oh, no, Master. She would never see harm come to him, I would wager my life on that."

Then where had she gone? "Bannon is a different question, though, is he not?"

Pen's eyes widened and he leaned toward Simon fearfully. "The man is a kill-cow, Master, a bully who will have his way no matter what. Those who anger him disappear and are never seen again." His eyes met Simon's, pleading for understanding.

"Peto would not want you to do anything to set Bannon after you. Nor do I want him after me."

"We will do what we can tonight. Afterward, I will not come here again." Finishing his drink, Simon ordered, "Leave now, as if you have gotten what you can from me and are going home. He will not put us together in his mind, so you will have no cause for worry."

Hannah marveled at Susan's health and serenity. The child showed no ill effects from her mother's recent trials. Only a day after her birth, her skin turned smooth and silky, her face rounded to perfection, and the black hair covering her tiny head shone with good health.

Another marvel was Janet's lack of concern for the child. While Hannah spent hours looking at the baby's fingers and toes and nuzzling its soft neck, the child's mother laid her down whenever possible. Despite her determination to like Janet, Hannah could not help but notice the girl saw the baby as an excuse to be idle. Only when a meal needed to be prepared or water carried did Janet snatch up the child and devote herself to it until Hannah had completed the task. She told herself she did not mind. Janet would grow to love the child with time.

For her own part, Hannah could hardly keep her hands away from the baby. Though she slept most of the time, the slightest sound from the bed drew Hannah to her as if a velvet ribbon connected them, pulling her to the child firmly but pleasantly.

While she was in the shop that afternoon, Susan began to fuss, then to cry. Pushing aside the curtain, Hannah found Janet standing in front of the polished brass mirror, wearing a necklace taken from a box of things Hannah kept for special occasions. Not an expensive piece, it was still lovely, with blue glass beads carefully painted with tiny gold flowers.

Janet started guiltily when she saw Hannah in the doorway.

"I was merely trying it."

"I see."

"It's a good color for me, don't you think?" She turned back to the mirror. "Not so good for a brunette, though. You should give it to me." Her tone was teasing, but her eyes were not.

Hannah was speechless, unable to fathom the girl's boldness. "It was a gift from Simon."

"Oh." Janet removed the necklace slowly, no discomfort apparent in her expression, and dropped it casually back into the box where she had found it. Hannah picked up the baby, confused and almost angry that she seemed more embarrassed by the incident than Janet did.

Switching topics as easily as she avoided work, Janet regarded Hannah critically. "I was smaller at the waist than even you before she came along." The slight emphasis on *she* made Hannah cringe. "I hope it has not ruined my figure."

Hannah looked down at the baby, content now she was cuddled. "But see what you got for your trouble! Is it not worth it to have such a perfect child all for your own?"

Janet did not bother to answer but went back to the mirror, touching her stomach and pulling the muscles as tight as she could. Janet did not seem to see her baby as worthwhile yet, but the girl would come to love being a mother. *What woman would not?* Hannah asked herself.

As soon as he thought enough time had elapsed to separate his departure from Pen's, Simon left the Bull's Horn. They had agreed to meet at a spot on the bank of the Thames, and he found Pen there, talking to some ducks that huddled against the riverbank. The conversation was interesting, albeit one-sided, for Pen told the mother duck what handsome children she had and spoke to the children about proper behavior. Some of them appeared to answer, at least as a duck might reply. Simon watched for a while, delaying the moment when they must take action.

"Let's be off, then," Pen finally said briskly, as if Simon dawdled with ducks and not he.

Moving quietly through the darkness, they headed to Southwark's wharf. Simon often looked back to see if they were followed, but it was impossible to tell. The streets were a maze, with many places a person could simply step into the shadows and disappear. He told himself that Bannon could not suspect them of anything. Pen was thought an idiot, and no one else here knew Simon had ever met Peto the Pope. It was likely they were safe, at least for tonight.

They passed boats of various sizes and purposes that lined up along the river's edge like mismatched serving dishes. The same motley assembly could be found on the other side of the river and on either side of the bridge as well. No boat could go under the Thames Bridge, for huge waterwheels built into the arches produced ferocious rapids between the piers. Only the most foolhardy types attempted to "shoot the bridge," and most of them drowned. This bridge, men said, was "for wise men to pass over and fools to pass under."

Along the wharf a short way, Pen stopped, holding up a finger for Simon to wait. Ducking between crates stacked for lading, he returned holding a lantern. "I thought we might need this." When he lit the wick, Simon saw that metal enclosed the lantern on three sides, showing only a single beam ahead of them to light the way. Pen had prepared carefully for their evening activities. Knowing Pen was more used to being an observer than a participant in illegal acts, Simon felt a little guilty. Still, the sight of Peto's man would reassure the smugglers, so Pen's presence was necessary.

They made their way along, footsteps echoing on the wooden deck of the wharf, as Pen stopped periodically to examine one boat or another. Finally he pointed at a trim little vessel that seemed empty, for it lay dark and silent except for the soft slap of waves against its stern. Approaching, Pen knocked at the bow, as if asking entry to a friend's cottage. After a moment, a voice called a response, the words unintelligible, but the meaning unmistakable: "Who is it?"

"A friend," Pen said softly.

"Amigo," Simon added one of his small store of Spanish words.

A hatch slid open, revealing light below, in the cabin. Simon guessed the ship was specially fitted to block inner light from showing outside. A man's head and shoulders appeared in the opening. The question he asked was again incomprehensible, but Simon thought he demanded identification. Pen seemed to understand, for he turned the glow of the lantern onto his own face. "You know me. This man"—he pointed at Simon—"is a friend." Pen repeated Simon's Spanish word. *"Amigo."* He shone the light on Simon, who raised his hands to prove he carried no weapons. "Peto is in trouble," he said in French, hoping they might understand.

The man said something to a person below deck. Receiving a response Simon could not hear, he stepped lightly onto the wharf and approached them. "I am Diego," he said. "I speak a little French. Enough, I think."

With a nod, Simon turned to Pen. "You should go now. I thank you for your help."

"I can wait, Master," Pen said, but he was already backing away. With clear relief at being dismissed from further action, he turned and disappeared into the darkness, his uneven footsteps sounding for a while before they were gone, too.

Simon and Diego found a place between two ramshackle buildings where they were out of sight and hopefully out of range of the hearing of anyone in the area. "Red John Cooper has been murdered," Simon began. "Peto is accused of the crime."

"We heard it." Diego's tone was angry, and he leaned closer. "Does Peto know who killed Red John and made it seem he did it?"

Simon felt a surge of relief. If the Spaniards were on Peto's side, they might be willing to help him. "He does. What he does not know is who in Southwark can be trusted."

"He trusts you?"

Simon shrugged. "I knew Peto long ago, so I relayed a message for him. That's all."

"I see." The man's gaze flickered over Simon as if the explanation confirmed what he had guessed, that Simon was no member of Peto's inner circle.

"How did you hear about the murder?"

"A man came this morning, one who has handled our cargo several times. He is family to Peto, I think. This man said Peto will hang, but the business will continue."

"With him in charge?"

"Yes." The smuggler paused. "I did not trust him. He seemed too pleased with the new way, even though he tried to appear sad."

Simon acknowledged that with a nod. "Can you help Peto?"

Diego shook his head. "I am sorry. He and I have long been friends, but we are strangers here. We would have no chance of rescuing Peto and would likely be captured ourselves."

Simon sighed, recognizing the truth of that.

Diego asked, "What will you do?"

He shrugged. He was an even more unlikely a rescuer than the smugglers: a lone man who respected the law despite sympathy for his friend. He tapped his fingers lightly on a nearby rail. "I do not see how Peto can escape, but if he manages it, will you take him out of England?"

Diego considered. "We meant to sail for home, but we can wait a few days more."

"I will get word to him that you are here, should he find an opportunity."

Diego clamped a firm hand on Simon's arm. "There is only so much scraping and swabbing we can do. Make your plan and get Peto here within three days' time."

Simon hesitated. While it was one thing to hope Peto could escape the hangman, it was quite another to make a plan to assist him. Could he do it? And should he?

Although Diego's expression was hard to read in the moonlight, Simon knew the man sensed his misgivings. *What a fool I am!* he thought. Not only was he unsure what to do, he could not even decide where his conscience led.

With a farewell to Diego, he started for home, still unsure how much he would do to help Peto the Pope escape hanging. He followed the river, heading toward the steeples of St. Mary's, easily seen from a distance, a sure guide to the Tower Bridge. At times rushlights burned at the front of buildings, but other stretches of Abbey Street were dark. Too late, he realized he should have hired a linkboy to light his way. The streets were uneven and crooked, and it was easy to become lost or trip over loose stones. The bridge would by now be closed for the night, and he would have to hire a boatman to take him back to London. Still, Hannah would worry if he did not return. He quickened his pace.

He did not see the blow coming, but some instinct, or perhaps a shadow of movement, warned him. Simon hunched, taking the impact on his shoulder rather than his head. He fell, striking his head sharply against the brick of a nearby building. Blackness reigned inside his skull as well as outside, and for a few moments, he could not make himself move. As his attacker bent to assess the damage, Simon, through eyesight that waved with nausea and faded in and out, recognized him. The man in gray Bannon had spoken to at the inn. Dimly, Simon understood he would soon be dead. He lay limp, hoping the other would believe he had accomplished his purpose and go away.

Suddenly he heard voices. The man who stood over him heard them too, for he tensed. Simon opened his eyes, hoping against hope that a rescuer had arrived, a night watchman or even a citizen with a stout cudgel in hand. Instead, in the light of a single torch borne by a lad who preceded them, three wobbly people approached, two men and a woman. They were singing, but their song stopped when they saw the tableau before them.

"What's this?" one man asked, his *esses* slushy. He either had no teeth or a gutful of wine.

Without a word, Simon's attacker faded into the darkness, his footsteps barely audible as he hurried up the alley.

"Help me," Simon managed.

"Awww, he's hurt." It was the woman, and despite her drunken slur, despite the smell of cheap perfume emanating from her like a miasma, she sounded sympathetic and therefore wonderful to Simon.

Haltingly, he told them what had happened. The woman turned to her two admirers. "We must help this man." At first, neither seemed much inclined to do so, but she added, "Once he is able to go on his way, we can get on with the showing of the duckies."

Both men seemed eager for that, and they helped Simon up from the cold earth. He found he could stand, although he was wobbly. His shoulder felt like a beaten drum, but he did not think it was broken or dislocated. "I must return to the city."

"We can see to that," said one of the men. In the torchlight, Simon saw they were both younger than he, while the woman was some years older. She had a professional charm, however, and the two seemed quite in awe of her, especially of her "duckies," large breasts that almost overflowed her dress.

The little party made its way to the river, where one of the men paid a waiting water taxi to ferry Simon across to the north side. The woman gave him a hearty kiss, embarrassing him completely. "Don't come to Southwark at night, young man," she said in his ear. "You ain't rich enough or strong enough to make your way here." Then she signaled the boatman, and Simon was on his way home.

Chapter Twelve

Hannah was waiting in the darkness, still dressed. She lit a candle as Simon fumbled his way into the house, gasping when she saw his disheveled appearance. Sitting him on a stool, she fetched a basin of water and a rag and began cleaning blood and dirt from his face. She moaned softly when her fingers found the lump at the side of his head.

"It is not a serious wound," he told her. "My mind is clear. No dizziness or nausea."

"Tell me how this happened."

She listened carefully as he told the story of his trip into Southwark. When he finished, she was silent for some time, which worried him. Although he valued his wife's opinions, Simon suspected she doubted Peto's innocence. She knew he had helped Simon in the past, but she also knew of his crimes. She had voiced no objections so far to Simon's activities, but the danger was no longer theoretical. Any wife might demand that her husband avoid further contact with Peto and his associates. In fact, most would.

Hannah was not most wives. If she doubted Peto's innocence, she must have sensed that Simon did not. She asked quietly, "What will you do now?"

"I will go to Calkin and tell him everything I know." Simon shrugged. "It is all I can do."

"You have done more than most would have." Hannah stroked his cheek. "Calkin can send someone to question folk about this Bannon, so that the truth comes out."

Simon did not speak his misgivings. Calkin would be more than reluctant to help a known criminal, especially with only Peto's word that he was innocent. And even if Calkin decided Peto could be believed, even if he found someone in authority in Southwark, someone willing to wade into a power struggle among thieves, who in that lawless spot would speak against Bannon, a man everyone feared?

Simon understood, however, that he was no force to take Bannon on. Tonight he had come as close to death as he wanted to. No match for the man in gray, certainly no match for Bannon, Simon would have to leave Peto to his own devices if Calkin could not or would not help.

Hannah watched him, almost as if she could see the thoughts progress through his mind. "You will not return to Southwark?"

"No."

"But you will go back to the Tower."

"Yes."

"To help the princess escape?"

"She will not hear of it."

Hannah hesitated, and he knew what she was thinking. Visiting Elizabeth was in its own way as dangerous as giving comfort to Peto the Pope.

Simon felt sick. Why could he not walk away from his two tragic friends? Why could he not keep to his own affairs? Why did he always feel he must do more?

He was too tired to think about it. Instead he ran his hand over Hannah's soft curls, freed from her cap and offering all the luxury a man could want. "Have I said that I love you, Mistress Maldon?"

She smiled. "Once or twice perhaps. But it bears repeating."

As Hannah tried to pin a straight hem, Janet turned this way and that to see how the skirt of her newest garment fell. The dress had belonged to the daughter of Simon's master, a girl who died tragically young. She had been tiny, like Janet, and the dress fit well. Hannah had only to lengthen it a little.

"Keep still, or the bottom will rise and fall like the tide!"

Sighing impatiently, Janet remained still for a while, but she was not silent. "It's so plain!" She fingered the neckline. "Could you add something here, a ruffle or some trim?"

"Perhaps, but not today. There is much we must do for the baby."

The young mother glared at the sleeping infant. "She doesn't care what she wears, but I hate looking like one of those awful reformers with their brown cloth made into ugly clothes!"

Hannah bit her lip to keep from commenting on Janet's ungratefulness. She had struggled all day with the girl's complaints and thoughtless comments, telling herself new mothers were often fussy and temperamental. Janet said their food was plain. She quickly became bored with the shop because most customers wanted no more than pain relievers and chest rubs. And there had only been one dress, and it was plain.

Janet kicked at the blankets she and her daughter had slept in. "The floor is hard, as I said it would be. The babe did not sleep well at all."

Despite Simon's late arrival the night before, Hannah had heard the baby cry only once. "I am sorry to hear it," she said stiffly. "I can have the loft ready for you and Susan today."

Janet gave the bed a speculative glance. "Perhaps you and Simon could sleep there."

Hannah was dumbstruck, but Janet continued her argument. "It would be more private for you, and when it cries, you won't be disturbed."

"I-I will see what Simon says," Hannah replied, her voice uncertain.

Janet looked at her, adding after a moment, "I'm so grateful to you for taking me in." She put a hand on Hannah's arm. "I don't know what I would have done."

Hannah hugged her. "You'll be all right now. And I'm sure Simon won't mind climbing up to the loft, at least until the little one sleeps through the night."

Despite his qualms and Hannah's fears, Simon went again to see Elizabeth. He was somewhat relieved to note the priest had quickly become a person of little interest. Mild-mannered, nondescript, and uninteresting, he seemed so earnest in his desire to catechize Elizabeth that he had no time even to look around him. It was, Simon reflected, a greater acting job than any they would ever see at a theater, for while his voice was a drone and his face held a pious expression, his hands shook and his insides felt like one of Hannah's holiday puddings.

The princess was a consummate actress. Although her eyes widened when she saw the bruise on his face, now a deep purple, her voice remained calm and her face composed.

After he had affected a blessing, she demanded in Latin, "Tell me what has happened, and I want to know all of it, or I shall ask for a different priest." Her lip curled in wry amusement. "I shall say this one is a drunkard who obviously walked into a door in his stupor last night."

Reluctantly, Simon told her the whole story, glossing over the attack and leaving out the Spaniards' reason for being in London. "I was not seriously harmed, and it is over now."

"It must be *completely* over," she said firmly. "Promise me you will stop dabbling in this criminal's affairs and let the law operate as it is meant to. If he is innocent, he will be found so."

As you will be? Simon wanted to ask. She had committed no crime, yet she might lose her head. How could she argue that the law was always correct?

"Highness—my lady, it is always wrong when the law misuses

a person." He did not refer to her situation, for it was treason to suggest that the queen was wrong. He stuck to the subject of Peto. "My friend did not kill this man."

"He is guilty of other crimes, so he must die. Where is the misuse?"

"Someone who is truly guilty of the crime will go free."

She waved a thin, white hand impatiently. "If the other criminal is caught at some point, we shall send him to justice, too."

Simon dropped the argument, seeing he would never convince her. Her own mother had been executed though she had committed no crime. Could Elizabeth not see that the law could be wrong? He should not have brought up the subject of Peto.

Elizabeth paced a few steps, feet scuffling softly, then turned and came back to where Simon stood, surprising him with her next statement. "Despite the fact he deserves to be hanged, it is obvious that someone tried to stop your inquiries into the matter. A clever plot has been hatched against your friend."

Simon's surprise was replaced by understanding as he glanced at their grim surroundings. Shut up here with the threat of death looming over her, the princess was desperate for something to occupy her mind. One who had always looked forward, never back, her way forward now offered little hope. Peto's situation was a distraction, something to ponder other than the Tower Green and the headsman's axe. Simon was gratified that his quest for justice in Peto's case might at least serve to divert Elizabeth's mind from her own problems.

It was an advantage for him as well. The mind that now dissected the story of what had happened in Southwark was like none other he had ever known. If anyone could find the weaknesses in the case against Peto, it was Elizabeth Tudor.

She lowered her head, possibly in prayer, but more likely

reviewing everything he had told her. "The outlaw claims the man was newly killed when he entered the room?"

"Yes."

"And it was as he said?"

"I went to the alehouse and saw it for myself."

"Simon in Southwark!" Her tone implied that was like a virgin entering a brothel.

Ignoring her amusement, Simon said, "The host claims there was no way a murderer could have been in the room before or entered unseen after Red John went inside."

"Then," she said with certainty, "he let the killer in at the rear door."

"Who would he have let in? And besides, Saddler swears Red John was asleep, which is borne out by the position of the body and the lack of any sort of struggle."

Elizabeth clucked her tongue in irritation, glanced at the others in the room, and took a moment to form a pious expression once more. "There are only two possibilities, since you insist your friend did not commit the crime. Either someone went in, avoiding the notice of a dozen people, or someone was already in the room when the victim got there. Without seeing the place myself, I cannot say which is more likely, but you have a mind. Figure it out."

Simon felt almost angry at her. Did she think he had not tried? He went silent, considering the two options. He could not believe that every person in the taproom had missed a killer entering the room. Were they all part of the crime, even the constable's men? Unlikely.

Then someone had been hiding in the room. But he had looked for himself and he said aloud, echoing his own thoughts, "There is no place a man might hide."

Elizabeth caught the flaw in the statement. "What of a woman? Or a child?"

The pale, pinched face of little Henry arose immediately before him, and Simon shook his head in wonder that he had not made the connection himself. "The boy!" he blurted, and then, as the guard and the women who sat gossiping in the corner looked up in surprise, he turned it into a chant, sounding, at least to his own ears, more like a lunatic than a priest. Elizabeth nodded solemnly and bowed her head as if receiving a very special blessing.

When the others went back to their own interests, he explained, "Peto's cousin, one Christopher Bannon, had a boy and a woman with him at the alehouse. When Bannon said he was home at the time of the murder, the boy seemed uneasy."

"Might you speak with him alone?"

Simon frowned. "Bannon keeps him close, and the child is obviously afraid of him."

"Then he is wiser than you, Simon. You endangered yourself, bringing your face to this Bannon's notice."

"I never thought he would recognize me with Pen at the Bull's Horn, but he must have."

"A clever criminal. He seems even worse than the one you call friend."

"Bannon is nothing like Peto," he insisted. "He operates by inspiring fear, while Peto has—had—the affection of those around him."

Elizabeth sniffed derisively. "Affection? For a criminal?"

"Peto is a kind of hero. Many benefit from his actions."

She nodded. "I know those who flaunt the law sometimes earn the approval of the common folk. They are bolder than others of their ilk, live more exciting lives, and, until they are caught, have the means to impress the crowd."

"Exactly." Simon tried to put into words the difference between an admirable outlaw and a despicable one. "Bannon takes what he wants and does not care who is hurt in the process. It is fear of him that now makes people unwilling to speak for Peto."

"I see. And Bannon seeks to take over Peto's role as leader of the criminals?"

"Yes. He arranged that the law should take Peto out of his way."

"And if he can tarnish Peto's reputation in the process, all the better for him."

"Yes."

Her expression turned thoughtful, and it struck Simon again that in one sense, Elizabeth was living Peto's nightmare. He said, "Bannon may find that while leadership can be achieved with an iron hand, it is difficult to maintain without affection."

Elizabeth saw the inference, but she never forgot the difference between royal and common blood, and her eyes flashed a warning. At that moment one of the attendants sneezed, which probably reminded her to moderate the tone of her reply. "Mary's position is not the same at all. Bannon is a criminal who longs to replace another criminal."

Simon would not argue with his friend, could not argue with a noblewoman. "I only meant that a benevolent thief is better than a malevolent one."

Elizabeth sighed. "Will you take heed? It is not your place to fight this battle."

He shrugged. "I know my limitations. I will not go to Southwark again, but I intend to tell Calkin the tale, so someone in authority knows Peto did not murder Red John."

"They will still hang him. Can you not see that?"

Simon thought, but did not say, that if Bannon were arrested, Peto's chances of escape from the Tower would increase. Once his name was cleared and his fearsome rival removed, Peto's friends might once again work for his good.

But Bannon's arrest was unlikely at this point. Calkin shared

Elizabeth's view that a dead criminal was the best kind, whether guilty of the crime he was hanged for or not.

Abandoning the argument, he prepared to take his leave. "Is there aught I can do for you?"

Her smile was sardonic. "Bring me wings so I may fly from this place."

"Would that I could! Are you sure—"

An impatient shuffling of her feet and a quick gesture silenced him. "Go home to your wife, Simon."

"I will come again tomorrow."

She wanted to forbid him to do so. He saw her struggle to say it, but she needed something to look forward to, even if it was only his visits. With a nod, she said, "I thank you."

As he left the Tower, Simon's heart felt a little lighter. He *was* doing something for Elizabeth. He had seen her relief at knowing she was not alone, that she had a friend.

Not friend, he reminded himself sharply. A princess was not *friend* to a man like him. Still, they were at ease with each other, and he thought she appreciated the fact that perhaps only he, among everyone she knew, wanted nothing from her.

Chapter Thirteen

After some thought, Hannah decided she would not ask Simon to give up his bed. He had been generous, letting Janet stay. He had made no objection when her contributions were minimal at best. He'd been polite with her obnoxious questions and inane comments. Janet was perfectly able to climb the ladder to the loft. When Hannah had mentioned the dresses stored there, she had climbed the ladder with no hesitation. Hannah suspected the girl's desire to sleep in their bed stemmed more from want than need. Much as she hated to admit it, Hannah had come to understand that Janet enjoyed manipulating others, seeing how much she could make them do.

As the girl sat in the doorway, watching the traffic on the street, Hannah gathered her courage and approached. "I have thought on it, and it is best if you sleep in the loft. The pallet there is comfortable, and I would not ask my husband to give up his bed."

Janet's head turned, eyes widening to a disbelieving stare. When she spoke, her words were carefully neutral. "I only thought to spare you when the child cries in the night."

"That is kind of you, but it matters not whether you are up and we are down or the other way 'round. The loft is more private, and Simon will sleep in the bed he made for the two of us."

The girl's lips pulled inward and she took breath to reply, but a customer entered the shop at that moment. Janet glared at the poor fellow as if he'd stepped on her toe.

The young man seemed ill at ease, whether from Janet's attitude or from his mission, Hannah could not say. She stepped forward. "Can I assist you with something?"

"Um, is the apothecary about?"

"No, but I am familiar with the medicines."

The man seemed reluctant to share his purpose with two women but saw the visit through. "I wondered if he has anything for, um—" He stopped, unable to say the word. Then he pulled off his cap, and Hannah saw his need. Though not yet twenty, his hairline was fast receding.

"Bald!" Janet's harsh laugh brought a blush to the man's face that made Hannah want to slap her.

She put a hand on his shoulder. "Do others in your family suffer thus?"

"My mother has three brothers who lost their hair early." He turned his body away from Janet and said pleadingly to Hannah, "Is there nothing to be done?"

"If he were here, my husband would tell you to crush a garlic bulb and rub it into your scalp each seven-night. Once that is done, wash the scalp in vinegar."

"That will help?"

"It is in the stars what happens to each of us. But if you keep your humors balanced and follow the treatment, it is the best you can do."

Hannah tried to refuse payment, a newly killed rabbit, saying she had given nothing but advice. The man insisted, and in the end she took it. "I thank you, for we have with us this young mother, who will benefit from a hearty rabbit stew."

Janet, staring out the doorway sulkily, did not acknowledge the comment. When the customer left, she said without looking at Hannah, "I see it is a hardship on you if I remain here. I will take my child and go."

Hannah hurried to her side, putting an arm around her shoulders. "You are no bother, and you can be a help, both in the house and in the shop." Her thoughts flew ahead: Susan gone from her forever, perhaps going hungry or living in a drafty house the church maintained for women with bastard children. How could she let the child go, whatever her mother's failings? "Stay a few weeks, and I will ask Simon if we might move to the loft. When you have recovered and the child is strong enough, then you can decide your future."

Janet was instantly warm again. "Oh, Hannah, you are the kindest person I ever met!"

A cry interrupted their embrace, and Janet moaned softly. "Will I never again have an hour's peace?" She went into the living area, brow furrowed. Hannah watched her go, unable to understand her detachment from her daughter. Then she reminded herself that Janet's lot was not an easy one. A woman with a child, especially a woman who had never been married, would not easily find a husband. Still, Janet was pretty, and she could be charming. Surely some man would take the child in order to have the mother.

Take the child. Hannah's heart wrenched at the thought of losing the child that was not hers. Susan would someday be taken away. She had to face that fact. She must love the little thing as much as she could today, for tomorrow, or at least too soon, the babe would be gone.

Simon could not bring himself to abandon Peto's cause without telling him what he had learned, although he did not inform Elizabeth of his intention. Once outside the Bell Tower where she was housed, he stepped into the shadows of an alcove. When he emerged, the cassock was gone and he wore instead a black wig, small rolls of linen in his cheeks, and his own sober brown clothing. In his good hand he carried a slate and some chalk.

Proceeding to the tower where Peto's cell was, he spoke to the guard. The rolls, although effective at changing the shape of his face, made it difficult to enunciate clearly, slowing his speech. It served to change his cadence, however, which was helpful in making him seem a different person.

"I am to make a drawing of this man for the news sheets." He raised his nose as if having contact with a criminal was the last thing he wanted, adding, "No need to open the door. I will look at him through the peephole."

Simon had deduced communication between those who worked at the Tower and those who sent people there was imperfect at best. Unless an individual nobleman paid particular attention to a prisoner, days might pass without anyone taking notice of him. The guards, therefore, made their own decisions on day-to-day matters. Peto was simply a man who would hang soon. Nobody cared who visited him, and nobody cared what the two of them said to each other. It would change nothing when the hangman got hold of him.

All over London, halfpenny news sheets offered the latest in news and the most scurrilous gossip, with drawings often included to add interest. For only the tiniest bribe, the guard accepted that Simon had been hired to add a picture of the notorious but mysterious Peto the Pope to one of them.

Led to the cell, Simon played his part, peering through the slot and then down at his slate, peering in again, then making corrections by rubbing out a line with the side of his hand. Chalk clicked and ground against slate, but it seemed the drawing did not go as he wanted. As the guard watched, he erased lines again and again, finally snorting with disgust and starting all over.

The guard became impatient. "Call me when you've finished, and I'll escort you out." The artist apparently listened with only half an ear, merely grunting in reply.

After the guard moved off, Peto approached the door. "For an honest man, Simon, you are wondrous crafty." Seeing Simon up close, his eyes narrowed. "What happened to you?"

"I was attacked in Southwark." He hurried to add, "Some revelers happened by and the robber ran off."

Even in the dimness of the cell's interior, Simon could read in Peto's expression the understanding there was more to the story than a botched robbery. "I did not intend this, Simon. Do not tempt the stars again."

Simon pulled from his pocket a cloth-wrapped meat pie he'd bought at a vendor's stall and handed it over. "I want to help."

Peto bit off a chunk of still-warm crust and spoke around it. The savory smell drifted through the bars, and Simon wished he had purchased two pies. "You must not put yourself in danger for my sake." Peto took another bite. "Did you find Pen?"

"I did. He went to your lodgings, but the woman was gone." To confirm Pen's assessment of the missing Frances, he asked, "Could she have had anything to do with this?"

"No," the other said firmly. "The girl is devoted to me." Peto's eyes clouded. "Almost too devoted. She would suffocate a man with her love, were he not careful."

Exactly as Pen had said. "Strange she is missing."

Peto frowned. "Was there any upset in my rooms?"

"No. The place was undisturbed."

"Then she has heard of my arrest and gone where none can find her." He sounded definite, and Simon guessed it was what he needed to believe, since he was unable to do anything for the woman in his present state.

"Tell me about Christo Bannon, then."

Peto smiled. An odd smile, full of knowing. "Tell me first what you know of him."

Simon told the story of his two visits to Southwark.

"I feared as much," Peto said when he was done. "Christo wants more than he has. He does not see the work it takes to build and keep an enterprise operating, only the possibility of taking what someone else has."

"What will you do?"

Peto raised an eyebrow. "From here? I can do nothing. But you, Simon, must stay out of Southwark. Christo is a hard man, and I would not have your death on my conscience." His eyes warmed a little. "You have done what you could for me."

Simon decided not to mention his plan to ask for Calkin's help. Instead he relayed the Spaniards' offer. "If you can escape from this place, you have a way to leave England." He tested the bars of thick iron between them, which did not move an iota. "I confess, I do not know how that might happen."

"Simon Maldon," Peto said, licking the remains of the pie from his fingers. "I thank you for looking to my future. But now I charge you: go back to your shop and remain there. If you do, my enemies will trouble you no further."

"Are you sure?" He'd had a frightening dream that the man in gray came to the shop and threatened Hannah.

"If they see no more of you in Southwark, they will be satisfied." Peto shook his head in frustration. "I knew Christo was ambitious, but I did not think he had the grit to take me on."

"He did not!" Simon said emphatically. "He acted as a coward, murdering your friends and murmuring lies to your associates. And rather than face you man-to-man, he framed you, hoping the law will do what he does not have the stomach for."

"You are right," Peto said thoughtfully. "I am at a disadvantage, but I am no coward." He seemed to take on a new sense of resolution. "Let us see what Peto the Pope can manage. If I am successful, Christo will have to find his courage, or he will pay with his life."

★ ★ ★ ★ ★

When Simon found him at St. James, Calkin was just going off duty. The two moved to a spot where they could speak without being overheard and, being a man who was seldom idle, Calkin took out a whetstone and began to hone the edge of his knife blade.

"It's rumored the queen will order her sister's execution soon," he said, brow furrowed.

"Renaud has returned from Spain?"

"He has. The marriage contract is made, and gossip says they will set about removing all impediments to Mary's rule. One of my comrades heard Renaud advise the queen to act 'for her husband's peace.' What else can it mean?"

Simon listened to the rasp of steel on stone. "When will the marriage take place?"

"As soon as Philip arrives, possibly by midsummer. But they will no doubt proceed with the execution as soon as possible, in order to give any resulting uprising time to die down before the duke arrives to see it."

"I thank you for telling me." It was not good news, but Simon was grateful for his friend's current knowledge. "My purpose in coming here was something different." Briefly he told Calkin about Peto, Bannon, and the murder of the man known as Red John.

When he finished, Calkin shook his head in disgust. "You risked your life to help Peto the Pope? Do you know how long the law in this city has been after that man?"

"Well, yes, but—"

"He is not worth putting yourself in danger, Simon. And don't tell me how you managed to visit him in prison. Simply knowing you did is enough to put my position in jeopardy."

Seeing his friend's anger, Simon tried to explain.

Simon floundered for an explanation. "But I'm sure Bannon is responsible—"

Calkin heaved a great sigh, probably reminding himself that Simon was his friend. He tested the blade with a finger and, satisfied, slipped it into the leather sheath on his belt. "I will report what you have told me to the justices in Southwark. If this Bannon is a criminal, they can collect him, too, put him in the cell next to your friend, and they can hang together. The crowds enjoy a double execution."

Simon pressed his lips together in frustration. If Bannon was under arrest he might breathe a little easier, but Peto would never be released. And now Elizabeth's situation had become more perilous. Should he abandon Peto's cause and concentrate on hers?

But what could he do for the princess? He knew no one who could intervene with the queen or one of her advisers. Every noble person he had ever met was either in prison or dead.

Prison! Robert Dudley was in a cell in the Tower of London, not far from Elizabeth's cell. Although a death sentence hung over his head, Dudley knew well the machinations of power. He might advise Simon how to proceed, how best to appeal to Mary.

Thanking Calkin and enduring patiently the guardsman's warnings that he avoid Southwark, he walked away, already planning his course. He could not visit a prisoner like Dudley in the person of a priest or an artist. He would have to find a more suitable disguise.

Chapter Fourteen

Hannah quickly became frustrated with Simon's lack of attention. Upon coming home he had gone directly to the loft and begun searching through the clothing stored there, sending up clouds of dust and lint that tickled her nose. In some detail, she brought him up to date on the baby's wondrous achievements, mostly yawning and digesting milk with various accompanying noises and smells. After a while she realized his distraction might be an advantage. She could tell him they were moving to the loft, and if he was not listening, she could claim later with all honesty that she had indeed told him.

Simon sat back in defeat. "There is nothing here that will do." He banged a knuckle gently against his teeth as he considered whatever was on his mind. After a moment he bent over the basket and began a second search.

With a sigh of determination, Hannah said to his back, "I have given Janet our bed."

He *was* listening, for he stopped and turned to look at her. Unable to meet his eyes directly, she glanced downstairs, checking to see if Janet was eavesdropping. "We can sleep up here." When he frowned she added, "That way you won't hear the baby cry."

Simon searched her face for a few seconds, apparently weighing the options. "I suppose that will be best for a few days," he finally said calmly. "Once her condition improves, Janet and her baby can move up here, and we will return to our bed." There might have been the slightest emphasis on the word *our.*

Hannah breathed out in relief. "Exactly my thought." She tried not to look at the tiny bed they would share up here, tried not to wonder just how long Janet would consider it necessary she sleep in the bed that should be theirs.

"He must be fitted properly, as you well can imagine," Simon explained to the guard outside the cell. "A person as important as Robert Dudley cannot go to his death looking like a scurvy knave." He had returned to the Tower, this time dressed in a suit he would never have chosen for himself. Finding nothing suitable in his box at home, he had stopped at a tailor friend's shop and managed, with promises he would be extremely careful, to borrow a suit of clothing and some fabric samples. It was lucky, he told himself, that Elizabeth, Peto, and Dudley were housed in separate towers. It lessened the chance he might be recognized when he visited for the third time in one day.

"Who sent you?" the guard asked gruffly. "We had no notice Dudley asked for a tailor."

Playing the role he had chosen, Simon tittered like a giddy girl and grabbed the man's arm. "Bless you, friend! He did not send for me!" He leaned closer, batting his eyes outrageously, and slipped a coin into the man's hand. "A certain lady took it upon herself to see to his attire for the occasion."

The guard's expression turned sly. "Who would such a lady be?"

Simon fluttered his hands as if he were shooing a chicken. "How should I keep my trade if I give away the secrets of my betters? The lady will remain anonymous, but she has chosen excellent fabrics." He indicated the pile of cloth he carried over his arm and added, "I will be glad to share with you the remnants once His Lordship has made his decision."

"No lord in there. Just a prisoner waiting to die." The

prospect of a bit of fine cloth seemed to please the guard, however, and he opened the cell door with a key from a ring on his belt. Simon smiled to himself. The entry fee was acceptable: a gold coin and a promise that would cost him nothing.

Simon entered the modest room where Robert Dudley sat playing chess with one young man while another looked on. All three seemed listless, probably bored half out of their minds. Prison, Simon had observed, was mostly boredom interspersed with periods of terror when one was reminded of the punishment to come.

The afternoon sun slanted in the one small, high-set window in the room, lighting little but a square of stone on the opposite wall. Dudley looked up, and one eyebrow rose at the sight of Simon, complete with tape measure, outlandish cap, and a long robe of the type worn only by old men these days. A ghastly shade of green trimmed with feathers, it covered him from neck to feet and ensured that few looked directly at his face. The heavy cap hid his hair and came low over his forehead, although it smelled of someone else's body and some sort of hairdressing he found objectionable. He had added a false mustache to further obscure his face and adopted an exaggerated walk, waving his hands dramatically and rolling his eyes when he talked.

The two men with Dudley tried unsuccessfully to hide their amusement at the figure before them. Dudley, however, looked at Simon closely, and a slight frown appeared between his brows. "What foolishness is this?"

"I am come to measure you for a new suit," Simon said, raising the tone of his voice higher than normal. "A gift from an admirer." He turned to the two men, brandishing his tape measure theatrically. "If we could have a few moments?" To Dudley he said, "I will be quick, and you will return to your game anon." He looked into Dudley's eyes as he spoke, trying to send a silent message.

After some hesitation, Elizabeth's longtime friend apparently received it. His gaze moved to Simon's weak arm as if confirming his thought. "Friends, please leave us. I promise you, I will make short work of this fellow."

The attendants smiled at each other with apparent enjoyment of the ridiculous figure Simon presented. Dudley smiled with them, as if relishing the joke as much as they did. Without haste the two men moved to another room, hardly closing the door behind them before Simon heard a burst of laughter. When they were gone, Dudley's brown eyes turned to Simon with purpose. "We have met before, I think."

"We have, Your Worship. I am Simon Maldon, friend to a lady of your acquaintance who even now is imprisoned here in the Tower."

"Elizabeth."

"Yes. I learned this morning that her execution grows more and more likely."

Dudley grimaced. "Mary wants her gone before the Spanish bridegroom appears."

"That is my fear."

The nobleman stood, walked a few paces, and paused before the tiny window. He was a handsome and impressive man, with the demeanor of one used to getting things done. "I wonder," he said, looking at the courtyard below, "if Philip understands he is best served if Elizabeth remains alive."

Simon's interest rose. "How is that, Your Worship?"

"Elizabeth and Mary are loved by the people, but Philip is not, being foreign. If Elizabeth is executed, they will put the blame on the Spaniard, not her sister."

It was human nature, Simon conceded, to attach the blame for evil deeds to a person already disliked.

"Added to that," Dudley continued, "the queen is thirty-seven, perhaps too old for childbearing. If Elizabeth remains alive, not only does Philip avoid the stain of Tudor blood, he has a second marriage prospect should Mary die." His lips tightened in a grim smile. "It worked for the old king, who married his brother's widow and begat Mary on her."

Simon looked at Dudley in awe. "I had not thought of that."

Dudley stood, sending the stool backward across the rough floor with a scrape. "You are not born and bred to it. For those of my station, life is a constant measuring of options." His tone conveyed grim amusement as he indicated the walls around him. "Mistakes are made, of course. One must forget the past, look to the future, and make the best of the present."

"Do you hope to live, my lord?"

"Hope? No, one cannot hope. It is too painful. Still, Mary cannot execute everyone who plotted against her, or she will have no competent advisers left at all."

But the Dudleys were her enemies, and Robert's father and brother had already gone to the headsman. Why would Mary spare Robert, Northumberland's cleverest son and Elizabeth's childhood friend? Simon wished it were possible, but he saw little hope of Dudley's pardon.

He returned his focus to Elizabeth's situation. His visit was already successful, for Dudley had given him an idea. Now he needed the doomed nobleman's help. "Do you think you might take a gamble on the future, Your Worship?"

Dudley smiled, spreading his hands wide. "What more can they do to me?"

"If you write a letter, explaining what you just told me but using the proper language and courtesies, I will see the Spanish prince receives it."

Stroking his beard, Dudley considered. "How will you do such a thing?"

"I recently met some Spaniards who will see to it."

The prisoner paced the room again, apparently considering

all facets of the matter. "It is not treason," he muttered, "for I propose no harm to the queen." He chuckled. "What matter, anyway? I am already sentenced to die. If I am successful, Philip might remember me when he comes to England. If I am not, some way must be found to get Elizabeth out of the country."

"She will not go, trusting in her sister's good will."

Dudley shook his head regretfully. "She was ever stubborn, that one. Still, if we appeal to Philip, she might be saved. Mary declares herself in love with the man, though she has seen only his portrait. They say she will do anything he asks."

He clapped his hands softly, apparently coming to a decision. "Return tomorrow at evening, and I will have a letter ready. It must be carefully thought out," he cautioned as Simon opened his mouth to object to the delay. "I do not think they will act before Pentecost, for royal murder would sully the holy season. We have some time."

He said it matter-of-factly, but Simon winced. How casually these nobles spoke of the axe! They seemed grateful for it, though one wondered why. Accounts he'd heard told that it often took several blows to sever a head from its body. Anne Boleyn had comforted herself with the comment, "I have a little neck." Indeed, her head had come off with one blow, but that was probably because a steel sword was used, not the usual iron axe.

Glancing at Dudley's strong physique and muscular neck, Simon guessed someone like him could only pray there were no misdirected blows or inept headsmen in his future. It was a terrifying prospect, one he did not allow himself to imagine for Elizabeth.

"Your husband lets you do all the work of this place." Janet's tone was scornful as she watched Hannah sort through a basket of herbs she had picked. "He has spent precious little time making physic since I have been here."

"He is usually very industrious," Hannah retorted, hearing the defensive tone in her own voice. The scent of coltsfoot drifted through the room as she began separating the flowers from the stems. She would make a syrup of the flowers, helpful for clearing mucous, and the leaves made a health-restoring tea.

Pinching off a flower, she added by way of explanation, "Simon has of late been preoccupied with the troubles of the friend I told you of."

Janet was immediately interested. "What kind of trouble does this friend have?"

Now Hannah was stuck. She could hardly admit to this relative stranger that she and Simon were acquaintances, if not friends, of England's recently disinherited princess. "A man he once knew has been arrested for murder."

"Murder!" Janet's tone was both horrified and intrigued.

"Simon is certain this man is innocent, and he wants to make those in authority aware of their mistake, so that justice is served."

Janet gave a scornful laugh. "Those in authority care nothing for justice."

Gathering up the flowers in her apron, Hannah replied calmly, "I'm sure it is not always the case, but when a man has a certain reputation, it is understandable that crimes might be laid at his door that are not his."

"True, but if they could see into a man's heart, they would know his motives are good."

Hannah did not argue the point, deciding that Janet's view of criminals was more romantic than realistic. She imagined her companions among the serving girls telling stories that colored her view. Besides, Hannah told herself, Simon would have taken Janet's side in the argument. He seemed to believe the reasons for Peto's crimes excused the crimes themselves. She disagreed, but she did not argue with Simon, either.

"Whose murder takes your husband so often from his work?"

After a moment's consideration, Hannah answered truthfully, judging it could cause no harm to tell Janet the story. "A man was killed in Southwark a few nights ago."

"That's not unusual," Janet retorted. At Hannah's questioning look, she explained, "One of the girls who once worked with me was sent away for stealing. She lives in Southwark now, but we see each other from time to time. She told me the place is both exciting and dangerous."

Hannah thought of Simon's visits to Southwark, hoping they were forever at an end. "The murder took place at an alehouse, and Simon's friend seems to have been the only one who could have done it. He is now locked in the Tower of London."

"Little chance he will leave there alive." Janet's tone was matter-of-fact, but after a pause it turned to something else. "I know someone who might help this friend of yours escape from prison."

"You do?" Hannah was a little amused, but she kept her face lowered, testing her preparation's consistency with a finger.

Janet looked slightly uncomfortable. "When I left the place I worked, I spent some time in Southwark, with the friend I mentioned, Ellie."

"You have been living in Southwark?"

"I had no place else to go when the old man put me out! I went to Ellie, hoping she would help me get r—" She stopped at Hannah's horrified look. "Until I could decide what to do with the child." She glanced in Susan's direction. "Ellie took me to a wise woman, but it was too late to, um, be done with the pregnancy. It would kill me, she said."

Hannah was dazed by this new information. Janet had lied. Janet had spent the last few months in Southwark. Janet did not want her baby. The last seemed most important.

Putting down her mortar and pestle, Hannah took hold of the girl's arms. "There are times when new mothers do not feel as they should toward their babes, especially when circumstances are hard. You have no husband, and you don't know how you will care for Susan. It is these things that keep you from loving her fully." She took the girl's hand in hers. "But you will come to love your child. Simon and I will help. Once you believe that, your cares will disappear, and you will see what a wonderful gift you have in her."

A gift I would give anything to have, she added silently.

Janet looked into Hannah's face for a few seconds. "You are right," she finally said. "With your help, everything will be well, for the child and for me."

"I'm glad." Hannah swept the leaves into her apron, and spread them on a board to dry beside the fire. "I must start the evening meal. Simon will be home soon."

Later that night, when they lay together in the loft, Hannah asked Simon, "Do you believe Janet told us the truth of where she comes from?"

Simon lay very still, and Hannah recognized his cautious mode, used when he knew a truthful answer would hurt her feelings. Finally he said, "What do you think?"

"She admitted today that much of it was lies." She didn't mention Southwark, knowing its reputation for harlots and prostitutes. "I did notice her hands."

"And I did not," he admitted. "What about them?"

"They are soft and white. No scullery maid escapes calluses from the work and redness from the strong soap and the cold water."

She hoped he would offer an explanation that could satisfy her doubts, but he did not. After a moment he said, "If she lied, does it matter? She told us what she thought she must to gain our sympathy for herself and our care for her child. I don't suppose we will throw her and the babe into the streets, no matter what the truth might be."

"No," Hannah agreed. "I would never want to lose Susan." She added a moment later, "Nor Janet either, of course."

Chapter Fifteen

Simon was busy in the shop at mid-morning when a customer came in. "Have you a remedy for deafness?" he called from the doorway, as if reluctant to enter unless assured of help. The way he leaned forward and turned his head to one side indicated the request was for himself. Waving the man in, Simon asked a few questions then began making a concoction that combined the gall of a hare with grease from a fox. "Warm a spoonful of this and place it in the ear each night before bed," he ordered. "And you must try to keep your humors in balance so you lose no more of your hearing. We cannot give back what is lost, so we will work to keep what you have."

The man nodded, accepting what he probably had already guessed. As Simon mixed the thick fat with the thin, sharp-smelling gall, he listened to a steady stream of gossip and commentary on the gossip from his customer. Simon agreed with a grunt that times were hard, but said nothing when the man expressed the opinion a woman could not successfully rule England.

"When have we ever had a queen and no king?" he asked, pointing a finger at Simon's chest as if Mary's reign was the apothecary's fault.

"Well, there was Matilda."

The man had obviously never heard of her. "Did she do well?"

"No," Simon had to admit. "But it was not all her fault."

A dismissing hand brushed aside explanation. "A woman on the throne is madness."

Deciding it was best to drop that subject, Simon repeated his instructions for the medicine's use. When he finished, his customer handed over a coin in payment. Testing the cord of the coin purse on his belt, the man commented, "One must keep his money well secured. They say Peto the Pope escaped from the Tower last night and is at large in London."

Simon continued putting away his ingredients, tying a string around the leather cover of the grease jar, though his pulse jumped at the news. "I had not heard it."

"Outwitted a guard, and he was away. There's no safety for honest men in these times."

Before the man could find a way to blame Peto's escape on the fact England had a queen and no king, Simon asked, "You are sure it was he, the notorious smuggler?"

The customer raised a hand, palm up. "Everyone has heard of Peto. Men say he is a leader among thieves." He snickered. "I suppose that is something like being a leader on the queen's council." He leaned toward Simon, brow furrowed. "Scoundrels are everywhere. A woman on the throne means trouble, whether in the alleys or in the palace."

No comment seemed appropriate, so Simon made only a noncommittal murmur.

"The queen should marry an Englishman, one who knows the people's mind and can manage the nation's business. A woman cannot do it, and a Spaniard will not." With that the man left, slamming the door in an apparent attempt to relieve his frustration over England's state.

Simon wasted no time heading through the curtained door, where he found the two women sitting side by side. "I must go out."

"What is it?" Janet asked the question. Hannah held the child, and he noted her serene expression, the sure gentleness of her hands as she patted the tiny body.

"A customer says Peto escaped from the Tower."

He was surprised at Janet's reaction. "Escaped! What do you mean?"

Hannah said, "I told you Simon's old friend—acquaintance—was arrested recently." After a moment she added, "Unjustly." Turning to Simon she asked, "He has escaped?"

"I will discover if this tale is true."

Janet's whole body tensed and she rose jerkily, taking a few steps toward the door. "Return quickly," she ordered. "And try to learn where he might be now!"

Hannah said gently, "He will not come here, Janet. You must not be afraid."

The girl spun toward them, eyes wide, bumping the table and sending the things on it rattling. "But he is at liberty, is he not?"

"Peto is not the sort of man who would harm you," Simon told her. "It is difficult to explain, but some, though they are considered criminals, are nevertheless good men."

Janet looked at Simon with an expression he could not interpret. It was no use, he told himself, trying to explain the difference between Peto and other criminals. He was not sure he knew it himself, but he *felt* that Peto was different.

"I will return anon." Kissing Hannah's cheek, he snatched up his cap and left the house.

It was almost midday, but the sun was hidden by low clouds that pressed ominously on those below them. Traffic on the bridge was dense and slow-moving. As he trudged along, Simon sorted his thoughts. He should not be doing this. If Peto was free, he could look to his own escape from England and did not need Simon's help. But Simon recalled Peto's threat against Bannon. He had to make Peto see that escape was his only option. In addition, if Peto sailed for Spain, he could take with him the letter Robert Dudley had promised, which Simon was to get from the prisoner this evening.

Penitence Brook would know where Peto was, if anyone did. He would find Pen, talk to Peto, then be done with Southwark forever.

When Simon arrived at the house, however, Pen was not there. "I have not seen him since early this morning," his sister said, her aggravation obvious.

"Where might I look for him?"

Her laughter was more harsh than amused. "Chase the wind. That's what he does." She eyed two baskets of laundry stacked on the floor beside her. "It's sure to rain this afternoon, I've wash to hang and a thousand other things to do, and he drifts away to see who might spend a few idle moments with him." With a baleful glance at Simon, she bent and took up the top basket.

Partially to help, partially hoping she might know something of Peto's escape, Simon lifted the second, balancing its weight on his hip to lessen the strain on his crippled arm. "I will help you. Perhaps Pen will return by the time we are finished."

Judith looked at him with surprise but did not object. Soon they were at the back of the house, hanging garments on a rope strung between two posts. From the variety of items, Simon guessed Judith laundered for her tenants to earn extra money.

"How did you come to know my prating toad brother?" she asked after a while. Her voice revealed no real curiosity, and Simon guessed she was only passing time with a stranger.

"We met some years ago, when the old king was alive. I had not seen him since."

Judith glanced Simon's way. "He sometimes speaks of his apothecary friend."

"I like Pen," he told her. "He is an honest man, and there are not enough of those."

"Hmph! Honest he might be. Helpful he is not. I count on

him for nothing. My brother is a fool, and he has been so since birth. I have always been his keeper, despite he is the older."

"He often claims he is a fool," Simon said evenly, "but I think him wiser than many."

Judith paused, the shirt in her hands forgotten for a moment. "Wise? I suppose it might be called wise to ignore useful work and the judgment of others."

"But you cannot?"

"No." Judith glanced over her shoulder. "All I have is this house, and it is all I can do to keep it." She shook out a linen cloth with a sharp snap before spreading it over the rope. "I know what folk say: 'Poor Judith, to have fallen so low!' I don't want their pity. All I want is for Pen to do as I ask and the others to pay what they owe. That's all."

"I'm sorry," Simon said, although he was not sure what he should be sorry for. "Life has not been kind to you."

"You might say that." Her voice vibrated with sarcasm.

Thinking the topic of her house might be safer, Simon said, "At least you have your home, so you have some security."

"It is no longer my home," Judith said through tight lips. "It is a gathering place for the lowly, and I am become their keeper, as I have always been for Pen. I wash their clothes and hear their complaints. I lose sleep when their babies are sick and give up a measure of cloth when their old ones die. I am mother to no one, yet I am responsible for them all. I am sick to death of it." More clothing slapped onto the line, underscoring the anger in Judith's mind.

Simon asked gently, "How did it come to this?"

Facing the line of laundry, she told her life story in plain words. "Our mother was a trull, raised in these parts but blessed with passing beauty. Before she was sixteen she had Pen, which was ill luck for her and for me, though I was not yet born. From the first his gait was odd, his face foolish, and his thoughts disconnected.

"When Pen was three, in a stroke of good luck, my mother met a rich man who fancied himself in love with her. I was born soon after, and when he built a fine new home for his legal wife and legitimate children near Hampton, Mother wheedled this place from him. Values were falling fast for such houses, because those who could afford them no longer wanted to live on this side of the Thames. I recall that my father was very pleased with his gift, and I was required to give pretty speeches of thanks whenever we saw him."

Simon imaged Judith having to bow and fawn on a man she did not admire or possibly even like. She had no doubt hated being unable to speak her mind, as she had from the first moment Simon met her.

"When he died," she went on, "there was no more money. As my mother often reminded me, I was not blessed with her looks, so there were no more rich men in our lives. We began to take in lodgers, and since she died, I have taken in more and more of them to survive." She grimaced. "Pen does not seem to notice, but I remember when the house was ours alone, with a maid to help with the work."

Simon looked away from the pain in her eyes. "I'm sorry."

Judith turned brusque again. "It's nothing to you, is it? You've got a shop, he says."

"A small one."

"Steady income, and no boarders getting into fights at midnight or running off without paying the rent."

It seemed that to Judith, Simon was a rich man. He supposed, in many ways, he was.

Their task finished, Simon looked around. Still no Pen. "I wonder where he could be."

"He could be here, helping me," she replied, dropping one basket inside the other. "But he isn't, and he seldom is." There were two sides to every story. Pen seemed unaware his sister needed help to run this place. Perhaps Judith was correct about him being unreliable, but neither was she a cheerful person to be around. Simon did not have to wonder why Pen stayed away.

While they waited for Simon's return, Hannah offered to show Janet what she had for the baby. She needed to forget the danger her husband might face, and it soothed her nerves to touch the tiny items one by one. In a box in the loft were things gathered in the years she and Simon had been married. Once hidden away because seeing them reminded her she had no child, now the clothes would be used. One by one, she showed them to Janet.

"I made this one," she said, showing a sack garment that tied at the bottom. "It will keep the baby's feet warm." She stroked the soft fabric.

"Very useful." Janet hardly looked at it.

"And these were given to me by a neighbor," Hannah said, taking out a small pile of blankets and wrappings. "Both his wife and the child died, but he said I should make use of them." Her eyes filled with sadness for a moment at the thought of that poor woman, who had lived only days after delivering a dead baby, and her stricken husband, left alone.

Janet's glance strayed to the curtained doorway. "When will your husband return?"

"I don't know any more about that than I did the first three times you asked."

"Will he find Peto, do you think?"

Hannah hoped not. She hoped the outlaw had left London the moment he was free, and they would never hear of him again. Then Simon would come home where he belonged and stop trying to be the man's friend.

Janet rose, the neatly folded baby things Hannah had set before her falling unnoticed into a heap as her skirts brushed against them. "I must know where he is!"

Hannah began picking up the things, noticing the smell of roses from the petals she had sprinkled between them before storage. "You must not worry about Simon, Janet. He—"

"Not Simon! I meant—someone else." She went to the ladder and turned to start down. Hannah saw there were tears on her cheeks.

"Janet—"

The girl did not answer, but a sob escaped as she hurried away. The sound of footsteps traced her passage as she crossed the living area and went into the shop. Unsure what to do, Hannah sat there for a while. Janet was hiding something, a secret that caused her great anxiety. How could she learn to care for little Susan when she was in constant turmoil? With a sigh, Hannah rose and went after her, determined to learn the truth.

When she got to the shop, however, Janet stood with her back against the door as if holding off raiding Frenchmen.

"What is it?" Hannah asked.

"There is a man out there." A moment ago she had seemed sad. Now she was afraid. Was this the emotional mix of a new mother or something else?

Then, with what appeared to be a great effort, Janet calmed. Expression drained from her face as if a magician had passed a hand over it. She let out a long breath and gave a shaky laugh. "He looked like someone I once knew, but that cannot be. I was mistaken."

Hannah angled to the window, peering out so she could see the street but not be seen. "The man in the tall boots and gray clothes?"

"He looks very like a man who used to—" She stopped, and Hannah guessed she could not think of a plausible lie. "At any rate, I see now he is not the one."

"I wonder what he's waiting for?" Hannah mused. "He keeps looking this way."

"I couldn't say." Janet's tone was casual now, as if the man did not matter at all.

Hannah took the opportunity to return to their former topic. "Janet, you said—"

The shop door flew open and a boy rushed in, his eyes wide with fear. "Goodwife, will you come? My mother needs you!" Knowing the woman was due to give birth, Hannah took up her bag and prepared to leave. She had a moment's regret that she would not get the chance to question Janet about her outburst in the loft. She would get to it, she promised herself. She would make Janet tell her the truth, though it would make not one bit of difference in the way she felt about her and her baby.

Chapter Sixteen

Simon did not find Pen at the Bull's Horn or any other place where Judith thought he might be. Without Pen's help, he had no idea where to look for Peto. Frustrated, he even went to the docks and found the spot where the Spanish ship had been anchored. It was gone. That was good, he told himself. Probably Peto had sailed with his friends, leaving England behind. If that was the case, he had done some good after all.

But the letter Robert Dudley was to write, what of that? If the ship was gone, he had no way of sending it to Spain. Simon tried to be content his friend had escaped death. Maybe Dudley could find another way to deliver the letter.

Not knowing what else to do, Simon turned homeward. His thoughts were so focused on the letter to Philip that he almost failed to hear a voice calling to him as he approached the crowded Thames Bridge. Turning, he saw his friend waving wildly on the far side of the throng. "You come on a wish, Master Simon," Pen said when they finally waded through the crowd and met. "I was sent to find you, but I feared I might miss you." He chuckled. "I thought this a likely place, since you had to pass both coming and going."

"I went to your house," Simon said. "Then I looked for you at the alehouses."

"None of that today," Pen said, his expression meaningful. "We have much to do."

A woman bumped Simon rudely, chiding, "This is no gossip post, Goodman!"

With apologies, they moved out of the bridge way and found a place where they could converse without being jostled. "We thought you would come to Southwark when the news reached you."

The "we" told Simon that Peto had sent Pen to fetch him. "I heard he was at liberty. Did he sail with the smugglers last night?"

Pen inclined his head and raised his palms. "I told him it was best, but—" He shrugged to indicate that Peto made his own decisions. "The Spaniards agreed to wait at a place he knows downriver."

"He should have left anon! It is a miracle he escaped the Tower."

Pen thumped Simon's shoulder excitedly. "A nice bit of work that was, was it not?"

"How did he manage it?"

"You helped, Master Simon, though you did not mean to." With obvious delight, Pen explained. "The guards thought you a priest that first day, am I right?"

"Well, yes."

"Peto made it seem that this priest had caused him to regret his sinful ways. He first tells the guard the priest said a man cannot be forgiven sins he has not atoned for. He asks the man to say nothing to anyone, but to discover how a thief might return something of great value to its owner. Of course the guard offers to take it for him, but Peto refuses, acting mysterious about what the item is and where it is."

"But they must have searched him when they brought him there."

"True. But then a second visitor came, an artist for the news sheets. After *he* left, Peto begins acting as if he has something to conceal." Pen craned his neck at Simon, a grin spread across his face. "Do you ken? He plants a seed in the guard's mind. Then he behaves odd-like. The guard decides he has something in the cell, the thing he spoke of returning to atone for sin."

Simon began to see. "Then Peto waits."

"All day, the guard peers in, hoping to see what it is and where it is kept. Peto appears not to notice. He stares into his own hands, at something he seems rapt with. And he prays."

"And the man begins to covet this unknown item."

"Yes, yes! You see it!" Pen almost danced with elation. "That night, Peto seems to go to sleep. Soon the guard opens the door and enters, quiet as a cat on the hunt."

"And brings no one with him, for he wants the valuable thing all to himself."

Pen clapped his hands, cackling, "You have a right mind, Master Simon! A right mind!"

"I would guess, then, that the next guard to come along found his fellow inside the cell with an aching head and a lie about how he was tricked and overcome."

"You are probably correct, though Peto was far away by then and cannot say for certain."

Simon had a moment of doubt. "But he left the guard alive?"

"The fellow came with knife drawn, greedy and willing to kill for the bauble he meant to steal from a defenseless prisoner." Pen clicked his tongue in disgust. "He is lucky Peto is not a bloodthirsty sort."

Simon wiped a hand over his chin, relieved that no more murders had occurred. "Well, he is free."

Pen's expression turned serious. "Peto intends to find Frances. And then he will right the wrong done to him."

"I fear neither of those is possible."

The older man shook his head. "He is not one to forget a friend, as you know, and he is not likely to forgive an enemy, either. Red John was his friend, and Bannon killed him. Bannon framed Peto. For that, he will be punished."

"But there are drawings of him everywhere. All of London is searching for him."

"He is safe for now."

With Elizabeth's words ringing in his ears and Hannah's face hovering in his head, Simon reminded himself he should take no further interest in this matter. Peto would do as he chose, whether it was wise or not. Still, Peto had watched over him once when Simon was too young and naive to realize the danger he was in. And there was still time to give him the letter to take to Spain. "Can you take me to him?"

Pen laid one forefinger alongside his nose. "It is what I was sent to do, Master, if you are willing."

Moving faster than Simon had ever seen him, Pen led the way across the bridge, back to London, with the last crowds of the day. Night was coming, along with a storm, by the look of things. Clouds that had blocked the sun all day turned from gray to black with occasional streaks of dark blue. The wind had picked up as they talked, and Simon felt it tugging at his clothes when they passed open spaces on the bridge.

Once on the other side, they turned west and walked through the darkening streets, passing shuttered windows where slits of light showed through. Simon took note of the route. Away from the Tower some distance, along the river and then northward perhaps a quarter mile.

He saw the church from some distance away, larger than the surrounding buildings and set back a little from the street. There was a bell tower on the nearer side, a churchyard on the other. Pen led the way past the church itself and paused to open a narrow gate leading into the churchyard. They stepped inside, and the dark became even darker. No light showed before them, and Pen slowed his pace as he followed a narrow path through the tombstones. Simon shivered as he brushed against one in passing. The dead did not frighten him, not really, but any man's hair might stand on end in a graveyard at night.

At the back corner of the burial ground, a small hut huddled against the iron fence, apparently a storage place for the mattocks and shovels needed for grave digging. Pen approached the tiny building, calling in a low voice, "It's Pen."

The door opened a crack, the dry leather of its hinges protesting noisily, and Simon saw a pale hand. There was a brief pause. Squinting into blackness darker than that outside, he saw a space crammed with shadowy objects. There was hardly space for a man to sit. Peto must be desperate to have taken shelter here.

The door opened wider. "Well met, Simon Maldon." Peto's voice was calm, whatever his situation might be. "Pen, where might Simon and I go to talk, now that we have night's cloak?"

Raising one finger as a signal to wait, Pen disappeared for a few moments. As the two stood waiting, Peto within the cramped space and Simon at the doorway, the rain began. The first drops thumped on the wooden roof like funeral drums, slow and separate. Simon felt his cap grow damp.

Pen returned, and with a hint of showmanship, bowed. "I invite you to St. Tristan's sacristy. The old priest is abed and deaf as a post. His housekeeper has gone out for a pint."

"Thank you, Pen," Peto said politely. "Simon, if you will follow, we will get you out of the rain and me to a place where I can move my elbows without overturning a shovel."

A small door at the back of the church stood open before them, and a soft light showed inside. Ducking as he entered, Simon followed Peto into a small, windowless room lined with shelves. The glow of a lantern lent enough light for him to see folded cloths, books, and an array of candles of different sizes and shapes, all unlit.

Peto dismissed Pen in low tones. "It is best if you appear in your usual haunts, my friend, so no one wonders where you have gone." Simon heard the clink of coins. "Take your lantern; return to Southwark by boat. Spend an hour at the Bull's Horn as if you have no care in the world."

Taking up the lantern, Pen asked Simon, "Can you find your way back home, Master?" At Simon's assurance that he could, Pen bowed to him, waved to Peto, and left, closing the door softly behind him.

The two sat for a moment, listening to the sounds of the old church. The rain came heavily now, and the wind outside made the building creak softly in a rhythmic cadence that was almost restful. Simon waited, letting Peto choose where to start the conversation. Instead, he heard the click of candles bumping together.

"They will not miss an inch of beeswax, I trow, and I dislike talking to one whose face I cannot see." Simon heard the scratch of flint, and a small light appeared. Peto found a holder, set the candle in it, and put it on a shelf at shoulder level. As the glow bathed his friend's face, Simon noted tightness around his mouth and eyes despite his apparent calm.

"Well, then," he said with a tiny smile. "Pen says you are determined to help me."

Simon nodded. "I will do what I can."

"Why, Simon?"

The question was difficult to answer. He felt he owed Peto something; that was true. But just as much, he disliked the thought of the wrong man being punished for murder. "I would see justice done." It sounded naive and he knew it. Elizabeth would have laughed aloud.

Peto did not laugh but turned, surveying the dark corners of the room. "There is no justice for people like me, not the justice you mean. And there is peril for those who dare to seek it. I asked Pen to find you when we heard you had gone to Southwark. You should not dabble in dangerous matters, my friend."

Simon set his teeth. "I am not helpless."

Peto shook his head. "Simon! Always fearful that someone will judge you less than a man because your arm is crippled. Do you not know your value to the world?"

He took a while to think before answering. "I know I serve mankind with my medicines. I know my wife loves me. And I know I have been at times of value to one whose name I will omit. But none of that means anything if I sit by and watch you imprisoned and hanged for a murder you did not commit."

Peto's sigh was deep, and he scraped a drop of wax from the candleholder and pressed it flat between his fingers. "It is my own fault, at least in part. I became too sure of myself, and forgot that a man has many acquaintances but only a few true friends."

"Your people fear for their loved ones, Peto."

"As do I." His expression turned bleak. "There has been no word of Frances."

"Do you think Bannon—?" Simon did not finish, unwilling to put into words what Bannon might have done.

"Perhaps she fled the city." A shake of his head followed, as if his body rejected his words. "I told her to go to Pen if ever I was caught. He is not a man most think capable of dissembling, and his sister's house is large. Although she does not know me well, Judith knows I would repay kindness she showed to a friend of mine." He paused. "She has birthed babies, too, so she will be a help should Frances's time arrive."

His words made Simon start, and Peto said, "What is it?"

"Your woman was with child?"

"She is."

Simon's lips tightened in what might have been humor, might have been self-reproach. The comment Pen had made about women "at certain times" and Peto's allowances for her behavior suddenly made sense. "She is very pretty, and blonde, of course?"

"Yes." Peto looked somewhat abashed. "I know they make jests behind my back, but blondes bring me luck." One eyebrow rose as he added, "Usually."

Simon smiled, leaning toward his friend. "I can ease your mind, I think. Frances is with me." He paused. "Rather, she and your child are with Hannah, at our house."

As she returned from overseeing a successful childbirth, Hannah decided she would have the truth from Janet. From what she could gather, Janet's child belonged to one man while her heart belonged to another whose affection she was terrified of losing. She seemed proud of her second conquest, while her feelings for the first, whatever they had been when she gave herself to him, had faded to a vague resentment for leaving her with a child to raise alone.

Then there was her unusual interest in Peto. At first Hannah had thought Janet was afraid of him, as any girl might be of a notorious outlaw. But in the spaces between her neighbor's labor pains, Hannah had time to reconsider what she knew and guess at the rest of it. Now she was determined that Janet would answer her questions, whether she wanted to or not.

Janet had found some walnuts, and the sound of shells cracking greeted Hannah as she entered the house. In the end, she confessed everything after Hannah posed one direct question. "Janet, are you acquainted with Peto the Pope?"

Dropping all pretense, Janet lifted her head proudly. "I am his woman."

"You are the paramour of an outlaw?" Hannah was shocked at the boldness of the statement. She struggled to understand the girl's point of view. Peto was a king among his people. Beside him, Janet must feel like a queen.

"So there was no noble lover?"

"No. Only my father's bailiff, who seduced me with pretty

words. I thought him a wonder until it became clear I carried his child." Her expression turned ugly. "There was a change! He disappeared like a wave on the strand."

"You are of the gentry, then. I thought you seemed unlike any serving girl I ever knew."

Janet took Hannah's observation as a compliment. "When he learned I was pregnant, my father ordered me to go to his estate in Scotland and remain there, a prisoner among his sheep, until the child came."

"He no doubt planned to give the child to one of his tenants to raise."

Janet blinked as if she had not thought that far ahead. "I did not care about that. But once my disgrace—that is what they called it—was over, they planned to wed me to a man my father has some business with in Edinburgh. He would be so happy to have a beautiful young wife, Father claimed, that he would not notice I am not a virgin or ask where I had spent the last year." She cracked a nut between two flat stones with more force than the task required. "Banishment to Scotland? Wedded to an old man? I ran away."

"To Southwark."

"Ellie, the girl I told you about earlier, was in truth one of our maids. She lives in Southwark since Mother sent her away for stealing, for no one will hire a maid with such a reputation. I left my parents' house early on the morning after they told me their plan. I found Ellie, who had a job working in a tavern. She said I could stay with her for a time."

Hannah wondered for a moment at Ellie's generosity, but Janet added, "I brought along whatever jewelry I could take, and we sold the pieces to buy our necessities."

That explained Ellie's willingness to shelter the demanding daughter of the people who had dismissed her.

Janet dropped the stones into her lap with a click, and her

face took on the glow that seemed to accompany thoughts of her lover. "I met Peto when he agreed to buy the goods. His offer was fair." She paused at the memory. "And he was charming. Nothing in my life before had prepared me for a man like him, for a love like ours." Her eyes shone, and Hannah thought how young she was. Thoughtless, selfish, and very young.

As Janet went back to harvesting nutmeats, never offering to share, Hannah wondered what Peto saw in this self-centered, immature girl. Beauty, certainly. Passion, probably. And maybe, Hannah thought, maybe he saw a chance at happiness with a woman totally devoted to him and him alone. She had known many couples, some very much in love, some companionably focused on similar goals, and some badly matched. What she had never been able to do was predict which matches would prosper and which made a household hell for both parties. Some who seemed ill-matched did well together, while others who should have made a strong pairing could or would not acknowledge each other's good points. Peto must have seen something in Janet that made him want her, whatever her faults.

The thought brought Hannah up short. "But you were carrying another man's child."

"Yes. At first, of course, it did not show. We had several weeks of pure happiness." She spoke of weeks as if they were decades. "I knew from the first I loved him, and I could hardly believe he loved me too." Janet caressed her lustrous hair. "I know I am beautiful; many men have said it. But Peto can have any woman he wants, and he remains faithful to me."

Her brows descended briefly, as if she was remembering the days they had been apart. She had probably been relieved to learn Peto had been in prison, locked away from the wiles of other women.

"When I finally told him about the child, Peto said it did not matter. He said he'd always wanted a son."

Hannah's opinion of Peto rose slightly, but Janet apparently had doubts. "Still, I asked myself, what man wants to raise another man's child?"

Many good ones, Hannah thought. *Possibly Peto, if Simon's opinion of him is correct.*

Janet took Hannah's arm again, this time more gently. "Once when we were talking, Peto told me about you and Simon. He mentioned where you live and said that Simon was these days an apothecary. He did not know you but had heard you served as midwife. He said he was told you were kind and beautiful." She laughed, touching Hannah's arm lightly. "Of course, he did not desire you, for Peto wants only blondes, like me. Still, you and Simon are good people. Those were his exact words."

Hannah wondered that Peto knew so much about a man he had not spoken to for years, but it was probably good practice for a criminal to know what his acquaintances were up to, where they were living, and who might be useful to him at some point.

Janet's next comment surprised Hannah more than all the previous ones. "When I decided I did not want this child, I thought of what Peto told me that day about you."

"You thought of us?"

"You are skilled in assisting with childbirth. Simon is a respected member of the community. I thought you would be able to find a home for her." With a look that conveyed more irritation than concern, Janet glanced at where her child lay. "I told Peto I had chosen a midwife in Millwick. When I return, I will tell him—" She stumbled, probably guessing what Hannah would think. "I will tell him the child was born dead." She clasped her hands together as if praying for Hannah's understanding. "We will have other children, Peto and I. Give this one to someone who wants her." She paused. "Maybe you want her." It was only half a question.

Hannah was thunderstruck. She thought about the events of

the last few days, reassessing now that she had all the information. Janet must have left Southwark, journeyed to their house, and hidden in the dovecote to wait for her pains to begin. Once she was in labor, she had judged it unlikely Hannah and Simon, those "good people," would send her away. And they had not.

Janet's lack of interest in the baby was because she had come intending to leave her with Hannah and return to Peto without the encumbrance of another man's child. She could not have predicted his arrest and imprisonment on the day she implemented her plan.

"Why did you not tell us the truth from the beginning?"

Janet stood up and shook the collected nutshells in her apron onto the fire. "I feared you might be too upright to take in a good fellow's doxy." Janet's use of the term seemed deliberate, to shock Hannah into seeing the world the way she, a criminal's mistress, saw it.

Hannah opened her mouth to object then hesitated. Would she have taken Peto's woman in? She thought she might have, but what if she had never held Susan in her arms? Would she have wanted the child? After a moment she said, "Whatever Peto has done, whatever you have done, it is not the babe's fault."

Janet stared into the fire, where the shells' combustion added heat and a pleasant scent she did not seem to notice. "I hope Simon finds Peto safe." She put a fist to her lips. "When he does, I will go to him."

This time it was Hannah who took hold of Janet's arm. "Wait. Think. Your presence can only complicate things for him at this time."

The girl paced a few steps then turned to Hannah. "Do you think he wants me to hide here when he is in danger?"

"He wants you safe, if he loves you." Hannah knew that even now, if Simon was successful, Peto might be on a ship to Spain.

"Your place is with Susan."

Ignoring the reference to her daughter, Janet began pacing again. "Did Simon help Peto escape the Tower?"

"No," Hannah answered quickly, and then amended, "At least I do not think he did. But he is determined to prove Peto did not kill this Red John."

Janet stopped in surprise. "It was Red John who was slain? That proves Peto is innocent, for he would never have hurt John!"

"You must trust Simon, who is very resourceful," Hannah pleaded. "And you must care for Susan. If you try, if you spend time with her, you will come to love her."

Janet waved a hand in the baby's general direction. "Don't you know someone who will take her?"

Hannah made an earnest plea. "Please, forget this plan to abandon your child. She needs you." Janet turned her face away, and Hannah went on, "Simon and I will help. No matter what happens, you will both be safe." She did not say there were no guarantees for Peto. Whatever his future, be it a trip to the gallows or a life far from London, Hannah would see that Janet and her baby did not suffer.

Janet looked at Hannah for a moment. Her face calmed, and Hannah thought the girl finally understood she was not alone. Suddenly she threw her arms around Hannah's neck. "You are a good friend, Hannah." Glancing toward the baby, she added, "Poor little mite has been lucky in that, if in nothing else."

"Will you stay here, then, and let Simon do what he can for Peto?"

"I will."

Hannah hid her sigh of relief. Janet seemed to be speaking truthfully for once, and she seemed willing to try to behave rationally, for the sake of her child.

CHAPTER SEVENTEEN

In the dank sacristy, Simon waited while Peto digested the news he had given. "She had the baby at your home?" he said in wonder.

"A little girl. The most beautiful one in the world, according to Hannah, although I must confess that all babies look alike to me, even yours."

"The child is not mine." As Simon struggled for a reply to that, Peto went on. "Oh, she tried at first to say I was the father, but two things made me doubt her. First, I have not fathered a child with any woman I have bedded. Second, Frances was farther along than she claimed." He looked at Simon. "I assume the child is full size."

"Hannah says she is one of the bigger babies she has birthed."

Peto twisted the candleholder, sending shadows moving across his face and into the corners of the room. "She came for Hannah's help?"

"It seemed to be happenstance."

"She told me she had found a midwife in Millwick who would let her stay at her home for a seven-night when the child came."

"Hannah is a midwife, though we do not live in Millwick. It seemed an accident, and she did not tell us she is . . . connected to you."

Peto gave a grim chuckle. "Actually, I feared she might leave the child on some doorstep." At Simon's look of surprise, he added, "She often worried it would make a difference to our relationship."

"Who do you—" Simon stopped, embarrassed to ask who the child's real father might be.

"Some fellow who worked for her father. Frances and her parents disagreed over her future and she ran away." Peto swiped at his jaw with one hand. "Frances has romantic notions about life on the wrong side of the law, but she is a rare woman." He cleared his throat with a nervous little cough. "She is well after the birth?"

"Hannah says all women should come through as easily as she did."

"I had some dread of it." Simon heard affection in Peto's tone. *What an odd thing love is,* he thought. A woman he found self-centered and demanding was apparently quite different in Peto's view.

"She and Hannah have done well together," he said, ignoring his own opinion that Janet used Hannah at every turn. "When we heard this morning you had escaped, she became upset. She was unaware of your arrest and asked a thousand questions." He shrugged, admitting, "If I had not been in such a hurry, I might have noticed they did not indicate fear of an escaped felon, but fear for your safety."

He recalled Janet—or rather, Frances—requesting a love potion a few days ago. Now he realized she'd been desperate to keep her hold on Peto, an outlaw who defied authority with style and recklessness. He wondered briefly what her father was like, for it seemed some young women chose lovers opposite to everything their parents stood for.

"If she is with you, then one of my biggest fears is eased," Peto said. "Bannon has not killed or captured her."

"No. And I do not think there is any way he could know where I live. Only Pen knows, and he would never tell anyone."

"You must be careful. Bannon is clever in his way, and ruthless as well. He will not hesitate to kill you if you pose a threat to him. No more crossing into Southwark, my friend."

Simon was more concerned for Peto's future, since he faced danger at every turn. "What will you do now?"

"I will ask one more boon of you. Will you bring Frances and the babe to the bridge tomorrow evening, just before curfew? Pen will meet you there and guide her to the ship so we can sail for Spain together." He looked down at his hands and smiled grimly. "No doubt all of England will rejoice when I am gone."

Catching the melancholy tone in his voice, Simon replied, "There are some who will be the worse for your absence, and I am one of them."

Whatever Peto might have said was interrupted by a scratch at the door. It opened with a soft creak, and the sound of the rain increased. It was pouring. Pen stepped into the doorway, hair plastered to his forehead and clothes dripping. He was agitated almost to panic. "You must be gone! Bannon and several men were crossing the bridge as I approached. From their stride and their turning, I fear they know your hiding place. They are surely right behind me!"

Peto was up before Simon could react. Clamping a hand on Simon's shoulder, he ordered, "Stay here for the count of two hundred then leave by the front gate. I will lead them the opposite way."

"Peto—"

"Do as I say. They outnumber us, and our only hope is speed, and you must return to your wife. Once more I thank you, but remember: this is none of your affair." The hand squeezed once, a sort of benediction, and Peto was gone.

As the sun sank in the west, Hannah became more and more worried. Simon had been gone far longer than it should have taken to learn the truth of the rumor of Peto's escape. Had he been arrested, caught up in the outlaw's crimes? She needed to do something. But what?

When the answer came, she wondered why she had not thought of it sooner. She did not know where to begin looking for him, but Her Highness might. Although she had been inattentive over the last few days as he talked of Peto and the problems he faced, Hannah did recall Simon mentioning what the princess had to say on the matter. Wrapping a gingerbread intended for Sunday dinner in a clean cloth, Hannah told Janet she was going to visit a friend, barred the shop door, and left the house, determined to learn what Elizabeth knew of Simon's activities.

By the time she reached the Tower, she had her story ready. "I am Hannah, once the princess' serving maid," she told a guard. "I do not expect to be allowed to see her, but I ask that you give her this cake, for she was ever kind to me."

The guard, whose teeth were both crooked and black, unwrapped the cloth, examining the contents suspiciously. "If you like," Hannah suggested, "you can cut it to see there is nothing inside."

Taking a knife from his belt, the man stabbed the cake several times. Apparently satisfied there were no weapons baked into it, he asked, "How do I know it isn't poisoned, then? Some there is that doesn't want her around, and you might be one."

"Cut a piece," Hannah said, "And I will eat it myself."

Again the man did as she suggested. After taking a bite, she offered the rest to him. Watching to see that she had swallowed her portion, he tasted the cake. "Good!" he mumbled, finishing the rest of the slice in one bite.

"Will you see she receives the rest of it?"

The guard called to another man who took the cake and disappeared down a narrow corridor. She heard his boots echoing for a while on the stone floor, then silence.

Hannah tarried, stalling until he returned. "You liked my cake?" she asked the first man.

"Tasty," he replied enthusiastically. "I wish my wife could make such things."

"It's made from honey, breadcrumbs, ground ginger and cloves. If you like, I could write the recipe down for you to take to her."

He scowled. "She has no use for reading, nor do I, for all folk say it makes a person wise. It is an idle pastime when there is always enough real work to do. Fools, I say, waste their time with books and paper."

Hannah nodded as if he had said something very wise. Just then her secret wish was granted when the second man returned and said, "The lady prisoner would like to see this visitor and thank her for the gift."

Elizabeth had guessed her purpose. She followed the guard through the Tower, trying desperately to ignore the feelings of dread that descended upon her. One bleak hallway after another, foul smells, cold, damp, and cheerlessness. How did one survive? Would anyone who had been imprisoned here ever be able to laugh again, even if she were allowed to live?

She was shown into a dull room lit by a single, smoking rush-light. Four dull-looking women sat in a semicircle around Elizabeth. Hannah almost gasped aloud at the change in her former mistress. She was dressed in white with no ornamentation whatsoever. Her color, always pale, was deathlike in the dim room. Her eyes were bloodshot, her cheeks sunken. It seemed loss of hope was sucking the life from her.

"Are you the girl who made this cake?" she asked. Her tone was neutral, as if it did not matter either way what Hannah answered.

"I am, Your—my lady." Hannah bowed her head and dipped slightly, not sure how to approach a disinherited princess. "I worked for a time at Hampstead Castle and recall you had a particular liking for such things."

"It is a kindness. I remember well those cakes and the cook who made them."

"Thank you, my lady."

"What is your name, girl?"

"Hannah, madam." She fervently hoped Elizabeth was pretending ignorance.

"Have you married since we last met?" Something in her face reassured Hannah, and she understood that they would speak in code. Elizabeth was asking about Simon.

"I had a husband, madam, but I know not where he is these days."

Elizabeth's brows rose and her shoulders tensed, but after a moment, she said, glancing toward her companions, "I have a similar problem. I am receiving instruction in the ways of the true church, but the priest has not shown his face today."

Hannah bit her lip, trying to maintain composure. She'd hoped Simon had been there and that Elizabeth would have some idea where he was now. That hope was gone. "Perhaps he is afraid, my lady. They say a desperate criminal, one Peto the Pope, escaped his cell in the night. He could be hiding on the grounds or in any of the Towers, even this one."

Elizabeth thought on that for a while. "If such a man escaped, he would no doubt go as far from this place as possible." She bent to pick up a clump of yarn she had apparently been winding onto a board. "I once knew a guardsman who claimed he could find anyone. Calkin, I think his name was."

Hannah got the hint and smiled gratefully. "I'm sure it is so, Your—my lady."

"Were I you, I would set this Calkin on your husband's trail. Or even the trail of Peto the—Post, did you say?"

"Pope, madam."

"Well, then. I thank you for the cake, goodwife. As you see, I am well, despite the gloom of this place." She smiled, looking directly into Hannah's eyes. "I well recall my stalwart friends from Hampstead Castle and hope they will all prosper."

Elizabeth stepped forward to give Hannah a kiss of dismissal. When her lips were near Hannah's ear, she whispered, "Your husband, Hannah, is a stubborn fool!"

"You were ever wise and good, my lady," Hannah answered. "I thank you for seeing me." She backed to the door, bowing slightly as the guard opened it for her exit. She had Elizabeth's advice on what to do about Simon's absence. The princess wanted her to go to Calkin and tell him the whole story. As the guard closed the door with a firm thud, Hannah felt that she understood Simon's need to help Elizabeth. It was an awful place, a horrifying situation, and the princess had done nothing to deserve it. Life was unfair, and she wondered why God let such things be. Saying a brief prayer of repentance, she reminded herself that it was not her place to question God. People were imprisoned wrongly. Men were accused unjustly. And women had babies who did not deserve them. It was not unfair. It simply was.

Following the guard out of the Tower, Hannah turned her thoughts to the princess' advice and what Simon would say to it. If Calkin went looking for Simon and found him with Peto, the guardsman was bound by duty to arrest the outlaw. He might even arrest Simon for helping a criminal.

But what if Simon was in trouble? Was arrest better than being pursued by a gang of violent men? What was she to do?

In the end, Hannah decided she would go home. Perhaps Simon was already there and the problem would be solved. If he was not, she could still go to Calkin for help. It would mean another long walk, but she felt sure that was how Simon would want her to proceed.

Thanking the guard, she started across the green toward the outer gate. Evening was approaching, and the shadows of the towers and the wall were even more oppressive than they had been earlier, as if the sun was glad to quit the place. When Hannah turned the last bend, she bumped into a man coming from the other direction. "Your pardon, sir," she said, dropping a curtsey. He carried himself nobly, and she was used to deferring to his sort, though the collision had been mutual. It seemed neither had been thinking about the path ahead.

"It is I who should beg your pardon," the man said smoothly, steadying her with a hand on her arm. "I was anxious to leave the shadows of this place, and my evening walks on the green are all too short." He glanced behind him, where two guardsmen followed at a respectful but businesslike distance.

Hannah looked up, recognizing the voicc. "My lord?"

Robert Dudley studied her face. "We have met, have we not?"

Having no idea how much he would recall, Hannah struggled to find the right words. "I served Her Highness Elizabeth for a time, during the matter of Lord Amberson's death."

"Ah." Dudley's expression showed remembrance and a glint of humor as well, as if he guessed he had never heard the complete version of that story. "With Simon Maldon, I believe?"

"He is now my husband."

"I see. Did he send you here?"

"No, my lord."

Dudley glanced at his guards. "You know he was here recently?"

"Yes, my lord."

"But you came tonight to see Bess. Is Simon in trouble?"

Hannah lowered her voice. "I fear so, my lord. I thought the princess might know where he went, but she has not seen him." She added softly, "We could not speak plainly, of course."

"The rules here are inflexible." His smile was ironic. "Except when they are not. My friends among the guards sometimes allow a few moments' conversation without fear of eavesdroppers." He gestured to the guards, who placed themselves between Dudley and the gate, tacitly giving consent for him to go on without them. Dudley turned to Hannah. "Will you walk with me? My time out-of-doors is short."

Although anxious to get on with her search, Hannah fell obediently into step with him. Blossoms from some unseen tree scented the air, and he sniffed appreciatively. As they walked, she told him what had happened, ending with, "I think Simon has gone to Southwark, but I don't know where to begin looking for him."

Dudley rubbed the stubble on his face, and she wondered fleetingly if no longer needing to be perfectly dressed and barbered every moment of the day was some small compensation for being a prisoner. Considering his likely end, that was doubtful.

Dudley's thoughts were more focused than Hannah's. "Did your husband mention an important letter he asked me to write?"

"He did not." Hannah despaired at the thought. She had been preoccupied with Janet and her baby. She had not been willing to listen, so Simon had not shared his plans. Now he was in danger, and she hardly knew where to begin to help him.

Dudley seemed torn. "It is a letter he was to take to some Spaniards whose ship is moored at Southwark. It is important to Elizabeth's welfare."

"I am sure he will come for it, Your Worship."

"There is, I think, a matter of time. It must be delivered soon."

"Oh." Hannah was at a loss. What was she to do? Simon was missing. But perhaps, her mind argued, he was not. It was possible he was at this moment home, wondering where she was. She made a decision. "I will take the letter, Your Worship, if you think it is best. I can give it to Simon when I see him."

"I think that is advisable, and I am somewhat anxious to be rid of it, in case . . ." He didn't specify. "If Simon is, uh, delayed, perhaps you can send someone else to deliver it."

She swallowed once, her throat tight, before answering, "I will try."

Dudley took her hand and raised it to his lips. She was surprised at the unusual gesture until she realized what he had in mind. As he lowered her hand, he clasped it in both of his for a moment, and she felt a rolled paper slide up her sleeve. Crooking her elbow to hold it in place, she bowed. "I must be on my way now, sir," she said in a tone the guards could hear.

"It was a delight to see you again," Dudley said, his tone casual and slightly suggestive. "Please give your husband my regards."

"I will." Anxious to be gone, Hannah nevertheless paused to say a final word. "I am sorry for your trouble, my lord. May God be with you."

His expression turned grim. "I fear that only He can help me now."

Chapter Eighteen

Simon counted slowly to two hundred after putting out the candle Peto had left burning in his haste. When he finished, he opened the door carefully, mindful of the squeak it had made earlier. The rain was slowing, and aside from the steadily lessening patter, it was silent in the churchyard. He saw no movement, only the glint here and there of a white tombstone.

Slipping out the door, Simon flattened himself against the stone wall and listened again. Nothing. The grass was wet, and his feet quickly became damp as he passed closely along the church wall until he reached the building's corner. There he stopped, waiting until his eyes adjusted to the dark.

His breath caught when, through the branches of a small tree that screened him from sight, he saw five men moving silently through the churchyard. He shuddered as they passed only an arm's length from where he stood. They were large men, crouched and ready for action, but their faces were hidden by hoods pulled low, either against the rain or to provide anonymity. From his stride, Simon thought the leader was Christo Bannon. Two of the men carried rough clubs, and Simon heard the clink of a chain as the last one passed his hiding place. With determined intent they stopped before the little shed, forming a semicircle around it. At a nod from the leader, one of them leaned forward and pulled the door open. When nothing happened, they moved in. Two flanked the exit and the others stood back, ready to prevent anyone getting by them.

One and then the other of the two at the door slipped inside the hut. Simon heard the tools rattle as they searched. A muffled curse, then a voice said, "Not here."

"The church!" The men hurried to the door Simon had recently exited. The process repeated, two going inside, three guarding the door. The search took longer this time, but eventually, they returned.

"Not in there, either."

"Light the torch and search the grounds." Simon recognized Bannon's voice. With light, how long before they found him? What would they do then? Kill him? Beat him into telling what he knew of Peto's whereabouts? Simon suppressed a ragged breath. At least they had only one torch. When they moved away from his hiding place, he would run.

The search seemed to go on forever. Three of the men circled the walled space, one carrying the torch and one on either side of him. They peered into corners formed by the buttresses of the church wall. They thrust their feet into every bush and kicked at every tombstone large enough for a man to hide behind.

Finally they came to where Simon huddled behind a bush that seemed to grow smaller by the second. He held himself very still, knowing movement, not sight, was the surest giveaway. Breathing shallowly through his mouth, he tried to quell the pounding of his heart. A sharp pain in his ankle almost made him cry out. One of the men had actually kicked him. He must have thought his foot hit the trunk, for he moved on. Simon bit his lip, resisting the urge to reach down and check for blood.

The searchers moved away, disappearing behind the church, but two men remained behind, guarding the front and back entrances to the churchyard. They seemed sure their quarry was here, and Simon wondered how that could be. More important, though, was getting out of there. He watched the man at the back gate, noting that he looked mostly in the direction his companions had gone. Human nature. His best chance was to slip by the man as he looked in the wrong direction.

Leaving his hiding place, he moved silently, feeling his way from tombstone to tombstone. Soon the watcher was a hulking shadow only a few feet away, peering at the spot where the torch floated near the base of the bell tower. Crouching, Simon felt around with his hand until he located a small rock. He threw it across the yard, hearing a satisfying crack as it hit a tombstone. With a grunt of surprise, the watcher took a step toward the sound. Taking advantage of the distraction, Simon slid out the gateway. Using the fence as a guide, he hurried away from Bannon and his men.

And tripped. Something—someone—lay in the way, back against the wall and feet stretching into the street. Simon went sprawling, feeling the scrape of earth on the palm of his good hand as he tried to break his fall. He landed with the sense of a small body under him, one that emitted only the tiniest grunt of pain. Quickly rolling to his feet, Simon made ready to run. Then sense turned to recognition. "Henry?"

The answer came in a whisper as soft as his own. "Yes."

"Are you all right?"

The child did not answer, for a voice called, "Did anyone pass, Hound?"

There was the briefest hesitation. Then the boy answered, "No. No one."

Bannon called out to the others, "He must be in the church. Look again."

Simon helped the boy up, and the two listened as the search moved away from them. Leaning down, he whispered, "Why?"

The answer came without hesitation. "You gave me your dinner."

Simon turned to go then halted, unsure of the way to the High Street.

"Shall I take you to the bridge?"

He hesitated. "Will it cause you trouble?"

Henry considered. "Not much." With a tug at Simon's shirt he moved off, going in the opposite direction he would have chosen. Trusting for no reason he could clearly understand, Simon followed.

When they were some distance away, Henry said, apparently in explanation, "Peto was ever good to me."

"I see. How did they learn where he was hiding?"

"A woman came and told them."

They reached a clearing in the buildings, and Simon recognized where he was. The bridge was only a short distance away. A turn north and he would be home in half an hour. Instead of setting off, however, he asked, "Why does he need you?"

A pause, and then, "I help him get into places."

"Did you help him get into the Bull's Horn the night Red John was killed?"

The boy's face was hidden in darkness, but the tone of his voice rose a note, as if tension gripped his throat. "He says they'll hang me if I tell."

"I won't hang you, Henry."

He thought about it then answered, "He bade me hide in the room. When the man went to sleep, I let him in the back door."

"How did no one know you were there?"

"I hold onto his leg, and he puts the coat on to cover me. He tells folk he has an injury from soldiering that pains him from time to time. But truly, it's how he gets me in somewhere."

"I see. You have done this many times?"

A nod affirmed it. "He knocks at the door of a fine house, pretending to be lost or looking for a relative. They let him in, 'cause he's got a silver tongue, he says, and I hide somewhere.

Other times he pushes me in through a window at night, and I open the door for him."

Simon knew there were a dozen clever ways thieves gained entry to steal a homeowner's goods, but he thought Bannon's use of a child the most reprehensible.

Henry went on with the story, probably relieved to have someone to tell it to. "That day, he told the host he wanted to see the room, to be sure it was safe. While they talked, I slid out from the coat and hid under the table. When they left, I crawled into a bin in the corner."

A spot Simon had considered as a hiding place but decided was too small. For a man, yes. For an underfed boy, no.

"So Bannon insisted on inspecting Red John's room and smuggled you inside." Simon imagined the child, cramped and afraid, waiting for Bannon's victim to fall asleep.

"I thought he was going to rob him, that's all." Henry was near tears.

"You did nothing wrong." Simon was not sure how the law would look at Henry's part in Bannon's crimes, but he intended to do his best to see that the law never learned of it.

Chapter Nineteen

Hannah approached home, hoping to see Simon looking anxiously out the doorway. Instead, she got a sense there was something wrong. The place seemed too quiet. Hurrying forward, she opened the door. Except for the faint glow of a dying fire, there was only darkness inside.

Where was Janet? With a sudden stab of fear, Hannah hurried to the bed, breathing a sigh of relief when she found little Susan sleeping peacefully. She bent to kiss the tiny head, breathing in her milky sweetness. The baby was here. Janet would return shortly, Hannah told herself, taking a seat beside the child.

But she did not return. Lighting a rush, Hannah added fuel to the fire and stirred the embers. She moved around the room, peering out each window and then closing the shutters. The shop was dark and silent. She closed the shutters there, too. As she started back to the room where Susan slept, she noticed the money box on the tabletop, its lid open.

It was empty. Hannah let out a little moan. As she turned her face away from the sight of betrayal, she noticed a fine powder spilled on the worktable. Bringing the light close, she discerned crude letters spelled out in the mess: *kepe hir.*

It took her a few seconds to understand. Keep her! The words, obviously Janet's, brought both fear and joy to Hannah's heart. Janet had gone, leaving the baby. Susan was hers.

Exultation did not last long. The child woke, obviously

hungry. When Hannah picked her up, she immediately turned her little head against Hannah's chest, mouth open. When no food presented itself, she became restless and fretful. Susan was unable to understand and unwilling to wait. Hannah tried everything: walking, singing, a rag soaked in milk, but the child wanted a more natural feeding. She became more and more agitated, and Hannah feared the baby felt her tension along with the pangs of hunger. What could be done?

An answer came, at least a partial one. Catherine, the neighbor with the newborn son, was a good person, clean, and kindly. She could feed the baby and tend her while Hannah went into the city. It was late: time that she asked Calkin to go out and look for Simon.

Standing where Bridge Street crossed his path, Simon tried to think what to do. Hannah was sure to be worried sick about him, and he should return home. But Henry had put himself in danger to help him escape Bannon and his men. What was he to do about the boy?

"Is there somewhere you can go, Henry? Somewhere safe?"

The hesitation was barely discernible. "O' course. Don't worry."

Simon felt sick. He wanted to be done with Southwark and Peto and all of it. He could not save the homeless, mistreated, poverty-stricken children of London. Boys like Henry were everywhere, crying out their masters' wares, squabbling in the streets, pleading for a handout. Many of them were probably likeable, as Henry was. Many were less fortunate than he, because they did not even have a Bannon to protect them. It was best, Simon told himself, if he sent Henry on his way. The boy would think of a story to tell, and in his own fashion, Bannon would take care of him. Bannon needed Henry. At least he needed a boy like Henry.

Still, Simon hated the idea the outlaw might punish the boy, might blame him for letting their quarry slip through. "Henry, if you're afraid of . . . if you don't want to go back, I can send you to the home of a friend. I think they will take you in if I—" He wasn't sure Judith would be happy about another mouth to feed, but Henry would make himself useful soon enough.

The boy's face was visible in reflected moonlight from the river, but Simon could not read the expression. "No. 'S all right." There was disappointment in his tone, but his words were brave. "He i'nt so bad. Bannon."

"All right, then. Here is a coin for the boatman. I am grateful to you, but I must go home now. My wife will be worried."

"Yes."

Even when it had been said, Simon found it difficult to walk away and leave Henry alone. The boy stood very still for a time, his scrawny body seeming to lean toward Simon without conscious intent. Then he shook himself slightly, turned, and hurried down the riverbank. He did not look back.

The rain had stopped, but the streets were wet and slippery. Hannah hurried from light to light, hating the dark areas of street in between. Catherine had agreed to keep Susan until she returned, assuring Hannah she had enough milk for three babies. Now Hannah was determined to get help finding Simon.

At the guardroom at St. James Palace, three yeomen were at work, each attending to equipment. One polished a sword, one mended a tunic with needle and thread, and one rubbed grease into a wide leather belt, testing its suppleness with his fingertips before reaching for more grease. They looked up in curiosity when she asked for their sergeant. Disconcerted by the knowing looks, Hannah explained that she brought a message from Calkin's friend Simon.

When he was fetched, Calkin approached Hannah shyly. She

had noted it before in unmarried men: faced with friends' wives, they were somewhat at a loss. Such men dealt easily with women as objects of desire but did not feel comfortable with them in other circumstances.

Calkin listened, however, and when she had told the story, acted quickly. "William!" he called to the young man who was polishing brass. "Can you locate some men who are off duty tonight and might take on an adventure?"

William grinned. "By my troth, Sergeant, you have only to ask."

"Do it, then, and quickly." Calkin went to a peg on the wall and took down a woolen jerkin which he put on, buckling a wide leather belt over it. Pulling on sturdy boots, he stomped a foot to settle the left one into place. "Madam, your husband is a fool. He told me nothing of this business, no doubt knowing he would get an earful of abuse from me. Why would he help a criminal like Peto the Pope?"

Hannah felt bound to defend Simon. "He would do the same if you were in trouble."

"True," Calkin admitted. "But I would deserve it." He turned to his preparations, apparently willing to help his friend even though he considered Simon's cause misguided.

In minutes, five capable-looking fellows were ready to cross the Thames with Calkin. "We are not the queen's men in this," the sergeant told them. "We go to find a friend of mine and bring him home to his wife." He turned to Hannah. "You, madam, must go home and wait."

"I—Yes." Hannah stifled her objection, knowing she could not go into Southwark with these men. She would be a liability, for one of them would have to see that she was protected from harm in the rough neighborhoods they would search. She must return home and face two empty rooms, but at least she would have Susan for comfort. "When you find him," she said to

Calkin, "bring—send him home as soon as you can."

After a moment's hesitation, Calkin nodded without comment on her shift of wording. Glancing around at the waiting men, he took six wooden clubs from a collection in a corner and handed them out. "We will find him," he said to Hannah as the men filed out of the room. "I promise, we will bring Simon back to you."

Hannah shuddered as they started off. Calkin had not promised Simon would be well when they brought him home. Or even that he would be alive.

Things got worse when Hannah reached her street for a second time that day. At her knock, her neighbor Catherine greeted her with surprise. "The little one's mother sent for her," she said, her eyes wide. "The man said you were with them."

"What man?"

Catherine pulled at the single braid that laid on her shoulder. "A stranger to me. He said the child's mother had sent him, and he was to take the baby to his sister's house." She tilted her head to one side. "He brought Janet's ring to prove she had sent him." She paused. "Well, it was your ring once. I recognized it, and I supposed you gave it to her."

Had Janet sent Pen for the child? "Was this man odd-looking, thin with wispy hair?"

"Why, no. He looked strong, though not tall, and dressed all in gray, like an overgrown mouse. Have I done something wrong?" But the question came too late. Hannah was already gone, hurrying southward, frantic to find Susan before Bannon's henchman harmed her.

Chapter Twenty

Simon trudged wearily home, hurrying as fast as his tired legs would move. He regretted the worry he must have caused Hannah. At the same time, he felt slightly guilty, knowing Peto might even now be fighting for his life against his enemies. What would happen to Pen, he wondered, now that Bannon seemed to know he was Peto's confidant? And Henry, that pitiful child. He did not deserve Bannon, but he had no one else.

But what could Simon do? Any help he might send to Peto's aid would arrest him when it was over. Both Pen and Henry were clever at surviving. He had to hope they would figure out a way to get through this crisis.

His concern turned to dread as he turned the last corner before home. His house was dark. Hannah would have left a candle burning for him, even if she had been able to fall asleep.

He hurried to the back door and entered their living quarters. Darkness here, too, except for the glow of the banked fire. He called out, but no one answered. Taking a rush from the pile in one corner, he lit it in the fireplace and searched the room. He climbed the ladder to the loft. Empty. He went into the shop and searched there. No one.

There was no sign of a struggle, no one sign of anyone. The second time through the main room he saw the two pieces of paper on the table, one rolled and sealed with wax, the other flat and weighted with two cups and a bowl. Lowering the torch, he examined the seal on the roll. Dudley. Somehow, Hannah had obtained the letter His Lordship had promised. Had she been to the Tower, or had Dudley found someone to deliver it? It didn't matter. Simon tucked the rolled paper into his shirt.

The other letter was from Hannah. Briefly she explained what he already knew, the truth of Janet's situation. The last part made his dread turn to fear. "After Janet left, a man in gray came and took Susan away. I have gone to get her back."

Brave, rash Hannah! With no time to waste, Simon left the house, closing the door firmly behind him. His wife was headed into danger. He had to stop her if he could, save her if he was too late.

Hannah struggled to remember what Simon had said about the location of Penitence Brook's house. Pen was her best chance to find Janet, and Janet might know where Peto's enemies took the baby. It was a starting point.

She hired a water taxi, using one of the coins she'd been saving to buy a gift for Simon's birthday. Janet had not found her little store, and Hannah had brought it all with her, willing to spend whatever she had if the man would return the child to her.

She had never liked the water, and the lurch of the boat as it left shore made her already nervous stomach flop alarmingly. She tried to focus on the opposite bank and the task ahead. The boatman was cheerful and talkative, spouting advice, snippets of gossip, and weather predictions. Hannah ignored most of it, but the thought did penetrate that Simon's mother would enjoy his patter. Mary Maldon, inveterate collector of information about the royal family, reveled in any scrap of minutia on daily life in the palace, impressions from visitors on the personalities of the two princesses, and rumors about absolutely anything. Hannah tried to remain pleasant as the boatman relayed gossip about the queen's marriage, adding his opinion that someday soon, everyone in England would be required by royal proclamation to speak nothing but Spanish.

When they reached shore, the boatman turned solicitous for her safety. "Goodwife, is there no one here to meet you? Southwark is no place for a woman alone, not a woman of good character, which I judge you to be. Shall I call for a linkboy to light your way?"

"I know the curfew law." Hannah showed him the pitch-tipped rush she had brought along. "I have light and a reason for being on the streets. The watch will find no fault with me."

"There are some about that's worse than the watch," the boatman warned. "You should hire some stout fellows to escort you to wherever you are going." He indicated a group of men standing on the wharf who seemed to her more like criminals themselves than protectors.

Hannah refused, assuring the man she had only a short way to go and knew it well. It was a lie, but she did not want to part with any more money than necessary. Putting on a brave face, she thanked the boatman, lit the rush from a torch burning nearby, and started confidently off, though she had no idea of the way to Pen's house.

Why had she not paid attention when Simon talked about where he'd been? He'd followed the course of the river to the west; she remembered that much. He'd said the house was at the end of a lane, a once-grand edifice with pockmarks on its front. But what was the name of the lane?

The main street of Paris Garden was busier at night than her own street was at midday. The crowds were noisy, relaxed, and for the most part, good-humored. Hannah began asking if anyone knew where Judith Brook's lodging house was. Most simply said no and went on, some looked at her askance, probably put off by her anxious manner. A few men made offers she could hardly believe, and she hurried past without reply.

Finally, she found an elderly woman who thought she knew Judith. "She's no friend to anyone," the old woman opined. "But she does keep a clean house, they say."

"Where? Where is it?"

"Down there." She pointed vaguely. "Follow the street, and when you come to the tavern with the daffodil sign, turn to the south. Go down the lane that twists and turns like a snake and finally heads back to the river. The last turning is Frog Lane, and Judith's house sits at the end."

With a quick thank-you, Hannah went on her way, following directions that turned out to be quite accurate. The Daffodil Tavern did not in any way call to mind flowers, although the sign was painted bright yellow. She could tell, even in the dark, because two boys stood outside the place with torches, ready to light the way home for any who had the means to pay them. From the amount of noise coming from inside, there would be many who needed guidance to find their way home, but darkness would not be the main cause.

Still following the directions, Hannah found the lane. It was quieter here, a residential area, though a poor one. A few people lingered outdoors, but the chill of evening would soon send them inside.

At the end of the lane was the house Simon had described. At its front, a torch burned in a holder near the top of the wide front door. Hannah rolled her own rushlight on the ground to quench its fire. *Please,* she prayed silently, *let Janet be here, and let it be true she sent someone for the baby. Even if she changed her mind about giving her to us, I will be content to know that Susan is safe.*

With that hope in her heart, Hannah knocked on the door of Judith Brook's house. A woman answered, holding a candle high as she peered at the visitor. Her eyes were cold and her manner stiff. Pen's sister, Hannah guessed.

"I seek a young woman with very light hair. I must speak with her."

The woman frowned even more. "Who are you?"

"My husband is the apothecary who is friend to Pen, your brother. We have been taking care of Janet for some days, and she left her child with me. I—" She stopped, unwilling to put into words what happened to Susan. "I must speak with her about the babe." When the woman did not answer, Hannah said, "If she is not here, I will go to the justices and tell them she is missing. Perhaps they will know what to do."

"She is here," the woman said quickly. "If you follow, I will take you to her."

Hannah stepped inside a house dimly lit and over-full with a motley assortment of furnishings, boxes, and baskets. She smelled onions, but they seemed to have been burnt.

Judith led Hannah past the staircase to the back of the house. Every door they passed was closed. Concentrated on Janet, Hannah didn't think about why, but it did seem odd, since most boarding houses she had visited were lively places. This one seemed quiet as a tomb.

At a room under the staircase, Judith knocked on the door. The door opened only a slit, and Hannah could not see the man who answered. "This is the apothecary's wife. She plans to go to the law if she can't see Frances."

"Does she." The door opened, and Hannah's stomach clenched. It was the man they had seen watching their shop, the one who had so frightened Janet.

Before she could turn to run, he grabbed her arm and struck her once, very hard. She felt herself falling, but she never knew whether she hit the plank floor or whether the Gray Man caught her in his arms.

Simon hurried back the way he had so recently come. How far behind Hannah was he? It was hard to know. He hoped to find her before she got to Southwark. He wasn't sure where she would go when she got there. Picturing his beloved Hannah wandering those dangerous streets made him frantic.

A water taxi was just arriving at the dock, and he took a coin from the bag of gold Peto had provided and returned the rest to the pocket inside his shirt. He had spent little of the money, and Peto might need it if he was to make a new life somewhere else. But Peto would not begrudge his using it in this case. Simon believed Peto knew now, perhaps for the first time in his life, what it was to love a woman and lose her, to be desperate to find her. Whatever it took to find Frances, Peto would do. Whatever it took to find Hannah, Simon would.

A noisy party of five got off the boat as he waited to get on. There was no shortage of trade, even at this time of night, and those who left the boat were drunken revelers, returning homeward with loud singing and raucous laughter. As the boatman prepared to shove off again, Simon asked if a woman had crossed recently. He shook his head, leaving Simon unsure if he meant no woman had crossed or that he refused to say. He was a cheerless sort, and their ride was silent except for the man's occasional grunt of effort at the oars.

When the little boat glided up to the dock and bumped gently against the piling, Simon stepped ashore, trying to plan his next move. Hannah would have no idea where to find Bannon, so where would she go? He decided she would have to begin with the woman she knew as Janet, Peto's Frances.

That meant finding Penitence Brook. Hannah knew Frances had been told to go to Pen for shelter if things went wrong for Peto. Hannah would hope Pen knew where Simon was, as well. Her starting point would be the house where Pen and Judith lived, the place he had described to her a few days before.

Simon turned east, toward Pen's, but a sound that might have been his name, might have been a cough, came from the darkness. He paused, peering into the shadows. "Henry?"

"It's me." The boy sat on a barrel, his back against a crate, his arms wrapped around his knees against the chill of night.

"What are you doing here?"

"I went home, but Bannon was away and Pearl was in a state: bloody and crying and screaming as she packed her clothes. I left her to herself." He looked briefly at Simon then dropped his head, apparently examining his shoes. "I didn't mean to bother you. I was surprised and spoke before I thought on it."

Seeing his doubt, Simon hurried to reassure him. "I'm glad you caught my attention."

"You are?"

"Of course. It's just that I have something very important to do right now."

"Oh. I see."

The truth of it was, he didn't. Henry thought he was being brushed off Simon's mind like road dust from a coat. "Henry." Simon came closer. "I will always be grateful for what you did for me tonight." He grinned. "Or was it last night? I don't know the hour." He searched for the right words. "I left Southwark intending—I am not—"

Speech failed him. How could he tell this boy that the people he knew, the world he inhabited, was not a place Simon Maldon ever wanted to see again? Did Henry know there were honest folk, men and women who did not cheat, lie, and steal for a living? "I meant to have no more to do with this place. But my wife has come here, and she is almost certainly in danger. I must find her, and I cannot—" He stopped again, unable to put into words the dread—no, the terror that had grown in him since reading Hannah's note. She might already be dead. A kitten walking among tigers has little chance of escaping alive.

"I can help."

"Henry, you—"

The boy hopped from his perch and landed with hardly a sound. "I know every street in Southwark. I can spot a bad 'un before he ever spots me, and I know how to hide where they will never find us."

Simon tried to think of a way to explain to the boy the danger that surrounded him and Hannah. Then he stopped as a new thought struck him. Bannon was the danger, and Henry knew Bannon as well as anyone. Henry had already proven he would stand for Simon against his master.

With a sigh, he said, "Let us walk, and I will tell you on the way what is afoot."

Chapter Twenty-One

When Hannah came to her senses, she was in a room strange to her. At first she could see nothing clearly, but then a glow of light resolved from a blur to three lanterns to a single lantern, set on a table a few feet away from her. She was lying on her stomach on the floor, and her hands were tied together around the foot of a bed frame. The ropes were cruelly tight, and her hands already felt numb. Directly in front of her was a hole in the floor with steps leading downward. A trapdoor rested against the wall behind it.

Turning her head awkwardly, Hannah looked around. The room was small, with sloping walls: an attic room. The wall on her left was decorated with carved birds hung from pegs, their colors dim in the lantern light. She could not see to the right, because the bed blocked her view. Pulling herself forward carefully, she peered around the end of the bed.

Janet sat beside a shuttered window, tied to a stool. Heavy ropes fastened her hands to her sides, running under the seat to keep her firmly in place. Her face was tear-streaked and filthy, and she slumped forward, as despairing a figure as Hannah had ever seen.

"Janet?"

She turned toward her anxiously. "Hannah! I was afraid you were dead."

"It's possible I would feel better that way," Hannah said in a poor attempt at levity. "Where are we?"

"At Pen's house. I came here, as Peto always told me I should if he was in trouble." She started to cry. "Bannon was waiting for me."

Hannah recalled the man who had knocked her senseless. "The man in gray came to my house and took Susan."

Janet seemed not to hear. "Bannon says Peto will not live through this night."

That was a chilling thought, made worse by the knowledge that they, too, were likely victims if they knew too much of Bannon's business.

They had to escape. Hannah surveyed the room. The only exits were the rough staircase and an octagon-shaped window. It might be large enough for a woman to wriggle through, but where would she be then? Hanging high above the ground? Over a friendly roof or near a climbable vine? She wished she knew.

She wriggled her fingers, trying to keep some feeling. How would she escape without the use of her hands?

Steps sounded on the stairway, and a man appeared, first head, then broad shoulders, and finally the rest of him, so tall he had to stoop to enter the room. He could only be Christo Bannon. Simon's description had been accurate, right down to the purposeful strut with which he moved to the center, where he could just stand erect at the roof's peak. Behind him, the man in gray came, catlike where Bannon was bullish, monotone where his master was splashed with color. Hannah wished she'd never had anything to do with either of them.

Behind the two men came Judith, her face expressionless. Since the room was too small for more people, she stopped on the stairs, arms folded across her chest in a gesture both defensive and defiant.

"The lovely Frances," Bannon said in a booming voice. "We are grateful to you for walking so neatly into our trap. Now you will be the bait that brings Peto into our waiting"—Bannon touched the knife at his belt—"arms."

The girl Hannah realized was not called Janet gave him a look that might kindle oak. "You may go to hell."

"Oh, I will be there, love, I have no doubt, so why not make earth as sweet as possible?" He regarded her for a moment. "You are a beauty, and I like a beautiful woman beside me." He glanced at the man in gray. "It happens I have need of a woman at the moment, do I not, Louis?"

"I think you made your wishes clear to the other," said the man in gray with a smirk.

"There. I am less one woman; you are less your man. You might throw your lot in with mine."

"I am Peto's woman and none other's, ever!"

Bannon chuckled. "And if Peto is dead?"

She rattled the stool angrily against the floor. "Then I would hate the man who killed him, until my dying day."

With a shrug, Bannon said, "A woman is a woman, and they are all the same in the dark. You could be an ornament for my days, but if you say no, I am content."

"Then let me go."

"Go?" He laughed heartily as the gray man smiled. Judith showed no emotion at all. "Pretty Frances, you are here to bring Peto to us so we may kill him." He grinned at her. "The best of it is, the officers of the law shall thank me for it. I might merit a commendation!"

"You—" Frances apparently could not think of anything bad enough to call him. "Someone will send for the law," she tried. "The boarders here must know something's afoot."

Bannon chuckled. "The boarders are ordered to stay in their rooms this night with the doors closed. They understand it is sometimes best for one's health to have blind eyes and deaf ears."

"We should get this business under way," the man called Louis prompted.

"Yes." The two men went to Frances, picked her up chair and all, and positioned her directly in front of the window. Louis dragged the table across the wood floor and placed it next to her. Bannon set the lantern in its center. "So your lover can see your pretty face."

Frances's lip curled. "When Peto comes, I will tell him to run. You might as well murder me now, for I will never help you destroy him!"

"Perhaps later," Bannon said casually. "Peto will look for you here. He said as much, did he not?"

"How do you know—" Frances stopped, her eyes sliding to Judith. "You! Peto was your friend, and you betrayed him!"

Judith made no response, but Bannon had one. "This one wants a better life, and I have promised she will have it."

"Traitor!" Frances screamed. Judith took a step back, but her chin rose defiantly. She turned toward Bannon, as if reminding herself that only what he had to say was important.

"Peto will be in some haste to be reunited with you and the child," Bannon said. "Thinking you are safe with friends, he will also be less than cautious."

"He will not know it is a trap if I am visible in the window."

"Lovely and clever as well." Bannon leaned toward Frances. "Now as to shouting a warning, you will not. We have your child, and now we have your friend here, Hannah, is it? If you warn Peto, she will die. If he escapes me tonight, I will suffocate his child as you watch."

Frances's next words came in a whisper. "I cannot let Peto be killed."

"You will do nothing to stop it." Bannon nodded at the man in gray. "Louis here will wait with you, out of sight. If you speak, even once, he will make short work of Hannah here."

Frances looked blankly at Hannah, almost as if she did not recognize her, and Hannah felt as if her bones were melting. Did she care enough what happened to either Hannah or Susan to do as Bannon wanted? He did not realize Peto was Janet's whole world. Would she sacrifice her child's life for Peto's? Or Hannah's?

"Gag that one," Bannon ordered. Judith looked around helplessly for a moment, but finally took the fabric belt from around her waist, knelt beside Hannah, and used it to gag her. As she worked, Louis made sure the ropes were tight. "She cannot raise her head high enough to be seen," he assured. "Frances will appear to be sitting in the room alone, waiting for Peto."

"There, my girl," Bannon said cheerfully. "You are the Judas goat, tied in place to draw the quarry into my grasp."

Louis moved the lantern closer to Frances. Hannah saw the effect they were after, a clear view of Frances's head and shoulders, the shine of her blonde hair, her lovely face. She would look worried, but that would be understandable. Peto would see only that she was where she was supposed to be, apparently waiting for him.

Once the scene was exactly as they wanted it, Louis sent Judith for a hammer and some nails. With short strokes he drove nails through the chair's legs, fastening them to the floor. When he finished, Frances was unable to rise, use her hands, or move the chair away from the window. After gauging the effect from several angles, Louis opened the shutter, carefully staying out of sight of those on the street below. "Now, we wait."

"You have the more pleasant part, up here with two beautiful women," Bannon said, "but I will have the satisfaction of seeing my cousin breathe his last." He went down the stairs, giving them a jaunty wave as he disappeared from view.

Louis took up a spot near Hannah, his rear on the floor and his feet on the steps. When he looked away, Hannah made an encouraging motion with her head, indicating Frances should try to get herself free. She worked whenever he was not focused on her, trying to stretch the ropes that lashed her to the bed frame. There did not seem to be any stretch to them.

For a while, Frances tried too. Each time Louis looked away, she strained against her bonds, twisting her body and hands awkwardly. As Hannah might have guessed, she gave up in frustration after only a few minutes. Instead she turned her attention to the street below, head turning from side to side as she scoured the night as if trying to prevent Peto's approach with vigilance. Hannah imagined her thought. The man she loved to distraction would be killed by his enemies, and she would be the cause. Tears rolled down Frances's cheeks, but she said nothing.

The room was deadly silent for some time, and Louis seemed uncomfortable with quiet. He began to talk, though Hannah could not answer him and Frances would not. "Do not fret so," he said when Frances began to make little sobbing noises. "Our men are waiting for Peto, and they will see him before you do. He is a dead man, no matter what."

How he thought that was comforting in any way, Hannah couldn't tell, but she felt a moment of relief. If Frances understood nothing she did could save Peto, perhaps she would not be tempted to risk her daughter's life, and Hannah's as well, in a futile gesture.

Relief quickly faded as reality returned. Whatever happened to Peto, neither she nor Frances would be allowed to live, knowing what they knew. And Susan? What would Bannon do with the child? Surely Peto's child, or what he thought was Peto's child, would be of no interest to Bannon. Pushing that thought away, Hannah returned to working on the ropes that secured her hands, despite her burning wrists and the blood that seeped into the ropes.

Chapter Twenty-Two

Simon led the way toward Frog Lane with little Henry hurrying along behind. The storm clouds, emptied of their burden, had dissipated, and stars peeped through. The moon appeared, too, and although it was less than half, provided some light. Even so, Simon had some difficulty finding Peto's house, having never been there in the dark. He made several wrong turnings but each time caught his mistake quickly and backtracked. Finally, he found the lane and started down it. He was caught by surprise when a hand reached out from the shadows, pulling him into the space between two buildings.

Before Simon could call out, he heard Peto's voice in his ear. "Quiet! It's me."

Peto's next utterance was an "Ow!" and a muted curse. Quickly, Simon moved between him and Henry, who had aimed a kick at Peto's leg with all the force he possessed. He caught the boy's thin shoulders, holding him back.

"Henry! It's only Peto."

The boy backed away, his face lowered and invisible in the dark, but his body reflecting something like awe.

"That's Bannon's boy, Henry," Simon told Peto. "He has been a help to me."

"Why would you help Simon?" Peto asked.

After a pause, Henry said softly but firmly, "He is a good man."

Peto's teeth flashed in the moonlight. "May you always be as wise as that, boy."

Henry turned toward him. "Your name is Simon?"

"I am sorry. There was never a good time for introductions."

Peto shifted his body impatiently, and Simon returned to business, telling Peto about Frances's flight, the baby's abduction, and Hannah's presence in Southwark. "I hope she will go to Pen's house. I was on my way there."

"We will go together," Peto said, "but cautiously. Bannon has eyes and ears everywhere, and I do not like how things have played out. How he learned of my hiding place at the church, I can't say. Pen was the only person who knew of it."

"Then he was followed."

"Possibly. But somehow Bannon knew enough to do that. We must be careful."

Simon looked around, shoulders hunching at the thought they might even at this moment be observed by someone with malicious intent. "I will follow your lead."

"And the boy?"

Turning to Henry, Simon said, "If there is trouble, you must run. Do you understand?"

"O' course. That's what I always do," the boy said, so like an old hand at avoiding trouble that Simon felt a wave of sadness for him. What a life the lad had led!

The three moved quietly down the lane, keeping to the shadows. The area was quiet, settled in for the night, with only the occasional sound of a door or a shutter pulled shut. When they were close enough to see the house, Peto put a hand on Simon's arm. "There."

High above them, a light showed, and Simon recognized the odd-shaped window he'd seen in Pen's room. A figure sat framed in the octagon of light. "Janet!" Simon whispered before he remembered. Not Janet, Frances.

She sat at the window, apparently waiting. Simon felt relieved she was alive and well. She must have slipped into Southwark without Bannon's knowledge, found Pen's house, and settled in until Peto could come for her.

There was no sign of Hannah or the baby, but the child might well be asleep on the bed behind Frances. It was possible, he told himself more hopefully than certainly, that Hannah was in the room, too, near the child she was drawn to like a butterfly to a flower. Peto would get his woman back tonight. He, Frances, and the child could escape to somewhere safe. And if what he hoped was true, Simon and Hannah could go home.

"There is something wrong," Peto said in a low voice.

"What?"

"She is unlike herself." He seemed unable to be more specific.

The front door opened and a woman appeared, holding a broom. She swept the entryway then the area in front of the door, her strokes brisk and efficient. Simon touched Peto's shoulder. "There. Judith is at her house tasks. That seems encouraging."

Peto watched as the woman assaulted the dirt that was her target. "A strange time of night for such work."

Simon didn't argue but thought of the widow a few doors down from his shop who spent most nights cleaning and re-arranging her house, carrying a candle from corner to corner to light her way. Some cleaned as a kind of emotional release. Judith might be angry at being in the middle of her brother's less-than-honest business.

When Judith finished and went inside, closing the door with a scrape that indicated it was slightly out of square, Henry pulled at Simon's arm. He bent down, and Henry said in his ear, "That woman told Bannon she could help him catch Peto the Pope."

Shocked, Simon repeated the information to Peto, who glanced briefly at the window before saying in a low voice, "Come away." He retreated into the night so quickly that Simon, who was looking directly at him, thought for a moment his eyes had deceived him. "Come!" his urgent voice repeated. With one backward glance at the waiting Frances, Simon followed, his mind a muddle of questions. Was Frances safe, threatened, or traitorous? Did she have the baby, or did Bannon or someone else? And most important, to him at least, where was Hannah?

Simon felt as if he were being torn in two. One part of him wanted to go off on his own, locate his wife, and forget Peto, his woman, and his problems. But another part reasoned that to find Hannah, he had to remain with Peto. From Frances, they were most likely to learn Hannah's whereabouts. Once they knew where Hannah was, Peto would help him find her and assure her safety. And Peto knew Southwark better than most people.

Elizabeth's words came to him, and Simon had a moment of doubt. Peto was a desperate criminal. Could Simon trust him to think of Hannah's welfare, or would Peto's own concerns take precedence? He thought Elizabeth was wrong this once. To her, Peto was not flesh and blood, but simply a man who broke the law. He thought if she knew him, she might trust him, as Simon had to trust him now.

Once they were a safe distance from the house, Peto said, "If either of us had knocked at that door, we'd have found an unpleasant surprise."

"But Frances is there."

"She is, but I fear it is not by choice." He glanced backward as if recalling the scene they had just left. "We need to alter our night's business somewhat."

Continuing down the street for a way, Peto turned, approaching a building that looked ready to collapse. It had once been a home of some grandeur, set off from others around it with a thick hedge on three sides and a strong gate across the front. Fire had destroyed half of it, leaving the other side blackened and probably unsafe. The smell of it lingered in the damp air, bitter and acrid. Someone had boarded up the exposed interior doorways to protect whatever was undamaged inside from the elements.

Signaling for Simon and Henry to wait, Peto circled the house cautiously. He checked the shutters, pulled at boards nailed across exposed spaces, and pushed at the doors on the undamaged side. Satisfied, he entered through the burnt portion of the house, motioning for them to follow. Moving cautiously to avoid the detritus left behind by the fire, Peto ducked under one of the X's nailed across a door. Simon and Henry did likewise. They entered a room that looked almost normal. Once-white walls were still bright enough to reflect moonlight and provided some visibility for the three uninvited visitors.

At floor level, only the lingering smell of smoke indicated that this room had been damaged by the fire, but Peto pointed upward. In one corner the roof was missing. "I keep track of places such as this to have a retreat in any part of town when necessary."

"Like the hut in the churchyard?"

"Exactly." Retrieving a cracked bench from one corner and an upended stool in another, Peto set them down, indicating Simon take the bench. Henry promptly plopped down on the floor beside it, mindless of the soot. Peto took the stool for himself. "Now," he said, "we shall make a plan while we wait for help to arrive."

"Help?"

Peto grinned. "If Pen did as I asked, we will soon be joined by the Spaniards you met on the wharf."

"They will help us?"

"They are good men. While they balked at taking on the Tower of London, they will work to get me out of Southwark alive, and they will help us rescue our women as well."

"You think Hannah is there, in Judith's house?"

"You said yourself she was likely to go there looking for Frances. If Bannon has Frances captive, and if he sent a man to take the child, he will not let Hannah interfere with his plans."

Dread hit Simon's gut like a blow. "Would he—" He could not say the words.

Peto's face was only a blur in the dimness, but he leaned toward Simon as if to lend strength. "He is cunning. He will keep all of them alive until he has done what he has set out to do. Until I am dead, they—and you as well if he can get his hands on you—are tools to use against me." He leaned back. "When I am dead, they are in real danger."

His friend's matter-of-fact acceptance that he might be killed gave Simon the courage to answer, "Then we must see that you do not die."

Peto chuckled. "That is my full intent." He rose, peering into the darkness for a moment before sitting down again. He cleared his throat with an unusual nervousness, as if he were considering how to say what came next. "This is not your fight, Simon. If your Hannah is in that house, you must take her and get away. Go back to the life you had." He added with emphasis, "No matter what."

After a pause Simon asked, "And what will you do?"

"I will free Frances, and I will kill Christo. If I can do those things before I am overcome, I count myself lucky." Peto's voice was cold, and Simon recalled the day his friend had revealed how Peto the Pope became a fearful force in Southwark by killing men who deserved nothing more than death. "Will you stay out of this fight, my friend?"

Simon swallowed once. "I will." He stood a little straighter. "If we find them together, shall Hannah and I take Frances and the baby home with me until matters are settled?"

Peto's gaze met his, unspoken between them the pledge that

if things did not go well, Simon would take care of his woman and her child. "I will be grateful for your help."

Simon tried to remain calm. "Well, then. How will we proceed?"

A soft whistle interrupted and the three froze. "Peto?" a voice called.

It was Pen. At a word from Peto, he entered the damaged house, followed by five men. Simon recognized the leader as the one he'd spoken to on the wharf, the Spaniard Diego.

There was a brief period of each side catching the other up; then Peto explained his plan, first in English, then in Spanish. The men crowded around him listened closely as he explained.

"We must assume Bannon has men stationed around the house as well as inside. We will first dispose of those outside. Pen, you will provide a diversion. Once the watchers are taken care of, you will get them to open the door and then take your sister to a place of safety."

"Judith, oh, Judith!" Pen was aggrieved to hear his sister had reported his movements to Bannon, but Peto insisted she might have been coerced in some way.

"Get her away from them. I would not have your sister harmed in this."

He turned to Simon. "You know something of the plan of the house. Your job will be to climb the stairs, free the women, and get them away as quickly as possible."

"What if there is a guard in the room with them?" Pen asked.

"I have my knife," Simon said. "If I am quiet about it, I can take one man. If there are two or more I will do what I can, and you must come as soon as possible."

Peto gripped his shoulder encouragingly. "My guess is that Bannon will have most of his men at the front door, where he expects me to enter like a lamb offering itself for slaughter."

"He is then," Pen commented, "a bigger fool than I ever was!"

"He thinks me friendless and desperate," Peto said, "and he is conceited enough to believe he has outfoxed me. We will let him believe it. Then we will surprise them all."

"Even surprised, he will be a formidable opponent," Simon warned.

Peto's voice was mild. "I, too, am a formidable opponent, when I have cause."

Ten minutes later, Simon peered across the lane at the quiet house. Frances still sat framed in light in the upstairs window. He realized now her position was too still, her arms too stiff, to be natural.

Now he had to admit Elizabeth Tudor had been right about something. His mind was not devious, as Bannon's was and Peto's must be. He had seen what he was meant to see and would have doomed himself with his own guilelessness. Luckily, Peto was not guileless. He had seen the trap behind the scene Bannon had set.

Chapter Twenty-Three

Pairs of Spaniards slid away into the darkness as Peto, Pen and Simon waited. Two sailors would circle around and disable (*kill,* Simon thought, but no one said it aloud) the guard on the east while two did the same to the west. Diego, the boldest of the Spaniards, went to take the man positioned at the back of the house. Peto himself would remove whoever watched the front door.

Henry, who had insisted he be given a role, was assigned to watch the street in case more of Bannon's men showed up. He had argued it was a milksop role until Simon reminded him that he was most likely to recognize Bannon's crew. The boy had to agree that was true, and they left him, small face turning slowly in all directions, determined to be of help.

The three men waited in the shadow of a nearby house. Simon heard faint sounds of normal life inside: a scuff of feet, the muted clang of metal on metal, a bump, perhaps a stool set against a wall too closely. For a moment he wished he were at home with Hannah, wished none of this had happened. Then he steeled himself. It had happened, and now he must deal with it. Courage, his father always said, was not lack of fear, but doing the right thing in spite of it.

It was time for Pen's contribution. At a nod from Peto, he left the shadows and staggered into the street, apparently unable to walk properly. Snatches of song escaped him, not loud, and not terribly clear, either. For some moments he appeared unable to make a straight line to his door. Had it been another time, the scene might have been hilarious and Simon might have admired his friend's acting. Taking a step forward, Pen reeled several steps back, swinging his arms as if to help himself navigate and shaking his head as if to clear the fumes of alcohol.

In only a short time they heard a muted call, somewhat like an owl but not enough like one to be real. Seconds later, a second owl hooted from the opposite direction. They stood tensed until the third call came. Pen was now talking to his cap, which had slid off and fallen to the ground. Signaling Simon to wait, Peto slipped into the darkness like a candle going out. Simon heard nothing for some time. As he watched Pen, who postured and reeled in a perfect rendition of drunkenness, Peto reappeared, his voice toneless. "Front is clear." He whistled softly, and Pen sat down near the front door, as if too confused to go any farther.

Simon caught movement in his peripheral vision, and Diego appeared beside them, the brief nod he gave telling all. Soon the other sailors rejoined them. One said something to Diego, who relayed it to Peto. "There is no more mans outside."

"Then," Peto said mildly, "let us go and see about the men inside."

It seemed to Hannah it had been days since she was captured. Her wrists were raw, but she had not managed to loosen the ropes at all. She guessed men like Louis could not afford to be sloppy about such things.

Frances seemed less and less in control of herself. Her eyes were wild and she bit her lips as if to force them to be silent. When Peto appeared below, would she be able to keep from calling out a warning? Hannah decided it didn't matter much. One man—even two, if Simon came with Peto—was unlikely to prevail against the men Bannon had gathered below.

Frances's eyes met Hannah's, wild with fright, but she did not seem to recognize her. She was close to complete madness, Hannah thought as the girl sobbed hysterically. Finally Louis said harshly, "Stop that."

She obeyed, going suddenly and completely still. Hannah watched, wondering how she was suddenly able to make herself calm. Looking at Louis, still seated in the center of the room, Frances spoke, a sly look on her face. "He will not come."

Louis looked up at her. "What do you mean?"

Frances sounded as haughty as Hannah had ever heard her. "I mean your precious Bannon is too stupid to guess that Peto and I have a signal. He will not come near, because I do not have the thing that lets him know it is safe to approach."

"What is it?"

"Why would I tell you that?" Her calm voice belied the panic Hannah had noted earlier. What was she up to?

Louis pulled the knife from his belt and leaned toward Hannah. With a half smile, he slid the blade along her arm, leaving a thin trace of blood. Hannah forced herself to remain quiet, but tears of fear and pain slid down her cheeks. Louis turned to Frances. "You think you're clever, but how much of your friend's blood will it take before you tell me?"

"No!" Frances was suddenly tearful again. "Don't hurt her, please!"

In answer, Louis took Hannah's fingers in his hand. "She's gagged. I don't suppose Peto will hear her scream when I cut off one of these."

Hannah gulped down a wave of nausea. She could not help but look imploringly at Frances. What was she doing, baiting a man who had no conscience?

"Wait! Don't do it!" Tears streamed down Frances's face. "It's a bird. The red one."

"What?" Louis had apparently paid no attention to the carvings, but Frances looked at the wall behind him, and he turned to them. "Those?"

Sobbing, Frances managed to speak. "He always calls me his little red bird, and he said I should set it in the windowsill so he would know it is safe to enter."

Hannah knew immediately Frances was lying. What purpose did she have in all this? As Louis moved cautiously toward the birds, making sure to remain out of the light, Frances focused her gaze on the lantern as if she had never seen one before. Hannah could almost see her intention in her eyes. Frantically, she shook her head, trying to get Frances's attention and making muted, negative noises. Frances paid no attention at all.

With a snap, Louis yanked on the carving's string, breaking it. Holding the bird, he crossed to the window, bent low to remain out of view. Frances's eyes never wavered from the lantern. "Nnnnnn!" Hannah moaned. "Nnnnnn!" When Louis reached out to set the red bird on the windowsill, Frances kicked the table leg with all her might. The table toppled, and the lantern fell, knocking against Louis's shoulder and continuing to the floor at her feet.

Arm and hip doused with fuel, Louis was immediately afire. He jumped up with a roar. "You stupid wretch!" he cried, beating at his doublet. "What have you done?"

"He will see it," Frances said, looking into the flames. "He will see it and run away."

Louis dropped to the floor, writhing to extinguish his burning clothing. He did not take the time to right the lantern, which rolled away from Frances's feet, spilling its oil onto the floor. Then, because its base was round, it rolled back toward her, lighting the spilled fuel, which went dancing across the wood as if happy to be free and well fed.

Frances watched as if fascinated, her expression triumphant. She had done exactly what she intended. Peto would know from some distance away there was something wrong at Penitence Brook's house. The fact that she and Hannah were helpless prisoners, the fact that her child slept somewhere in this house, did not appear to matter.

Hannah watched helplessly as Frances caught fire, first her skirt, then her sleeve, then her hair. When the screams began, horrible and almost inhuman, Hannah looked away, sobbing. The seconds that followed were all too real and yet unbelievable. Frances's anguish did not last long, and Hannah knew she counted her life no cost at all as long as Peto was saved.

The fire sent fingers outward, lapping at the overturned table, the floor, the chair. Pulling the blanket from the bed, Louis beat at the flames, cursing. But there was much to feed on in the old house, and soon flames licked the wall under the window. It was not a battle he could win. Looking around at the fast-growing inferno, Louis decided to save himself.

"Help me!" Hannah tried to call out, but Louis did not even slow. He hurried down the steps, pulling the trapdoor closed behind him and ignoring her muffled cries.

Try as she might, Hannah could not free her hands. She felt the wetness of blood on her wrists as she twisted in every direction, trying to sense the slightest weakness in the rope. Smoke began to gather, and the temperature in the room rose quickly. She struggled to breathe. Her desire to live strong, she lowered her face to the floor to gulp in relatively smoke-free air.

From that position, she was looking directly at the bedpost, and a thought came to her. If she could raise the bed a little, she might slide the ropes under the post and free herself.

Stretching out as far as she could, Hannah slid her body under the bed frame. It was difficult to find a position where she could apply upward pressure with her hands tied. Rolling onto her stomach, she raised her rump, pressing it against the boards of the bed. Nothing. She forced her mind to calm and ordered herself to think. When Simon lifted a large rock out of their back garden, he used a board as a lever and a log as a fulcrum. The fulcrum, he said, must be as close to the target as possible. Wedging her shoulder under the bed frame, Hannah lifted her upper body. Nothing moved. The wooden plank pressed sharply into her back but stayed put.

She sobbed once, drawing in smoke-filled air and coughing it back out again. She had to try again, but her eyes stung from smoke and her mind teetered on the edge of despair. Pulling her legs up under her rump, she wriggled the strongest part of her shoulder directly under the bed frame and pressed upward a second time. The bed rose slightly, but not enough for her hands to slip under the post. For a moment she rested, gathering strength for another try. She feared it would be the last, for the room had become a miniature hell, with clouds of black rolling toward her. Once the straw mattress caught fire, she would not escape. Could she do it?

Setting her shoulder against the frame once more, Hannah pushed with all her might. The bedpost rose a few inches! She eased her hands toward her as she supported the weight of the bed with her back. The rope caught briefly on the rough wood, but with a final tug, she was free.

Chapter Twenty-Four

At Peto's signal, the Spaniards split into two groups: two stayed with Peto and Simon; the three others would enter at the back of the house.

"Remember," Peto reminded Simon, "your task is to find the women and the babe. Take them down the back stairs, and pay no heed to anything else." Simon nodded understanding.

They flattened themselves against the front of the house. Simon felt the solid wall beneath his hands and wished he never had to let it go. Peto stepped up and knocked boldly on the door.

Judith answered. "You know who I am," Peto said. "Is there someone inside awaiting me?" Simon shook his head at the double meaning of Peto's question. How could he jest at a time like this?

"She is here," Judith said in a flat tone. "Come inside." She opened the door wide, and several things happened at once. Peto grasped her arm and pulled her outside, where Pen grabbed her skirt and jerked, causing her to fall to the ground with a grunt of surprise. Peto ducked into the house, immediately stepping to one side. The two sailors were right behind him, each with a belaying pin, no doubt borrowed from their ship, held ready for action. Taking a deep breath, Simon followed.

The scene inside Judith's house was almost comical. Off to one side of the entry stood two men, their faces frozen in surprise. To the left, two others rose from a small table where a pair of dice lay between them. Behind them stood Bannon. His expression, at first sly, changed when he saw Peto was not alone. Hands moved, weapons slid noiselessly from sheath and belt hooks, and bodies tensed for a fight. "Go!" Peto ordered, and Simon headed for the stairs.

A rushlight burned in a sconce at the first landing. Simon thought it was poorly made, for the smell of acrid smoke filled his nostrils. Halfway up the first staircase he met a figure all in gray. The man who had tried to kill him two nights ago now hurried downward, unaware of Simon as he looked over his shoulder in fear. One side of his face was scorched, and one sleeve was burned away, revealing a blistered arm.

Simon grabbed the man's collar as he passed. Slamming him against the wall, he brought his knife up threateningly. "Where are the women?"

"Let me go!"

"The women!" Simon pressed the flat of the blade against his neck, putting pressure on the windpipe.

"The attic! A fire! Now let me go!" Simon released the man, who hurried on, tripping in his haste, apparently unconcerned with Simon. For a moment, Simon looked after him in confusion. Then his words penetrated and Simon realized it was not the rush that caused the strong smell of smoke.

Pulling the gag from her mouth, Hannah gasped for air that was less and less breathable. She began groping for the stairway, now hidden by dense smoke. All sense of direction was lost, and she reached out blindly, certain the hole in the floor was nearby but unable to find it. She sobbed, crawling on her knees, and flailing before her only to find she had reached the rough surface of another wall. Weeping in frustration, she began to search again, her bound, numb hands groping for cracks that would reveal the trapdoor.

Suddenly she heard a loud thump behind her. "Hannah! Hannah, are you here?"

Turning, she saw a dim square of light through the clouds of smoke. "Simon! Here!"

Soon his hands, searching in the blackness, found her shoulder. "Tied," she croaked, holding up her hands.

"Janet?"

"Dead. She set the room on fire to warn Peto, and she—" Hannah choked back a sob. "She died because of it."

Simon did not answer, but she felt his hands on hers. In seconds, the ropes parted and she was free. "Can you manage the steps?"

She rubbed her wrists, trying to regain feeling. "Yes."

"Hold onto my coat. We will find our way out of here." Closing the trapdoor behind them, he led her down the stairs to the third floor. Fire raged above but down here, no one knew of it. What they heard, the boarders ignored, and the floor was quiet. Judging from the crackling above them, it would not be for long. The fire would make its way quickly through the house.

Hannah's voice was raspy. "Susan! She is here somewhere."

Where would they have taken the child? Simon said, "When I was here before, there was a young woman with a newborn baby. They might have given her the child to tend."

He led the way around the staircase, selected a door, and knocked. An old man peered cautiously out. "Is there an infant here?" The man shook his head. Pointing to the staircase where smoke billowed downward, Simon said, "You must get everyone out. The house is on fire."

Gray brows rose almost to the hairline. Simon asked again, "The child?"

"Next door down." Pushing past Simon, the man headed for the stairs.

Simon knocked on the next door. In a few moments, a sleepy-looking woman answered. "Are you keeping a baby for Christo Bannon?"

The woman's brow furrowed and she opened her mouth, undoubtedly with a denial. Hannah stepped in front of her husband, warning him to silence with a glance. "The house is on fire," she said. "Get your children out, quickly."

Immediately the woman turned back to the room. Hannah followed her inside as the woman woke a child of perhaps three and took him by the hand, scooping her own infant up and clutching it to her chest. Hannah located Susan on a blanket in the corner and took her up, grateful to feel her warm body once more. She returned to Simon, tears streaming. "I have her."

He hugged her to his chest, briefly enclosing Hannah and the baby in his protection. Releasing them, he said, "We must hurry."

As they headed for the stairs, a man opened a door and stepped into the hallway as if to stop their passage. "There's a fire," Simon told him. "Get the people out."

The man's answer was a bellow. "Fire!"

Immediately, sounds of skittering came from every room in the house, and soon people poured out of other doorways. The man turned and shouted "Fire!" into his own room, and in no time three children and a woman raced toward the stairs, one clutching a kitten and another an armful of clothing. The woman carried a china teapot and a small cloth bag that clinked as she hurried past them. Others streamed around them, coming from rooms down the long hallways that stretched in front and behind. In only moments, the whole floor was emptied. Popping from above signaled wood being consumed at a faster and faster rate. Smoke began to waft down the stairs, as if shyly following the humans' path.

Hannah started for the last set of stairs, but Simon stopped her. "Peto and Bannon have joined battle down there, and I don't know what we will find. We will go down the back stairs. Outside, I want you to find Pen and tell him I said to take you and the child home."

"But you will be with me. Why do I need Pen?"

"I'm not sure what I will do," he answered. "Peto—" Knowing her husband's sense of honor, Hannah quelled the argument she wanted to make. She knew he could not run from danger if a friend was in trouble. "If I do not follow, I will come when I can." Biting her lip, she nodded. Simon turned to lead the way down the stairs.

Chapter Twenty-Five

The staircase at the back of Judith's house was meant for servants, not for ease of use. Crowded and cramped, it turned on itself in a dizzying manner. Simon reached back, steadying Hannah, who was encumbered with the baby and weak from the ordeal that had not ended yet. Most of the house's tenants had already escaped, but they did come upon an elderly couple, the woman hobbling, the man supporting her as best he could on his own unsteady legs. Simon helped the old people, calming the woman's timid questions with words of assurance.

When they reached the bottom, he heard grunts, cries, and oaths at the front of the house. The battle was joined, and the combatants seemed unaware the house was burning over their heads. Simon ushered Hannah to the back door. "Circle to the front and find Pen," he repeated. "He will see you get home safely."

Clutching the child, her wrists raw and bloody, Hannah hesitated only a moment before doing as he said. She must have known he needed her safely away, and she also knew she was the baby's only protection. She followed the elderly couple, looking back only once as tears streamed down her cheeks.

Simon hurried to the front of the house, unsure what he would find. As he went, the sound of fighting quieted. Chaos turned to vague rumbles, threatening but less overt than before. When he got to the entryway, he saw why. The melee was over. The battle to the death was about to begin.

★ ★ ★ ★ ★

Hannah slid through the narrow space between Judith's house and the one next to it. Susan had awakened and begun to fuss, unnerved by the noise. Hannah shushed her softly. "We will go home soon, little one."

On the street in front of the house, people milled anxiously, peering upward to where the fire lit the night high over their heads. Here the fire smelled almost pleasant, a woody aroma mixed with fresh night air.

At one side of the crowd Judith stood like a cornered rooster, hackles up and claws ready. Before her stood Pen, his face knotted in question. "Why?" he kept repeating. "Why, Judith?"

"Money, you fool!" she answered. "You think your precious Peto is perfect, but did he ever offer to pay you for all you do for him?"

"He sees I am rewarded," Pen said, his tone uncomprehending. "And what I received I shared with you, each and every time."

"A pittance now and then!" Judith scoffed. "Bannon will—"

"He will use you and throw you away," Pen interrupted sadly. Glancing at the house, he added, "If he lives out this night, you will learn the sort of man he is."

Pen saw Hannah then and turned away from his sister. "Mistress Maldon, is it not? We have not been introduced, but I am ordered to see you get home safely." Turning away from his sister as if she did not exist, Pen offered Hannah his arm in a courteous gesture. "Peto even thought to give me money for the boatman."

Simon received little notice when he entered what had become an arena of combat, but he could read what had happened thus far from the tableau before him. On the floor, two men who were strangers to him were dead, judging from the casual splay of their bodies. Another leaned against the front wall, blood streaming from a gash on his head. One of the Spaniards held a kerchief to a wound in his side while another held one arm against his body as he fashioned a sling from his kerchief using his good arm and his teeth. Peto's men seemed battered but whole.

In the center of the room, Peto squared off with Bannon. Each man held a knife; each leaned forward a little, lifting his weight onto the balls of his feet. Simon gasped and moved toward his friend, but Diego put a hand on his arm. "He say, 'Stay out of it,' so we do."

Horrified, Simon looked to Peto, who gave him the merest nod of confirmation. "Bannon and I will settle this."

Bannon shifted the knife in his hand. "I will settle it. You will simply sink."

Peto made no reply but crouched even lower. The difference in the two men's size was considerable. Bannon towered over Peto, outweighed him by a third, and had a reach that could span the distance between them without moving his feet. Peto seemed unaffected, watching the big man's eyes with an expression of what appeared to be mild interest.

Bannon lunged, swinging the knife in a wide arc. Peto's backward step was graceful and effective. Chuckling, Bannon said, "You are heedful, which is good for one's health."

Peto remained silent, and Simon saw the man who had for a decade held sway over Southwark, the outlaw feared even though he was also admired, respected, and often loved. This Peto was lethal, without posturing, without threatening, without speaking. Death was in his eyes.

Bannon feinted right but tossed the knife to his left hand and made an upward thrust that would have opened Peto's stomach had he not danced sideways. As he retreated, he sliced Bannon's arm lightly, as if in warning. Gasping in pain, Bannon looked down at the line of blood that oozed up from the wound. For the first time, his smile faltered.

What followed was both terrible and impressive. Bannon was nothing if not willing. He tried a dozen different moves, each of which Peto easily defeated. When he tried to use his superior reach, Peto slipped beyond it. An attempt to use his greater weight failed as well.

Simon's skill with the knife did not include close combat. He could throw with great accuracy, but it was different face to face, as Peto and Bannon now fought. Quickly Simon saw the difference in their approach to the duel. Bannon was used to overpowering opponents. Peto seemed able to outthink them. Simon was fascinated by Peto's ability to move just ahead of Bannon's knife. Time and time again the bigger man attacked, but Peto was not where he thought he would be. Despite his horror, Simon could not take his eyes off the scene: Peto's cool vigilance, Bannon's increasing frustration and anger.

Watching closely, Simon saw the merest flicker of movement in Bannon's eyes. They moved to the right, and there was some sort of message in them. Turning, Simon saw Louis creeping toward Peto, knife in hand. Where had he come from? It didn't matter. His intent was clear.

Simon reacted from pure instinct. His own knife was out in a heartbeat, and it flew across the room. The throw caught Louis squarely in the chest and he cried out, the arm he'd intended to stab Peto in the back with suddenly nerveless. Simon's quick action slowed his approach but did not stop it. Instead of the fatal blow he intended, Louis managed only a weak thrust. Still, his blade sliced into Peto's thigh as he fell to the floor.

As Louis's breath left his body forever, everyone froze, unsure what result this cowardly attack would bring.

Bannon's face took on a look of cunning. "Shall we continue, Cousin, or are you too inconvenienced to face me?"

Peto's teeth were clenched with pain. His breath came from deep in his chest, releasing in stuttering gasps. Putting out a hand, he motioned to Diego, who approached. Peto removed the kerchief the smuggler wore on his head and tied it over the wound on his thigh, wrenching it tight with a knot.

"I am ready," he told Bannon.

"Peto—" Simon could not believe this was happening. "You can't do this!"

Peto did not even look at him.

"You are at a disadvantage," Bannon said, his tone gloating. "You cannot dance away from me now."

The comment brought only a grim smile from Peto, who crouched forward, ready.

The fight began again. With his maneuverability hampered, Peto was in real danger. He narrowly missed the blade of Bannon's knife several times, pulling himself away just in time. His face revealed the pain he was in, not in its expression, but in the set of his jaw and the sunken look of his cheeks.

"Do something!" Simon urged Diego, but the fellow shook his head.

"Peto is much a man."

When the end came, it was so quick Simon almost missed it. Bannon, his confident grin once again in place, made a feint to the left, forcing Peto to lean back and to the right. Taking advantage of Peto's unbalanced position, the big man stepped forward and made a fierce upward jab meant to split his opponent's insides. But Peto guessed Bannon's intent and with a quick twist on the injured leg that must have been agonizing, spun out of the way, thrusting his own weapon forward as he moved. Bannon's momentum and weight drove Peto's knife directly into his heart.

For a few moments, the room was silent except for Peto's jagged breathing. Then the Spaniards cheered. Simon suddenly remembered where they were. "The house is on fire."

The truth of his words was evident, had they not been focused on Peto's struggle with his enemy. Smoke hovered on the staircase, and shouts could be heard outside as people formed the legally required bucket brigade.

Diego looked at his men. "We go, Peto."

"Yes."

"But your leg," Simon objected.

"Diego will take care of me." He paused. "The women and the baby, are they safe?"

Simon pressed his lips together. "Hannah and the child, yes. Frances was dead when I found them." How much should he tell? That she had given her life to warn him of danger he had sensed from the start? Peto did not need to know that. "Pen took Hannah and the baby home."

Peto paused, his expression betraying pain both physical and emotional. Finally he said softly, "Will you see the child finds a good home?"

Simon swiped a hand across his forehead. "I think she already has. Hannah loves her—"

"Peto!" Diego's voice was urgent.

With a half smile, half grimace, Peto moved to the door. "Come, Simon."

One of the Spaniards handed Simon his knife, which had been wiped clean. *"Bueno,"* he said, his expression admiring. He tried it in English. "Is good."

A crack from above startled them, and one of the men muttered something that might have been prayer, might have been oath. "The place will collapse on itself soon," Peto said.

Simon looked out a crack in the shutters. "How will we walk away from this place? There are dozens of people out there."

"We simply do it." Peto smiled grimly, pulling himself erect. "The key to dealing with a crowd, Simon, is appearing to have the right to do so."

Simon put his eye back to the slit. Peto might manage to walk through a crowd of dazed boarders and curious onlookers, but what if Jenkins the constable was out there?

What he saw was much worse. People at the front of the crowd were jostled aside, and Calkin strode into view, followed by several strong young men who wore no uniform but were surely guardsmen. Calkin had come to Southwark, no doubt looking for Simon. Now Peto and his men were trapped.

Simon quickly conveyed to Peto what he saw. The outlaw's brow furrowed, and he translated the news for the Spaniards. The conversation that followed concerned Simon; he could tell by the looks that slid his way as Peto explained. He knew if it were not for him, the men would have chosen to fight their way out of this. It seemed the Spaniards argued for that very thing, but Peto demurred. It seemed he would not fight the friend of a friend.

Outside, Calkin began taking command of the milling crowd. The law required every household to have a bucket of water on the doorstep and every able-bodied citizen to turn out to fight a fire. Too many old, close-built wooden structures meant large sections of a city could be lost in a single fire. Everyone was expected to work to prevent such catastrophes.

By now the roof of this house must be fully engaged, but no man with a bucket could reach those flames. The would-be helpers were unsure what to do. Under Calkin's command, men who had been frozen with confusion became an efficient force to fight the fire.

"Come this way!" he called to those who stood at the front of the crowd, indicating the side of the house. "You, over here. You, stand next to him. Keep the buckets coming!" People followed his commands without question. In the chaos, someone was making order. The crowd did not know the guardsman, but they recognized a voice of authority.

The other guardsmen helped to organize the bucket brigade, setting onlookers into a place in the line and assuring they did their part. Simon's heart filled with dread when he heard Calkin order, "See what can be salvaged, William."

They were coming inside! Peto, who had taken up a spot on the other side of the window, turned to his men and said something in Spanish. They tensed, taking stances that indicated they had no choice but to attack. Peto shook his head in a negative gesture, glancing around the room. Another crack above was followed by a crash. The upper floors had started to give way under the fire's advance.

"Let us find a better place," Peto said mildly. He jerked his head toward the back of the house, and they moved past the staircase and down the hallway. At the back of the house, things were worse. Flames had licked their way down the servants' stairway, which glowed with fire that was obscured by smoke. The crackling was louder than Simon had imagined such a thing could be, perhaps because he had never been inside a fire.

The front door burst open, and they retreated to the sidewall, out of view of men who, from the sound of it, were removing what they could carry of the inhabitants' belongings. As long as they stayed at the front of the house, Simon thought, Peto was safe. But how was he going to get away from here?

As Simon moved his feet nervously, his leg bumped against something hard yet yielding. Stooping down, he felt the side of a basket and inside it, clothing. The laundry he had helped Judith hang—was it only yesterday?

"Peto!"

Peto limped to where he stood, fingering the various items. "Have you found a way to escape this hell?"

When Simon explained his idea, Peto laughed. "You and your disguises, Simon Maldon! Will you have me take up your methods?"

Simon touched his friend's shoulder. "It is either that or a fight with these men, Peto, and I would not have any more death tonight."

Peto paused. "All right, then." He turned to the Spaniards, explaining briefly as Simon handed out skirts, shirts, and blankets that would transform them from trapped outlaws to terrified tenants escaping their burning home.

In a very short time, Peto and the five Spaniards looked very like four women and two men, one of them so old he had to lean on another for support. One of the sailors found near the back door several shawls, some hats, and a cloak for Peto that hung low enough to cover the blood-soaked cloth on his leg.

Simon had a moment's doubt about his plan. "Even if I can distract the guardsmen," he asked Peto, "what if someone in the crowd realizes you are not really tenants?"

"The area is blanketed with smoke, and tonight you have seen these people's ability to ignore what is not good for them to see," Peto told him. "They will not question us, even if they notice that the women are uglier than any they've seen before." That was certainly true, for one of them had a full beard, although it was covered by the shawl "she" draped across her face.

When they were ready, Simon gave Peto a nod and stepped out the back door, running as if desperate to escape, which in truth, he was. Staggering forward, he approached the two men who had come with Calkin. "I am Simon Maldon," he told them. "I have important information for the sergeant."

"He is at the front," one of the men said.

"Please, take me to him." Simon appeared to faint, and the two men caught him before he fell, supporting him with their strong arms as he lolled, apparently helpless. They helped Simon make his way to the front of the house. He dared not look behind to see if the last escapees of the house were challenged as they hurried out the back and through the line of firefighters.

Calkin's face lit with relief when Simon was practically lifted into his presence. "Simon!" he said. "Your wife sent me to find you, but I feared I would find only your charred corpse in this coil!"

Quickly Simon gave him an edited version of the night's events: Bannon's takeover of Judith's house in hopes he could catch Peto, his kidnapping of Frances, and his death.

"How did he die?" Calkin asked. "Was Peto the Pope here?"

"I went upstairs to try to save the woman," Simon said, sticking to the truth as much as possible. "Frances was already dead, having set the place on fire to thwart Bannon's plan."

"But where is your friend the outlaw now?"

Again Simon answered honestly, at least in the strictest sense of the word. "I don't know where he is. He might have died in the fire, for all I know."

"We caught two suspicious-looking characters," Calkin said. "We will turn them over to the constable, but they don't appear the type to tell the truth about any of this." His eyes met Simon's. "I will depend on you for an honest account."

"I will tell you what I can," he replied, telling himself the word *can* had shades of meaning. One *can* tell all, or one *can* tell what he thinks he must. Simon sighed. He was starting to think like Peto the Pope.

Calkin was not satisfied, but the crash of a collapsing wall sent people scattering at that moment, and he hurried forward to help rescue a man caught too close and pinned under a beam. "It's too dangerous now to go inside," he called. "Concentrate on keeping the fire from spreading to the neighboring homes!"

Simon caught the sleeve of one of the young guardsmen. "I am feeling better now that I can breathe fresh air. Please tell the sergeant I have gone home, but I will find him tomorrow and answer his questions."

The young man asked, "Are you certain you are well enough to walk home?"

"I have friends nearby," Simon told him. "They will see that I get there."

Chapter Twenty-Six

He was only a block away when a soft whistle alerted him to Peto's presence. With the stealth he had come to expect from them, Peto and the Spaniards appeared around him, clapping him on the back. Peto remarked, "We stayed to see they did not arrest you for helping a fugitive escape. We would have fought for you had the need arisen."

Simon opened his mouth to reply, but a figure stepped from the darkness and touched Peto's sleeve. Judith's face was half lit by moonlight, and tears streaked down her cheeks. "Peto!" she sobbed. "You must know I meant you no harm."

Peto did not even turn to look at her. "Were you not Pen's sister," he said to the air, "you would be as dead as your friend Bannon." With that he led the way down the street, leaving Judith alone, backlit by the conflagration that had once been her home.

When they reached Bridge Street, Peto shook Simon's hand. "You will go your own way from here." He put a hand on Simon's shoulder. "I thank you, my friend. And I'm sorry for what you've been through for my sake."

"Will you leave England?"

He nodded. "I have a bit of money put away, and I speak tolerable Spanish. I will prosper, and I might even become an honest businessman who need not look over his shoulder in dread of the law." His gaze met Simon's in the dim morning light. "We will not meet again."

Simon raised a hand to his forehead in salute. "Be well, Peto." He lightened the moment by asking, "Should I return the lucky piece you once gave me, to keep you safe?"

Peto grinned. "I will find some Spanish luck when I reach the end of my journey."

That reminded Simon, and he took the letter from inside his shirt. "We spoke of this letter. Will you see that Philip of Spain gets it?"

"I will." Putting the roll of paper inside his own shirt, Peto gave Simon a courteous bow and turned away, a limp marring his jaunty exit only slightly.

As Peto and his comrades disappeared down the wharf, Simon heard a sound behind him. Still tense from the evening's events, he whirled, drawing his knife at the same time.

Henry's pale face showed uncertainty. "Is all well, Simon?"

He had completely forgotten the child. At a loss for a moment, he finally stammered, "I have lived through a long night, much thanks to you."

"That's good, then." The boy paused, apparently waiting, as Simon tried to decide what he needed to know.

"Bannon and his men are . . . they are dead."

"I saw Peto just now," the boy said, as if that explained everything. "I think I saw your woman, too. The foolish man took her and the baby somewhere."

"Home," Simon said, feeling somehow uncomfortable at the word. What would happen to Pen now? He had no home, and his sister had betrayed him. Would he go back to Judith? Would they struggle on together?

And Henry. He had no home, and now, he did not even have Bannon. What would happen to an orphan boy in Southwark, undersized and unprotected?

Simon reminded himself that Peto had once been the same. Peto had survived, using his wits. Henry, he thought, possessed a good mind. He would also survive. Somehow.

He looked down at the boy, so small, so young, so wise beyond his years. As Simon watched, the thin shoulders slumped and Henry took a step backward. "I wanted to see you made your way home all right." He pointed to the river's edge. "There's a boatman down there."

"Yes." Simon turned to look at the brightly painted boat waiting in the mist of morning.

"Have you money for the fare?"

Simon almost smiled. The child sounded just like his father. "I do."

"Well, then. Good-bye to you, Simon." He turned away quickly, head held high.

Simon tried to form words of farewell, but they would not come. Instead he called out, "I have enough money for two fares, Henry."

Chapter Twenty-Seven

It was late the next day when Simon went to the Tower. Aside from their exhaustion, he and Hannah had had many things to discuss. He was not sure she liked the idea of Henry coming to live with them, and Simon could not blame her. The boy was lousy, undernourished, and totally tongue-tied in Hannah's presence. When she tried to ask where he came from or how he had come to live with Bannon, Henry merely shrugged. Simon thought it was embarrassment and perhaps fear of her. Hannah said little, but the set of her jaw indicated she thought him recalcitrant and possibly dull-witted.

Simon wished she could see that Henry had learned to appear slow in order to protect himself and that he probably feared women. He'd seen how the unlamented Pearl had treated the boy, and he doubted Bannon's other women had been any more loving. He would explain Henry to her over time. At the moment, Hannah was so caught up in Susan that she hardly saw anything else. Henry would make an excellent apprentice, and the thought of teaching what he knew to the boy made Simon quite content. Nevertheless, he took Henry with him when he went to the Tower, unsure how the boy would fare alone with Hannah.

As they walked, he explained to Henry he would be playing a trick on some friends, a ruse that required dressing up like a priest. "You will wait outside, and I will return in an hour."

All went well until Simon reached the White Tower. "She is

gone, priest," the guard said. "Did no one tell you?"

"No, um, I fear not, my son. Where have they taken her?"

The man laughed, more a guffaw than real humor. "To the block for all I know. Do you think they tell us anything?"

Simon's heart skipped a beat. That could not be true!

Footsteps sounded behind the guard, and a man appeared, followed by one of the women who had served Elizabeth. "That's the man!" she said. "That's the priest who has been teaching the queen's prisoner her catechism!"

"By whose authority?" The man was a functionary, it seemed, for he was plainly dressed and officious in manner.

"He has a letter from the queen," the guard said defensively. "It has a seal and all."

Simon stood frozen. He could not produce the letter he had forged, for this man could probably tell the seal was not Mary's. Should he say Elizabeth had asked him to come? He was reluctant to do so, lest he intensify whatever trouble she might be in that caused her removal from the Tower.

"I was sent to try to teach the Boleyn woman the True Faith," Simon began, hating the use of a term that implied Henry Tudor and Anne Boleyn had never been married.

"And who did the sending?"

He searched his mind for an answer that would not get anyone else in trouble. He was probably done for, caught in a lie with no way to escape. Who could he say ordered him here?

"Father! Father, come quick! There's been an accident and a man is dying!"

They all turned to see the boy who had apparently come in search of a priest. Simon was both shocked and relieved to see it was Henry. He turned to the guard. "They said to fetch some men, too. His cart fell on him, and they need help lifting it off."

Henry's manner and message threw Simon's questioners into chaos. The guard turned to call for help. The woman put her hands over her face, imagining a scene that did not exist. And the officer of whatever-he-was seemed flummoxed, at a loss to be of help. Finally he began repeating orders the guard was shouting, so that "Get some rope" and "Bring some logs" echoed like words called down a well.

Simon took his cue. "Take me to him, lad. He might need last rites." Henry turned, and Simon followed him through one gate and then the next, as quickly as they could manage without running. Once outside the walls of the Tower, Simon slid between two buildings and took off the cassock. Handing it to Henry he said, "Stay here until I tell you to come out."

It took only a few minutes for the official and two burly guards to pass by where Simon sat, but by then he had spread his wares out on either side of him and covered one eye with a leather patch. When the men stopped before him, he pushed his jaw forward, changing both the shape of his face and his manner of speaking.

"Where is the accident?" one of the men asked.

"I don't know, Your Worship. I have been here all morning and heard of no accident."

There was craning of necks. There was cursing. There were questions about a priest and a boy. The street vendor claimed to know nothing. After a while, the disgusted group returned to the Tower. The vendor waited a while before calling out, "We are safe, Henry."

The boy came out from between the buildings and helped Simon pick up the goods he'd set out as his impromptu alibi.

"How did you know I needed help?" Simon asked.

"I'm not sure," Henry replied. "I just thought you might, going in a place like that."

"What you did was very brave," Simon said. "Foolish, perhaps, but brave." He grinned at the boy. "I've been known to do a foolish thing or two myself, as Hannah will tell you."

"She doesn't like me."

He could not deny it, but he could not let it lie, either. "She does not know you yet. When the two of you become better acquainted, she will see your value."

Henry thought about that. "It doesn't matter. As long as you are content to have me around, what others think or say will not concern me. Even her."

Chapter Twenty-Eight

Hannah was alone in the shop when the man came in, for which she was forever grateful. As good as Simon was with disguise and subterfuge, he was not one who could easily lie to another man's face.

"Can I help you, sir?" she asked the stranger. He seemed an old man, not so much in years, but in manner. He looked like joy had been squeezed from his face, leaving it stiff and dry.

"I hope you can, goodwife. I am looking for my daughter."

It was as if Hannah had been holding her breath for three months, waiting for catastrophe. Now that it was before her, she found she could face it. "Your daughter, sir?"

"She ran away from home some time ago, and we have had no word of her." He stopped, pinched his lips together, and added, "She was carrying a child."

"Oh, how sad, to lose both a daughter and a grandchild."

The man heaved a great sigh. "It would be, if the child were a boy. We have an abundance of girl children in our line, but no males." He frowned. "It is my fondest desire to have a grandson, so much so that I would forgive Frances everything."

"Why do you come here, sir?"

"After months of searching, we found her trail in Southwark, where a woman who once served in our house now lives. She said Frances planned to go to a midwife in Hampton to have the child and then give it away. There was some nonsense about a lover who is apparently dead, his body found in a house with several others after a fire."

"I see."

"When I asked in this neighborhood, they said you had a young woman living with you for a time, and she had a baby. I hoped it might be Frances."

Here is where Hannah was glad Simon was in the back. She answered very carefully. "The girl we took in was meant to help out in the shop, but she, too, died in a fire."

"And the child?"

Hannah hesitated, but finally she said, "I'm sorry, sir, but I can assure you, the child our maid bore was not your grandson."

She felt somewhat guilty when the man had gone. To assuage her guilt, Hannah decided she would make something special for tonight's supper. Henry liked whatever Simon liked, so a tart of scallions would please them both. Having done it often, she worked without conscious thought, boiling the scallions, draining them, and then mashing them to a paste as she settled with her conscience. Frances's father had not come for Susan. He wanted a grandson, and it was clear he wanted no more girl children to raise and provide dowries for.

They were a family now, she told herself. Simon, Susan, and she belonged together—and Henry too, of course. Adding fresh cheese, saffron, and several eggs, she put the tart in to bake.

Hannah wasn't sure how she felt about Henry, but the boy and Simon had become almost inseparable. That was probably good, since she was so busy with Susan, but it was odd that after years of having only each other, each of them now had another person to care for.

The thought of Susan made her take a moment to check on the baby. She was playing with her toes, talking to them as if they were quite entertaining. Hannah smiled at the child then went back to work. Henry was certainly no trouble, and if Simon wanted the boy to stay, she would treat him well, even if he could never hold her heart the way Susan did.

★ ★ ★ ★ ★

Simon was in the apothecary shop with Henry, teaching him the basics of medicine. "Humors are what make us," he explained. "The phlegmatic man is prone to idleness, the sanguine to lust and overindulgence. Choleric types are covetous, and the melancholic person is prone to deceit and envy. Out of balance, humors make us sick, and we must right them with diet and physic."

The door opened and a woman stepped inside. Everything about her was lavish: her clothing, the abundance of dark hair topped with an array of decorations, even her figure, sharply outlined in velvet and silk. There was a foreign cast to her face, dark eyes and long lashes that indicated southern influences; Italy, perhaps, or Spain. Despite her sumptuous clothes and expensive accessories, her manner was tentative. "Are you Simon Maldon?"

"I am."

"I am Isabella Caldwell, once de Marcia. Elizabeth Boleyn and I knew each other when we were but girls."

Simon was instantly irritated by the reference to Elizabeth by her mother's surname rather than her father's. She was obviously important, however, and he kept his expression blank as he waited to hear what she wanted.

The lady seemed curious about him, for she took a moment to study his face before she spoke again. What was she looking for? Some apothecaries could be bribed into making poisons, and some nobles used such things to advance their careers or rid themselves of troublesome relatives. He pressed his lips together. If that was what she'd come for, the woman would be disappointed.

When her study was complete, Isabella said, "I have a letter for you."

"A letter, my lady?"

"From Elizabeth." Reaching into a silk purse at her waist, she pulled out a roll of paper. "As I said, we met some years ago. I was engaged at the time to a man who turned out to be, um, unsuitable. She was very kind to me then." Her gaze dropped to the floor and she took up a different sentence. "Now things are hard for Elizabeth. She is illegitimate, of course, and was raised a Protestant." The word sounded like a curse in Isabella's mouth. "Still, she and I were once friends, so when I passed near Woodstock recently, I stopped to see her."

"How kind of you." He kept the sarcasm from his voice with diligent effort. He remembered now where he had heard of Isabella de Marcia. She'd been engaged to the first man Simon killed, a madman who had murdered several women.

The thought of killing distracted him for a moment. The count was now two men dead at his hand. Simon did not like to think of himself as a killer. In both instances, he had been forced to kill to protect another person. He hoped God understood both his need and his regret. Men like Peto might feel justified in such actions. Simon felt sinful.

His visitor held the rolled papers, tapping them nervously against her hand as if unsure whether to give them up or not. "Elizabeth told me nothing of what is in this letter."

Ah, there's the rub, Simon thought. The woman feared treason, yet she liked Elizabeth well enough that she did not want to believe her capable of it.

"My wife and I have long been acquainted with the princess," Simon said, careful to speak only the truth. "I was at first charged with helping her practice her languages. My wife served as her maid, which is how we met." He put his hands on the table, for they seemed determined to reach out and snatch the letter from her. Giving his most disarming smile, he forced a light tone. "I think Lady Elizabeth feels she had a hand in our courtship."

"I see," she said. "Elizabeth assured me there is naught here that would harm anyone."

Again keeping his tone casual, he said, "We often correspond so that she can continue practice of her Latin or Greek, but we speak of mundane things." He waved a hand at the shop. "She is very kind, taking an interest in our lives here and the little things we do each day."

Isabella raised the papers like a rod, pointing them at Simon. "I find it odd she would write at such length to"—Simon sensed what she might have said, although she changed it at the end to something less insulting—"old acquaintances."

"She says her tutors insisted a foreign language is a skill that must be practiced to keep it sharp."

"As you say." The woman finally proffered the letter. Simon took it, giving her a pretty speech of thanks, though what he wanted most at the moment was to see her gone.

When she left, he turned to Henry, who was grinding garlic for a poultice. "Watch the shop, son. I must share this with Hannah."

Something in Henry's eyes made him pause, and Simon realized what he had called the boy. Yes, he had come to think of him as his son. The look on Henry's face said more than Elizabeth's letter possibly could. Ruffling his hair as he passed, Simon felt a swelling in his chest. He and the boy did well together.

He found Hannah digging in the back garden. "We have a letter from Her Highness."

"I hope she is well." Hannah wiped her hands on her apron.

"It is in Latin, so I will read it to you," he said.

Master Maldon,

I write to thank you for the toothache remedy you provided. I am now at Woodstock, the hunting lodge my grandfather favored. Here I pass the days pleasantly, away from the bustle of the city, although the place is in such sad disrepair that I am lodged in the gatehouse.

"Under house arrest," Simon muttered. They had learned of Elizabeth's removal to Woodstock a few days after his last visit to the Tower. Her situation was an odd balance of imprisonment and freedom, and the queen seemed unwilling even to hear her sister's name. Calkin, who had after great effort abandoned efforts to get the truth from Simon about the night of Frances's death, still served as Simon's source of information. He reported that after Elizabeth had written Mary several letters of complaint about her treatment and conditions at Woodstock, Mary had angrily ordered the man who was essentially Elizabeth's jailer to stop sending them.

"At least she is alive," Hannah said.

Since I last came to you for physic, I have had many adventures. I was housed in the Tower of London for some time, as you may have heard, but since I am innocent of crimes against the queen, I was set free. Officers remain with me here in order to prevent foolish plotters from using my name to foment treason.

"In other words, she is watched constantly and suspected of all sorts of evil."

"It is the way of things these days," Hannah said. "I wonder if there was ever such a wicked time as this, with the government in shambles and the economy so weak."

Simon did not argue with his wife, who tended to think whatever was happening at a given moment was unique to mankind. Having studied history, he believed chaos was constant, and only the type of chaos changed with time. He went on reading.

During my time in the Tower, a priest came each day to teach me the ways of the True Church. He was most earnest, but it was discovered later he had no right to be there, having no orders from the queen or the council. No one knows where he came from or where he went, but I can only deduce he had my best interests at heart and intended to provide for my salvation.

Hannah chuckled. "Imagine their confusion. A priest no one sent that nobody can locate." Her expression sobered. "You were lucky, Simon."

"We make our luck by careful planning," he said, though he knew she was correct. He returned to Elizabeth's words.

Since I have much time to think and little to think on, I have set my mind to the questions you raised when last we met. You were concerned about a certain girl your wife had hired to work in your apothecary shop, and you were also concerned about a friend of yours who had disagreed with his cousin and wanted you to help bring him to justice. After some thought, it seems to me suspicious that this young woman appeared looking for work at just the time your friend became embroiled in trouble. I think the two are connected somehow, and though the matter is probably settled by this point, I charge you to look past the outward appearances of these two and see what advantage they seek in coming to you. I would add that you should do this in all your dealings with folk, for you are ever too trusting.

"What a mind she has!" Simon said, shaking his head in awe. "Without ever meeting Peto or Frances, she connected them. Of course, she imagines an evil intent, but Her Highness never accepted that Peto's cause was just."

"As you say, she had a clever mind." Hannah's face was expressionless, but Simon sensed she agreed with Elizabeth's condemnation of Peto.

The letter ended with these words:

I do not know if we shall meet again, Simon Maldon.

(Simon added Hannah's name to that sentence as he read, not wanting her to feel left out.)

No man or woman knows when death will come, and whatever God and our Queen decide is not for such as we to judge. I will tell you, then, that I am grateful for your care for my health and your kindnesses of the past. Be well, and may you and your wife be blessed with the children you want and deserve.

E.

"I wish she might know we have our little girl now," Hannah said, quickly adding, "and Henry, of course."

It was probably not wise to write a return letter to Elizabeth. Who knew what plots were hatching around her at this very moment? Philip of Spain would arrive any day, and many Englishmen resented the coming marriage.

"The queen's bridegroom comes soon," Hannah said, echoing his thought. "Perhaps when she is married, the queen will look more kindly on her sister."

Simon thought of the letter Dudley had written to Philip, outlining the reasons he should protect Elizabeth's life. Had it reached him? Was he willing to accept advice from a Protestant nobleman under sentence of death? Might he use his influence to save both Elizabeth and Dudley, seeing their possible usefulness?

If the letter had reached Philip, and if he was convinced, Simon had done his part to protect the princess he admired, as had the criminal she despised. She was alive, though a virtual prisoner. Peto, too, was alive, though an exile forever from his homeland. Simon had done what he could for them both. Rolling the letter and placing it next to his heart, he returned to the house, where the happy Susan played and the solemn Henry worked. He had a family now.

And Elizabeth? Only time would tell what was in store for her.

AUTHOR'S NOTE

Elizabeth Tudor was released from the Tower of London May 19, 1554. I shortened her time in prison by a few weeks, being a merciful sort and needing my story to move along at that point.

Evidence indicates Philip of Spain did indeed plead for Elizabeth's life, and of course Mary would deny him nothing. Robert Dudley also credited the Spanish bridegroom with convincing Mary to pardon him. Of course, I have no proof that an apothecary and a smuggler had anything to do with the matter.

ABOUT THE AUTHOR

Peg Herring lives in northern Lower Michigan and writes mysteries, both historical and contemporary. When not reading or writing, Peg loves travel and directing choral music. She and her husband also garden, mostly for the benefit of elk, deer, rabbits, and birds in the area, and work to keep their century-old farmhouse from crumbling around them.